LYONS SEVERED THE PLASTIC CUFFS AROUND HIS ANKLES

He reversed the knife and sawed at the wrist loop, then flexed his fingers to get the circulation going.

The Able Team leader knew he was far from safe yet, and as if to prove the point he heard someone shout nearby. He recognized Rick Teeler's voice. Lyons grinned, the expression that of a caged animal back on the loose and ready to take on anything that came his way.

Dark figures moved toward Lyons's position, armed and determined. He backed away, seeking a better place to make his stand. The Militia Men didn't know it yet, but the war had started, and they had no idea what was coming.

Other titles in this series:

DON PENDLETON'S

STONY

AMERICA'S ULTRA-COVERT INTELLIGENCE AGENCY

MAN®

DEFENSIVE
ACTION

the Slingshot Project
BOOK 1

A GOLD EAGLE BOOK FROM

WORLDWIDE®

TORONTO • NEW YORK • LONDON
AMSTERDAM • PARIS • SYDNEY • HAMBURG
STOCKHOLM • ATHENS • TOKYO • MILAN
MADRID • WARSAW • BUDAPEST • AUCKLAND

First edition August 2002

ISBN 0-373-61944-8

DEFENSIVE ACTION

Special thanks and acknowledgment to
Mike Linaker for his contribution to this work.

Printed in U.S.A.

DEFENSIVE
ACTION

PROLOGUE

Liberty Flats, Dakota

Rosario Blancanales pushed open the door of the Shanty Bar and walked inside. The interior of the timber building was dim and smoky. A jukebox in one corner pounded out a foot-stomping tune that rattled bottles on the shelves behind the bar.

The bar was the local haunt of members of the Militia Men, a hard-nosed organization that made no secret of the fact that it was strongly antigovernment and despised anything that smelled of the federal authorities.

Conspiracy theories, black ops, the nation under threat—these were all high on the Militia Men's manifesto. The American government, according to the group, was liable to plunge America into chaos and global conflict. Individual freedom was a thing of the past. Government surveillance and ultrasecret planning were undermining the whole U.S. Membership of the Militia Men had grown in the months leading up to the millennium, and continued to grow as disenchantment within a section of the population increased. That disenchantment became paramount as the government continued its militaristic stance, pushing for expansion of its defense strategy.

The Militia Men, isolated and angry, organized and armed by Hubbard Tetrow, its bellicose leader, had its headquarters in the Dakota badlands. Based at Tetrow's ranch, the HQ, with its self-sufficient capability and underground facility, prepared itself for what Tetrow saw as a need to fight back against the federal monolith.

Twenty miles from the ranch the town of Liberty Flats was where the Militia Men obtained their supplies. The town had little to offer in the way of anything else—except for the Shanty Bar. A sprawling timber construction, much added to over the years, the Shanty offered cheap food and liquor for anyone who stepped inside. Long-haul truckers bedded down in the basic dormitory, where beds could be had for the night, and for a few dollars more a woman to share it with. Many of the truckers were sympathizers, bringing in information and often supplies for the Militia Men.

Legally there was little the authorities could do. The Militia Men weren't guilty of anything. Despite their protestations about loss of personal freedom, they were still able to voice their thoughts about the government, practice their military drills and fire their weapons within the boundaries of the Tetrow ranch. They often came under the watchful eye of the federal authorities, who sent out the FBI to take photographs and observe. There were files on the group in the FBI computers, and every man who joined up became a suspect. That was as far as it went, because the Militia Men hadn't broken any laws.

All that was in Rosario Blancanales's mind as he crossed the room and bellied up to the bar. He had drawn a degree of attention from the occupants, but no tangible threat had been made. Blancanales ordered a beer and took it with him to an empty table, where he was able to sit with his back to the wall and observe.

He was waiting for someone.

Dressed in work clothes, Blancanales looked like any one of a dozen men in the place. Though he might have looked the part, manual work was the furthest thing on his mind at the moment. Interest in him faded after a while. Blancanales drank his beer, politely warded off the attentions of one of the bar's working girls and settled back.

Twenty minutes later a group of men walked in and stood at the bar. There were six of them. Blancanales had eyes for only one—a strongly built man with blond hair and blue eyes, wearing faded Levi's jeans and a weathered leather jacket.

Blancanales drained his beer, placed the bottle on the table and pushed to his feet. He sauntered across to the bar and stood behind the blond man. One of the blonde's companions noticed Blancanales and nudged him.

"Feller here seems to have taken a shine to you, Jag."

The man named Jag turned around and eyed Blancanales. Almost immediately his face hardened and he swore bitterly.

"Thought I'd seen the last of you, Agent Rimmer," he said.

"Agent?" one of Jag's companions said. "This bastard's a Fed?"

Jag nodded. "Well, ex-FBI. They took his badge away."

"I figured there was a stench in here," someone said.

"Who is this pansy ass?" another man asked.

Jag grinned. "This is ex-FBI Agent Jack Rimmer," he said. "Son of a bitch has been on my tail for months. Like a goddamn stalker. Got some idea I done something wrong. Won't let go. Even after he was thrown out of the Bureau. That's right, ain't it, Jack?"

"Like I said, Jag, maybe he took a shine to you."

Blancanales ignored the others. He stood face-to-face with Jag.

"You and I need to talk."

"The hell we do," Jag said. "Now, I just came in here with my buddies for a quiet drink. Don't want no hassle. You don't have any jurisdiction over me, Rimmer, so get out of my face."

There was a round of laughter from the assembled crowd. A shuffling of booted feet at they edged in, scenting a possible kill.

The barman leaned forward.

"Fellers, no trouble in here, now. You know Tetrow's rules."

Jag nodded. "That's right. Okay, Mr. Lawdog, we'll do this outside. We drink in here. Settle our differences out back. If you got the guts, of course."

"Whatever I have to say can be said outside."

Jag led the way through to the rear of the room and pushed open a door. Blancanales followed him, and they walked through the trash-strewed back lot. Beyond the building the land lay hot and dusty. There was a graveyard of abandoned cars and trucks, empty packing cases and barrels.

A few of Jag's companions trailed in their wake, still clutching their cans of beer, chuckling to themselves as they watched the confrontation.

Jag and Blancanales were at a distance now, voices raised in argument. Of the two, Jag was the more agitated as he waved his arms about, pointing here and there to emphasize some point or other. Then Blancanales jabbed a stiff finger in Jag's chest, pushing him back a step. The action enraged Jag. He stepped in close, reached under his jacket and pulled a gun. Without a moment's hesitation he aimed it at Blancanales and pulled the trigger twice. Blancanales stumbled back, slumping against the side of a wrecked car. He hung there for a moment, then slid to the ground and lay still.

Jag waved to his companions.

"What the hell you do that for?" one of them asked when they reached him. "Jesus, Jag, you don't go around shooting fuckin' Feds."

Jag smiled. "Why not? They work for the government, don't they? Hell, Joe, this is the enemy. You forgot or somethin'? How many times do I have to tell you this one is freelance now. He's not a Fed anymore."

He reached in his pocket and took out the keys to

his truck. Tossing them to one of the men, he said, "Arch, go bring my truck around here."

Bending over the still form on the ground, Jag searched Blancanales's pockets. He located a wallet and an automatic pistol. He stuffed the wallet in the back pocket of his jeans and tucked the pistol in his belt.

"Son of a bitch ain't going to have any use for them," he said. "Not where he's goin'."

He rolled Blancanales over. Blood stained the front of his shirt, the cloth around the wounds black from muzzle-blast. Taking hold of Blancanales's collar, Jag hauled the body upright, then over his shoulder.

The man named Arch arrived with a battered Dodge pickup. Jag rolled the body into the back and covered it with a tarp. Turning, he handed a set of keys to Arch.

"This loser's truck will be out front. Go dump it somewhere. Burn the goddamn thing. Just make sure you don't leave any prints on it."

"Where you goin', Jag?" Joe Warner asked.

Jag climbed into his pickup. "I'm going to give Lawdog a burial. Where he won't be found for a long time, if ever. See you boys back at the ranch."

He fired up the engine and swung the Dodge around, heading for the highway in a cloud of dust.

Warner watched the pickup vanish. He snapped into action, rounding on the others.

"Deke, you follow Arch. When you done losing that car, head home. I better go tell Tetrow what the new boy went and done."

"You figure he's going to be upset?"

"I'll tell you later."

Militia Men HQ, Tetrow Ranch

HUBBARD TETROW listened to Warner's account of the shooting in silence. When Warner finished, Tetrow hauled his bulk out of the massive leather chair behind his desk and crossed to the tall cooler that stood against one wall of his office. He yanked open the door and reached in for a chilled can of beer. He opened it and took a swallow, pausing to stare out the wide picture window overlooking the ranch yard.

"I knew that boy had it in him the day he showed up," he said. "We could do with a few more like him round here."

"Hub, I'm not talking about his style. For Christ's sake he just axed a fuckin' Fed. Okay, ex-Fed. That ain't smart. They get peeved about that kind of thing back at Quantico. Next thing you know we'll have an FBI task force all over Liberty County. How's that going to sit with our comrades?"

"The man was out on his own, Joe. The FBI isn't going to waste time keeping tabs on a loose cannon they threw out of the job. Sounds like he was stepping on Jag's tail and did it once too often. So Jag did what he had to do."

"I still don't know," Warner grumbled.

Tetrow stared at him, a slow smile edging his mouth. "Lighten up, Joe. You're starting to sound like my old man. He was always whining about something or other. Which is why he never amounted to anything. Let the damn world trample all over him. Stood back and let the government yank his land out from under his feet and didn't do a damn thing except use a 12-gauge to blow his brains out. Day I saw him do that I knew I'd found my enemy. Bad enough what they done to this country. Took away the individual's right to think for himself. Put in their damn subversives to poison everyone's mind. Now look at the damn country. Run by a bunch of idiots in Washington who fuck up everything they touch. Drag us into wars all over the place. Let America fall apart while they go trample all over some godforsaken regime in the back of beyond and try to make them dance to Uncle Sam's tune. Time they stayed home and sorted out the mess here.

"Now they want to build this fuckin' defense setup. Radar in Alaska. Missiles all around the country. Satellites. Christ, before you know it we'll be back in another cold war. Damn Chinese and Koreans will have the excuse they need to start in building up their missiles. Russian military, too. Gives those damn hard-liners a reason for cranking up the pace. And we don't have a say in this. Washington decides and the American people have to take it like whipped pups."

Tetrow swung around, his face creased with anger. He shook his head.

"No way it's going to happen, Joe. Not while I got the Militia Men around."

"We're with you on that, Hub. You know that. I was worried Jag might have—"

"Don't you worry about Jag. Tell him I need a

word when he gets back. I'll figure this out. You see to it we got everything we need for our guests.''

Warner left Hubbard Tetrow with his thoughts.

There was an almost peaceful expression on Tetrow's face as he settled behind his desk again, leaning his solid bulk against the padded back of his chair. He swung it around and gazed out the window, deep in thought.

His mind flitted from one thing to another. He had a lot to think about at the present, what with the up-coming visit from the Russian militia group and the business that would go with it. On top of that there was the ongoing problem with the authorities. It was a battle of wits, with the cumbersome machine of the federal government moving as slow as all hell. That never changed. The Feds, with their power base in Washington, had to follow all the petty rules set down by the authorities. By the time they had the where-withal to carry out some operation, the matter was over and done with, most probably forgotten by the originator of the request. The local boys had the Feds down as a bunch of jokers, full of bullshit and about as much use as a wooden chain saw.

Tetrow saw deeper than that. He knew about the covert operations that went on behind all the fussing over the Feds. The boys in black, with their helicopters and surveillance cameras, they were the ones to watch. Running illegal ops behind the backs of every-one, the shadow squads, working directly for the President and the military, were planning and scheming, just waiting for the day when they got the order to move in. That would be a black day for America.

When the nation's real enemy showed his face, and it would come as a big surprise to some. Not Hubbard Tetrow. He'd been waiting for this for a long time. Planning and rehearsing. Readying his people. The day they came to Liberty Flats the bastards would get one hell of a surprise, as well as a bloody nose.

First off was the problem of the antimissile defense system. Information had started to come through almost a year back, and the information had the militia up in arms. Just when the international situation seemed to have calmed down, with Russia having dumped the Commies and the nuclear threat easing off, there was the U.S. government announcing it was going to start building missile sites again. The mealy-mouths in Washington tried to smooth it over by calling it a protective measure for the American people. It wasn't offensive, simply a defensive system that would only be used to destroy incoming missiles.

Bullshit!

The government was up to its old tricks again, using every twist and turn it could to hide the fact the military-industrial lobby in Washington was snapping its collective teeth and pushing to gain the advantage. Get the missile system up and running and the U.S. was back on top, able to flex its muscle and wave the big stick at the rest of the world. The federal machine was gearing up to start waving the U.S. flag again, pushing in where it wasn't wanted, just to guarantee that the American way became the way for the rest of the world. Overnight the Russians started yelling. So did the Chinese and the Koreans, who all saw the

American plan as simply a devious way of rearming themselves with nuclear missiles.

The damn fools in Washington turned a deaf ear to the unrest their acts were causing. Terrorist groups, especially in the Islamic countries, would see the move as another threat, and would step up their violent resistance to the nation they had named the Great Satan. More Americans would die as a result, slaughtered in indiscriminate terrorist attacks. Bombings, shooting, kidnapping. It would accelerate as the American missile system became a symbol of U.S. imperialism.

And did the government ever ask the American people what they wanted? Whether they wanted a ring of missiles threatening the stability of world peace? Tetrow knew the answer. No! They never had. Because if they did, the overwhelming majority of *real* Americans would tell them no. It was why decisions were made in the Capitol, away from grassroots America. Well clear of the silent, honest, hardworking Americans who had sweated and slaved to build the nation into what it had become. America didn't need a foreign policy. She was big and strong enough to exist on her own terms, without all the political, economic double-dealing that went on in secret, behind closed doors and unseen by the people.

Right now the government was playing with lives. Not foreign lives, but those of patriotic Americans who wanted nothing more than to stay home and live their lives the way the Constitution had it laid down. As free men, in a free land, able to control their own destinies by their own efforts, and not through the shadowy dealings of a government that wasn't *of the people, for the people.* If the federal authorities went ahead and built their missile system, they were inviting hostile reactions from distant nations who judged America by her actions and would see this new proliferation of missiles as an out-and-out threat. Something had to be done. It was up to ordinary, decent Americans to do something to stop it. Before it was too late and the inevitable happened. The terrible day when the missiles would be coming in from every direction, reducing America to a wasteland of radioactive ashes.

Tetrow saw nothing alarmist in that imagery. The chance of a finger hitting the button came closer every time the nuclear threat rose. Safeguards were supposed to prevent it happening, but Tetrow knew how close that day had come on more than one occasion. He had written proof of false alarms and near misses from the old cold war days. With the intended missile system American could find itself back on the edge, and this time there were enough rogue states around to make the standoff even more fragile. All it took was one group of fanatics to decide the day of reckoning was on them and the skies would be full of missiles. Once it started, the whole damn world would go button crazy, each blaming the other of treachery, while in the end the innocents would be dying in their millions.

Hubbard Tetrow had no intention of allowing that to happen. Not as long as the Militia Men were around to do something about it. They had to do something to prevent their great country from being bombed into oblivion.

The contact with the Russian group, initially made over the Internet, had made Tetrow aware that there were like-minded organizations in other countries. In Russia, despite the move to democracy, there were those in the government and the military who had the same objectives as the U.S. They didn't want the same things as the general public, and the secrecy and subterfuge in Russia was deeper than anything in America. They still had a strong grip on the public, controlling information and the media to a degree that was frightening to an American used to the overwhelming amount of media information that flooded the airwaves.

The Russian group had made it clear that it was desperate to put a stop to the U.S. missile system. If it came online, the Russian military would have the upper hand in resurrecting its own defense policy. The arms race would start up again. The Chinese and the North Koreans would take great delight in pointing the finger, saying they had been correct all along, and the Americans weren't to be trusted. It would be their way of plunging back into the missile business. The self-perpetuating monster would be reborn, shaking off his treaty restraints and opening the floodgates for all-out weapons development.

For that reason Tetrow had entered into a dialogue with the Russian group, the culmination being the upcoming historic meeting in the next few days. If things went well, Tetrow's Militia Men could very well team up with their Russian counterparts in an operation to sabotage the work on the radar installation in Alaska. It was going to be an interesting time, Tetrow thought.

He had known this day would come. A time when all the talk would be over and action was needed. The Militia Men had been created for such a confrontation. Some called them traitors, working against the legally elected government. The Militia Men wanted anarchy to overthrow the federal government and snatch back the reins. Part of that was true. Tetrow did want the government out of the way, but for the simple reason that the Washington monolith was draining the nation, stifling the inherent strength of the American people and turning them into obedient drones who danced to their federal jig. America, once the proud bastion of individual freedom, true democracy and the right of the people to set their own goals, had become a soft, listless organism. Washington set the rules and had slowly stolen the American backbone from its citizens.

Political correctness had even denied the right of people to speak their mind. Now the thought police listened and pounced on hapless individuals because they used the wrong phrase or the outlawed name. The woolly liberals, the do-gooders, the self-appointed counselors had the nation in its grip, slowly turning America into a like-minded, like-thinking marshmallow monster. It was happening, but most people were already so far into the mire they couldn't see it.

The Militia Men knew what was happening, and they weren't going to stand back and watch it happen.

There was too much at stake. In fact the whole damn country was at stake. It didn't need enemies beyond the borders. America was creating its own destruction, turning in on itself. The death was by strangulation. Slow, maybe, but certain to happen unless someone blew the wake-up call and put the country back on the right track.

Ringing the country with missiles that were controlled by satellites in space was like painting a huge target across the land and inviting every loose cannon in the world to take a shot. It would happen, as sure as day followed night, Tetrow saw.

The crazies were running the country. It was time to hand things back to the sane. The government went right ahead and initiated its wild schemes without as much as asking the American people if they sanctioned it. That was wrong. The American people had a right to know what was being created in their name, and there had to be good reason to bypass them. Tetrow thought about that and changed his mind.

There *was* no good reason for what was being planned. America didn't need to continue its worldwide role. It was time the government concentrated on the problems at home. Let the rest of the damn world go about its business. There was enough here to keep them busy. Who the hell appreciated it anyway? No one. The minute the U.S. reached out to help, someone, somewhere would start whining. As far as Tetrow was concerned the rest of the world could go to hell. The battle was here, and it was time something was done about it.

He knew what was going on. Involve America in

trouble abroad and take the minds of the people off homegrown problems. Distracted them so that they didn't notice the happenings in their own backyard. Like the move to disarm the American people. The antigun lobby was hard at work, using shadowy tactics to take away the right to bear arms. To say to Americans, "You have too many guns. We'll take them and decide who should have them." That was all bullshit. Once they had the weapons, they had the country at their mercy. More than ever the government would be able to call the tune, and slowly the God-given rights of ordinary citizens would be stolen right from under their noses.

Just the thought enraged Tetrow. There was no way the American people would allow that to happen. So they had to fight back. Show the government that ordinary citizens were united in their refusal to let it happen.

First on the list was the missile system, with its radar and satellites, making America a target for every nut with a grudge. It wasn't needed, and the Militia Men were going to be on the front line to show just what could be done. There was no way the project could be allowed to reach completion. All it would do was harm the current manageable peace throughout the world. The dominoes would start to fall once the project went online, and missile threats would be coming in from every nation capable of mounting its own programs. Paranoia would run riot as the imagined scenarios grew bigger and wilder by the day. Gun control in America would pale into insignificance against the return of global meltdown. The military hawks would be rubbing their sweaty palms together as they envisaged secure futures for their careers. The military-industrial complex would be back in business, and the ordinary citizens of America would start looking to the skies once again, wondering when it might start to rain destruction on their heads.

But at least there was a solution. Drastic, maybe. That didn't worry Tetrow. His mission was risky. It would probably cost the Militia Men dearly. But they all loved their country to a man, the hell with what the others might think. They were true Americans. Patriots. And every man of them was willing to go that extra mile to prove it.

TETROW HAD CALMED a little by the time Jag arrived back at the ranch. He even managed a smile when the man was shown into his office.

"Story goes you did a little housecleaning earlier today," Tetrow said.

"It was something needed doing. The guy was like a damn shadow walker. Every time I looked around he was there. I didn't want him poking around here."

Tetrow offered Jag a drink, then sat down behind his desk.

"So what's the story with Rimmer and you?" Tetrow asked.

"Ex-story," he said. "Remember I just took care of it."

"Humor me."

"Ever since Rimmer got on my case about four years back he never let go. Every time I turned around he was there. The guy made me his mission in life. Got so he was falling behind on his other cases, so the FBI hauled him in and chewed his ass off. Problem was, it just made him more determined to prove he was right. In the end I hired a lawyer to go to the Bureau. Harassment. Denial of personal liberty, all that crap. It worked, though. Rimmer was given an ultimatum. Let go or he was out of the FBI. He wouldn't let go, so they fired him. Took away his badge and his gun. He took a half pension, and still wouldn't leave me alone."

"Jag, why did this guy have such a hard-on for you? What did he think you'd done?"

"He had me down for a couple of heavy bombings on federal buildings. One in San Francisco and one in Boston."

"They the ones about five years back?"

Jag nodded. "Rimmer was certain sure I did it, but he couldn't prove it. And that was what stuck in his craw. He just didn't like the fact I was walkin' around guilty as all hell and there wasn't a thing he could do about it."

"So did you do them?" Tetrow asked.

"Hell, yes, I did them. And Rimmer knew it. But he couldn't prove a damn thing. What got to him was knowing I was guilty and not being able to touch me. I guess I would have felt the same in his position."

"Son of a bitch, Jag." Tetrow grinned. "I like it."

Jag raised his bottle. "Here's one for old Rimmer and a kick up the ass for the Feds. It's time we did something to show those Washington high rollers who really runs this country. Jesus, we need to do something to make them take notice.''

''Don't you fret about that, boy, 'cause we're going to do something real soon that's going to rattle their goddamn cages all the way up the fuckin' Potomac.''

''Sounds interesting,'' Jag said.

Tetrow studied the blond man, considering his next words. Before he asked what was on his mind he leaned forward and fixed Jag with a steady eye.

''Why the Militia Men, Jag?''

''No other choice. I read your manifesto on the Internet. You had the guts to say what a lot of people only think. And you make sense. Time this country saw what's really going on. I been around. Seen a lot and done a lot. This country is being screwed by the government, but the people don't see it. Too busy making their money and enjoying life. Ain't nothing wrong there. Free country and all. Trouble is, they don't see what it's costing them. Life's too easy. Too comfortable. Nobody wants to rock the boat, Hub. They're all happy just to let the government run the country as long as it doesn't stop them watching TV and eating a take-out pizza. They need to be shown what's really happening. From where I stand the Militia Men are the ones to do it.''

''Boy, you talk some. Sure you ain't a fuckin' politician?''

''Steady, Hub, I can take a joke with the best, but that doesn't even come close to being funny.''

''I was born and raised in this country. Seen good and bad times. No shit, Jag, I tried to live my life straight and honest. Makes me want to cry when I see what's being done to this country. Lot of folk have forgotten how this nation started out. Built from the dirt up by folk who wanted nothing more than a chance to live free. They broke their backs doing it. Worked themselves until they dropped. Laid the foundations for what we got today. They came here from all over the damn world, looking for the end of the rainbow. They fought and died for it. Stood up for what they believed in. This country has started to forget that. I ain't, Jag, and I never will. Day we do, this country is on its way to hell in a handbasket.''

Tetrow pushed up out of his chair and crossed to a filing cabinet. He opened a drawer and took out a thick file. Returning to his desk, he opened the file and laid it out in front of Jag.

"This is what we got to deal with, Jag."

The file comprised copies of government data. There were stamps on the sheets, declaring that the information was classified. Top secret. Sensitive. There were photographs, schematics, drawings. Every item showed the same logo—Project: Slingshot.

"You didn't pick this stuff up from the Internet," Jag said.

"Not everyone in Washington is a brainwashed federal kiss-ass," Tetrow said by way of explanation.

"This is good," Jag said as he read through the file. "Christ, it points the way, Hub."

"Don't it just."

"Going to take some planning."

"We're already into that. And we got help flying in tomorrow. You see, we got friends abroad with feelings similar to ours who want to help. Maybe soon you can meet them, Jag.''

''It's what I joined up for.''

Tetrow held out a powerful hand and shook Jag's.

''Welcome to the club.'' he said. ''You want another beer?''

He crossed to the cooler and took out a couple of fresh bottles. After taking a long swallow, Tetrow raised the bottle in a salute to the latest member of the Militia Men.

Acknowledging the gesture, the new recruit drank from his own bottle. The way things were going, he would probably need a couple more before the day was out.

Although Hubbard Tetrow knew him as Jag, his real name was Carl Lyons, leader of Stony Man's Able Team.

CHAPTER ONE

"You want to kick this off?" Hal Brognola asked Barbara Price.

Price nodded.

"I'll make this as easy as I can," she said. "For the past three weeks Carl has been working undercover. His mission has been to infiltrate a right-wing group called the Militia Men."

She used a hand control to bring up an image on one of the monitor screens set in the wall.

"That's Hubbard Tetrow," Gary Manning said. "I'd recognize that face anywhere."

"As long as it isn't behind the barrel of a gun," Rafael Encizo said.

"Tetrow is well-known for his opposition to the government and anyone belonging to organizations that work for, or are in any way connected to the federal authorities," Price added. "He's smart and slippery. Always a step ahead. His views are extreme. He makes no bones about his dislike of the government and blames it for every ill that strikes the U.S.

His claim is that he's a patriot and his intentions are to protect the American homeland from federal interference and the stupidity of Washington's expansionist policies."

"Sounds as if that came from the Militia Men charter," Manning said.

"Militia Men Web page actually," Price informed him.

"Nuts on the Net," Manning murmured. "So what have the Militia Men done that puts them under our spotlight?"

"Standard surveillance of the Militia Men by the ATF some weeks ago fed this into the intelligence system."

Price brought another image to the screen. A shot of three men standing beside a parked car in an isolated lot.

"Two of the men are militia," Price said. "The third man is the important one here. His name is Paul Curtis. Civilian employee in the Department of Defense. He's an analyst. Works on predicting the performance of high-spec equipment allied to missile systems. His current assignment is working on the Slingshot project."

"The same Slingshot the late Colonel Li Cheng tried to duplicate?" Encizo asked.

"Yes. What we are talking about here is the second phase of that project," Price said. "If you recall, the initial missile tests in the project didn't rack up much of an impression. There was a lot of shouting in Congress about money being wasted on a project that was dead in the water. Public polls showed that there wasn't a great deal of favor toward it.''

"Wasn't the project put on the back burner?'' Encizo queried.

"Officially, yes,'' Brognola said. "In reality the President stuck out for keeping the project, but in a slightly different form.''

"It was discovered recently that the North Koreans have an advanced missile program under development,'' Price explained. "Top secret, but one of our deep-cover agents, based in North Korea, smuggled out information. Not as detailed as we would like, but we can't blame the guy on the ground for that. Not after he died getting the stuff to us. His body was found in a back alley in Hong Kong three days after we received the information.''

"What was in the message?'' Manning asked.

"It isn't the fact that the missiles are under development,'' Price stated. "It's no secret the Koreans have a continuous program under way. It's just that they appear to have been working on some cloaking technology that will hide the warheads from surveillance.''

"These are Koreans we're talking about,'' McCarter said, "not Klingons.''

"Until we get additional details, we can only guess,'' Price admitted. "Military analysts are thinking along the lines of stealth bomber technology. The theory exists. If you can hide a missile from radar, it would be one hell of a big step forward.''

Brognola tapped the file in front of him. "I had a meeting with the President this morning. We both agree that this new strategy could leave us with egg on faces as far as the antimissile project is concerned.''

''Slingshot is supposed to be how we counter incoming missiles,'' Encizo said. ''So why the worry?''

Brognola picked up a phone and punched in a number. ''Aaron, you ready to join us now? Five minutes. Fine.''

Let's take a break, people,'' Brognola said, pushing away from the table.

Price and McCarter joined at the coffee station. While the big Fed and Price helped themselves, the Briton turned to the minifridge and helped himself to a bottle of Coke Classic. He rejoined them, taking a swallow from the frosted bottle.

''Hal, this undercover mission Carl is on. Can he keep in touch?''

Brognola frowned. McCarter had asked one of the questions he didn't have comforting answers for.

''We know he was fine three days ago, which was the first contact we'd had with him for over a week. Since then, nothing.''

''How did he contact you?'' McCarter asked.

''By 9 mm bullet,'' someone said behind him.

McCarter turned.

''He shot me with a couple,'' Rosario Blancanales stated.

''Will somebody explain all this bloody nonsense?'' McCarter demanded.

Blancanales and Schwarz had entered the War Room together. After helping themselves to coffee, they joined the others at the table.

"I saw Carl at the Shanty Bar," Blancanales explained. "It's a meeting place for the Militia Men in Liberty Flats."

"Carl had joined the Militia Men, using the cover role we devised for him," Price said. "They know him as Jag. According to the details we put on nationwide police and federal computer networks, Jag is a suspected bomber with a heavy background. We gave him a profile as a loner who hates all kinds of authority."

McCarter chuckled at that. "Pretty much like he really is, then."

Price gave him a stern look that immediately shut up the feisty Briton. He suddenly became very interested in his bottle of Coke.

"We knew Hubbard Tetrow would have Carl checked out, so we did as much as we could to make his cover believable," Price continued. "It needed something physical to show Jag's personality. Pol came up with the idea of having someone show up to put Jag on the spot. So we invented ex-FBI Agent Rimmer."

"I'd been dogging Jag against FBI orders. In the end they fired me, but I still kept following him around, trying to prove him guilty on a couple of bombing charges. I turn up at the Shanty Bar and we have words. We go outside and Jag pulls a gun and drops me. Then he puts me in his truck and buries me where no one will ever find me. And all in front of his Militia Men buddies."

"And you call me crazy," McCarter said. "How did you pull it off?"

"I wore a vest fitted with blood bags. Carl used blanks and the imagination did the rest. It happened so fast none of them figured to question it. Carl used the moment to take charge. Get *them* doing things while he dumped me in the back of his truck. He drove away fast, took a route we'd worked out previously and I hid out for a few hours to give him time to get back to Tetrow's HQ. Later on Jack picked me up and choppered me away."

"Only now you can't get back in touch with Carl?" Manning asked.

Brognola shook his head. "That was an agreed part of the cover right from the start. We couldn't risk anything that might weaken Carl's story. No wires. No tracers. He went in on his own."

"It was the way he wanted it," Hermann "Gadgets" Schwarz said. "Carl accepted it was the hard way to do it, but to maintain credibility he had to be on his own."

"The Militia Men are up to something. The only way we can be up to the minute is to have someone on the inside," Brognola said. "Since he joined up, Carl managed to telephone twice. We have to wait until he does it again. If he's convinced Tetrow, he might be allowed in on whatever they're planning."

"A lot of bloody ifs in there," McCarter said. "Well, I always said that bloke was mad. Now he's gone and proved it. I hope I get the chance to shake his hand and tell him to his face."

Schwarz grinned. "I think he did it just to get away from Pol and me."

The door opened and Aaron Kurtzman rolled his

wheelchair into the room. Behind him was Yakov Katzenelenbogen, the former leader of Phoenix Force. Since his retirement from the field the Israeli had accepted a position as the Farm's tactical advisor, where his years of intelligence and combat experience were proving invaluable to the SOG.

Kurtzman wheeled his chair to his usual position, giving him access to the panel that controlled video and computer input. He busied himself keying in the commands that would bring up the information he had been preparing. In the meantime Katz helped himself to coffee, poured one for Kurtzman and placed it beside him. Moving around the table, Katz seated himself next to Barbara Price. McCarter noticed this and attracted Katz's attention.

"There's an empty chair next to me," he said. "How is it you always sit next to Barbara?"

Katz raised his head to stare at the Briton, a slow smile edging his lips, as he looked his way, then slowly turned to the young woman.

"Did he really ask that question, my dear?"

Price nodded. "He just doesn't understand."

"You people ready?" Kurtzman asked.

"Go ahead," McCarter said.

Kurtzman activated his monitor, giving a running commentary as the simulation played.

"The concept of the stealth application is nothing new. What we're actually talking about is camouflage. A means of hiding something you don't want the enemy to see. It's been going on since conflicts began. Now it's extending itself to another role. First the stealth aircraft, now the missile that can't be picked up by the target defense. This was bound to come. Once development of antimissiles had been perfected, it meant that surprise attack started down the road to being redundant. So the next logical step was to make the missiles invisible to the enemy radar.''

"This is what the Koreans have been working on?" Blancanales asked.

"Looks that way," the computer expert said. "As of this moment, we can't be certain just how far down the road they are, but we have to look at it from a military point of view. Which is why Slingshot is an important part of future U.S. defense."

"Slingshot has changed, though?" James said.

Kurtzman nodded. "It appears that from the word go Slingshot was conceived to be ongoing, changing with the defense needs of the moment. If requirements demanded a drastic alteration in the concept, then Slingshot could be made to fit the new specification without a great deal of downtime."

"Sounds impressive," Hawkins stated.

"Believe me it is," Brognola said. "I was given the chance to look at the simulation planning. The President is worried that because of recent intelligence feedback we've had, the overall security surrounding Slingshot may have been compromised. Part of it goes back to our late comrade Colonel Li Cheng. When you broke up his offshore base and took him out, it appears that certain information wasn't recovered. The computer disks you picked up had eighty percent of the stolen data on them, but our analysts realized that encoded data wasn't present."

"And this had to do with the next stage of the Slingshot project?" McCarter asked.

"That's right," Price said. "One of the Chinese who copied the original information included it. He might not even have been aware of its importance. It was only when our people did a full check into the computer system that they found this section had been copied. It seems they have a program built in that can record and store what has been copied."

"That's okay, then," Manning said. "As long as we know it's been stolen, there's nothing to worry about."

"I hope you're not about to tell us the China mission was all a bloody waste of time because we're no better off," McCarter said.

"David, the China mission achieved its purpose. The result was what we expected. This new problem is only connected because of the new direction of Slingshot. No other reason, so don't go thinking you didn't achieve mission priority."

"Why don't we let Aaron complete his briefing, then we can discuss the upcoming mission, give ourselves a little breathing space," Katz suggested.

"Go on, Aaron," Brognola said.

"We need the radar system in Alaska because it's an important part of the Slingshot setup. It receives signals from an orbiting satellite sensor cluster. The exact number hasn't been decided on yet, but it could possibly run to fifty or so. These would be linked to the ground-based radar, orbiting analyzer satellites and finally missile launch."

"And how far has this project got?" Manning

asked. "Are we talking actual hardware, or just a paper project?"

Brognola interrupted. "Aaron can't answer that."

"Can you?" McCarter asked.

"Satellites are already in position. The President gave the okay for the deployment some months ago. It was kept out of the public eye and the media, for obvious reasons. Three weeks ago a simulation was made and the result was exceptional. Based on that the President has sanctioned the second phase."

There was a hush in the room as the information was absorbed. Glances were exchanged. No one spoke for a while. Kurtzman brought up some more screen images on the monitor.

"This was released to us by the President. It's a detailed mock-up of the way the system works. Just to give you guys an idea of the scope of Slingshot."

They watched in silence as the digital simulation, interspersed with actual footage, followed the launch, radar pickup and satellite coordination. Once the threat of the missile had been encoded the satellite interceptor locked on, passed the information to a ground-defense system that in turn activated and fired the interceptor missile. The simulation ended with the destruction of the enemy missile during its rising arc and well before it reached its target path.

"That's how it *should* work," Kurtzman said. He switched off the monitor. "The problem is that we don't know what information Paul Curtis has passed to his contacts in the Militia Men."

"How much would he know about the system?" Katz asked. "If it's as hush-hush as you suggest, just how many people would be privy to the level we've just seen?''

''Hard to say,'' Brognola admitted. ''With a project as complex as Slingshot, it can't be completed without a fair number of people being advised.''

''This is getting us nowhere,'' McCarter snapped, his exasperation breaking through. ''All I can see is another bloody mess brewing because Washington can't keep its people under control. And as usual we have to go chasing all over the bloody place cleaning it up.''

Brognola cleared his throat. ''David has clarified the situation with his usual erudition. I hate to say it, but he's just about right. The debate over the rights and wrongs of new missile programs is going to be with us as long as there are missiles.'' Brognola said. ''Each country wants its own way. The various agreements and pacts to control future missile development and deployment were fine at the time. Due to the current state of global threats, the U.S. administration has deemed it the right time to concentrate on defending ourselves. And the minute you start doing that, the whole damn world starts shouting foul.''

''It's a no-win situation,'' Katz added. ''If you compromise to satisfy one party, there will always be a second one saying he's being discriminated against. In the end every nation state has to look to the safety of its own people and infrastructure. Do nothing you could be caught napping, if the day came. Arm yourself and you are branded a warmonger, just waiting for the right moment to shower the world with nuclear missiles.''

"And no middle ground." Manning said. "Make a stand for one or the other you still end up the bad guy."

"So where do *we* stand?" McCarter asked.

"Where we always stand," Brognola said. "Out in the open with every opposing side using us as the damn target."

"We need to neutralize all these factions," Price said. "The Militia Men, and this Russian group because we just don't know what their plans are. But you can bet your pension it isn't going to be good for us. If we have the Chinese and the Koreans to deal with, as well, this could turn out to be a difficult time for the project."

"Able can look into the stateside implications for the moment. We have to let Carl run with Hubbard's group because there isn't a great deal we can do to help until he makes contact," Brognola added. "Let's hope he makes that sooner rather than later."

"Amen to that," Schwarz said.

"Aaron will provide any technical detail you need," Price said. "I've put information in these packs for you. Everything we have on the people we've identified. There may be others we don't know about yet. We may not until you come across them in the field."

"What about this Paul Curtis?" James asked. "Is he still on the loose, or have the authorities pulled him in yet?"

"We decided to let him run for the moment," Brognola replied. "If we haul him off the streets now, it could alarm his contacts. They could pull back into deep cover and change their plans. Or vanish and we might lose all contact. He's being closely watched, and at present his work detail is being edged away from the highly confidential work he previously handled.''

"Isn't that going to make him suspicious?" Manning asked.

"Maybe, maybe not," Brognola said. "It's the best compromise we could come up with in the short term."

One of the telephones rang. Brognola picked it up, accepted the call and listened for a moment before indicating to McCarter that he should pick up his own extension.

"Mei Anna for you," the big Fed said. "Calling from London."

McCarter identified himself and heard Mei Anna's voice. At any other time he would have welcomed a call from her, but the subject of her message did nothing to ease his mood.

"Listen, Anna. Don't do anything. Stay out of sight until you hear from me again. I'll get to you as quickly as I can. Right now I'm out of the country."

McCarter replaced the handset.

"Shun Wei is making some deal with the Russians and the Koreans according to Anna. Part of it is to do with the Slingshot project. Hal, we need to talk to her soon."

Brognola glanced across at Katz. The Israeli had been taking in everything being said. He gave the briefest of nods in the big Fed's direction.

"Mei Anna gave us a lot of help during the previous mission. She knows Shun Wei and her contacts in Asia are better than ours. If there's the remotest chance she can help, we'd be foolish to ignore her.''

Mei Anna and her group, resisting the hard control of the Chinese authorities, had joined up with Phoenix Force during their mission to locate and destroy the island complex of the late Colonel Li Cheng. Using stolen U.S. technology, the man had created a duplicate of the American missile-control facility and been intending to use it to neutralize the initial Slingshot system. Although the mission had been a success, with the complex destroyed and Li Cheng dead, his mistress, a ruthless, ambitious Chinese woman named Shun Wei, had escaped. It appeared now that she had taken some of the computerized data on the Slingshot system and was making her own deals.

''Barbara, make the arrangements,'' Brognola said. ''See if you can get the guys on a military flight to the UK. That way they can at least go in armed. David, how many?''

''I'll take Cal and T.J. Gary and Rafe can liaise with Aaron and pick up all the information they can on the mission brief.''

Price pushed to her feet and turned to leave the room. ''I'll get right on to fixing your flight, guys.''

Brognola nodded. ''Okay, people, let's go. Looks like we have our orders.''

CHAPTER TWO

London

Time and place always mattered, McCarter thought. Especially when the person you were going to meet was someone special. The importance was in the memory that would linger long after the actual meeting. And when the person being contacted was Mei Anna, the memory would be extra special. McCarter hadn't seen the young woman since their frantic dealings with the late Colonel Cheng. Not since they had finally parted at the end of the mission, McCarter returning to Stony Man and Anna taking up her self-imposed struggle against the repressive actions of the Chinese government. Anna's subversive struggles were fired by a deep-seated sense of justice and a need to right the wrongs being inflicted on her people. In her heart she knew the enormity of her battle. It made no difference. Mei Anna had the will to wage her war, and she would continue her efforts no matter what the personal cost. The stubbornness of the aging and isolated men of power in Beijing holding on through fear of change was the only glimmer of possible victory. That alone was enough to spur Mei Anna on.

The call that had reached McCarter, rerouted via Stony Man had been both pleasant and a surprise. Anna's brief words had made him aware of the urgency, and the risk, and Stony Man had pulled out all the stops to get McCarter, James and Hawkins to London.

In the early morning, south of the Thames, mist still hovered over the water that lapped against the damp pillars of the bridges. The traffic was thin, only a brief couple of hours away from the congestion of the rush hour.

McCarter had parked his car and locked it. He stepped away from the curb and crossed the street, zipping his leather jacket against the chill. On the corner was a café, windows steamed from the heat of cooking and boiling water. McCarter pushed open the door and went inside. The place was starting to fill up. Workmen sat at crowded tables, busy with their breakfasts, plates of bacon, eggs, sausage, thick slices of bread, mugs of scalding tea. They ate, some smoking the first of many cigarettes as they read the morning papers and digested the latest tabloid sensation. The smell of the food hit McCarter's nostrils as he paused to check the place over. It was something he missed when he was away from England. The hell with unhealthy diets. The rich smell of good bacon and eggs always got to him.

He saw Mei Anna almost immediately. She was at a table near the window, her back to the wall, below a poster advertising a pop concert. She wore dark pants and a light roll-neck sweater under a suede jacket. Her black hair lay soft and thick against her shoulders. She caught his stare and nodded briefly. McCarter joined her after ordering himself a mug of tea. He spooned in milk and sugar, carried the mug and crossed to sit facing her.

"Hello, Clancy," she said, using the cover name he had gone under during the earlier mission.

McCarter grinned. "You'll never let me live that down."

"I may forgive you one day," she said, reaching out to lay a slim hand over his. "You look well."

"You look..." McCarter paused, then his honest nature took over. "Anna, you look like you haven't slept for days."

"And they say the British are not romantic." Mei let her shoulders slump a little. "Actually I think it's more like weeks. Do I look that bad?"

He studied the dark smudges under her eyes. The strain was etched into her lovely features.

"What have you been up to?"

"Shun Wei is alive and still working for the Chinese government. It appears we failed to destroy all the data Li Cheng had. Shun Wei is using it to promote a project to destroy the American antimissile system that none of us are supposed to know about. You know which one I'm talking about?"

McCarter nodded. "It isn't exactly a big secret. The Russians don't want it, and the Chinese and the Koreans have been making threatening noises."

"Behind the scenes they're doing more than make noises. My group intercepted information being passed between Shun Wei and interested parties. They're cooperating on some scheme to sabotage the radar facility to be built in Alaska.''

"How the bloody hell did you get all this, Anna?''

She smiled. "Lots of skulking around. Following Shun Wei from China to Russia. Siberia to be exact. It wasn't much fun.''

Mei leaned over and picked up a leather file. She unzipped it and took out a number of photographs, which she spread on the table.

"Shun Wei. Talking with some Russians. We haven't identified them yet, but the way they acted made me believe they were ex-military. Now this one has Shun Wei at a meeting with an American.''

"Where was this taken?'' McCarter asked.

"Khabarovsk. Why? Is there something you know?''

McCarter tapped the image of the American. "I've seen his face before. Rick...something. Rick Teeler. He's second in command of the Militia Men. It's one of those crazy American organizations that believe the U.S. federal government is out to get them. They call themselves true patriots. The real Americans. They live out in the isolated back country and have weapons and survivalist supplies stashed away. They train and wait for the day the country goes down the drain.''

Mei made a face. "They sound weird.''

"They believe in what they're doing. I can't fault them for that. But conspiracy theories and secret black ops being waged against them make them look paranoid. The trouble is, a lot of Americans have sympathy with them. Especially in the isolated rural areas.''

''Are they a threat?''

''They would be if they amalgamated. But they tend to stay in their own little groups. Each cell goes its own way, has its own grievances and every top dog wants to stay in charge of his own bunch.''

''So what are the Militia Men doing in Russia, talking to Shun Wei and ex-military Soviets?''

McCarter took a long swallow of tea. ''Adding it all up, I'd guess they're tied in with this sabotage attempt on the Alaskan radar site.''

Mei showed him a batch of written reports she had compiled. She explained that the data had come from a number of sources sympathetic to her struggle, including a contact in Siberia, and she hadn't yet been able to analyze it all. A low buzzing caught McCarter's attention. He reached into a pocket and pulled out a compact transceiver. He activated the unit and put it to his ear.

''What?''

''You're being watched, and if I'm not mistaken, overheard, as well. A car parked across the street has a probe poking out of a rear window in your direction. Probably a parabolic mike. Okay?''

''Right,'' McCarter said, then broke the connection.

''You ready to go now?'' he asked Mei.

She placed the photographs and papers back in her file and closed it. They made their way out of the café and walked to where McCarter had parked. He unlocked the car and they got in. The Briton started the engine and put the car in gear. He eased away from the sidewalk and drove off, keeping well within the speed limit.

Mei Anna stirred restlessly in her seat, glancing across at McCarter, then out the window.

Before they turned the first corner, McCarter spotted the car following them. It was a big, heavy Bentley, some years old but built like a tank, and it would have a powerful engine under the hood. He grinned. The Bentley was a class car. It was for comfortable driving at sustained speeds, but it was no pursuit car and it wouldn't have the performance of the powerful Rover he was driving.

"Looks like some of your fans have followed you."

Mei took the news badly, frowning as she twisted in her seat and studied the car trailing them.

"I can't believe I let this happen."

"Nobody's perfect. Let's hope they haven't realized *they're* being followed."

McCarter eased the car through the quiet streets, making his way toward the river and the road that ran parallel to it. He knew the area well, and used his knowledge to take them into an area where residential streets gave way to industrial drabness. There were deserted buildings, where business had closed down, and the warehouses and storage facilities were dark and empty.

Checking his mirror, McCarter saw that the tail car was still with them. He couldn't see T. J. Hawkins and Calvin James's car, but he knew they were somewhere close by, staying out of sight until the right moment.

"Can you lose them?"

McCarter shrugged. "I can try."

The tail car suddenly accelerated, the driver deciding he didn't want to spend any more time racing through the streets. The vehicle surged forward and cut recklessly alongside the Rover. Without any warning it swung in and broadsided the Rover, pushing it across the sidewalk and against the brick wall of a warehouse they were passing. Paint was burned away by the friction and a trail of sparks erupted along the side of McCarter's vehicle. The tail car eased away, then swung in again, pushing McCarter back against the wall. He fought the jerking wheel.

"*Bloody...*" McCarter began, and then abruptly stamped down on the brake. The Rover reduced speed with a vengeance and the tail car shot ahead. Swinging the steering wheel, the Briton came up behind the tail car, rammed his foot on the gas pedal and slammed the rear end. He dropped back, then repeated the action. Rear lights shattered.

"*David!*" Mei yelled in warning as she saw a man's head and shoulders emerge from one of the rear windows. He held a gun and began to trigger shots at the Rover. The windshield cracked.

McCarter hauled on the wheel, braking, and let his vehicle slow. In his rearview mirror he saw Hawkins and James bearing down on them fast. Their car shot past him, swinging wide. James leaned out the passenger window and opened fire with his autopistol. He put half a magazine into the tail car, concentrating on the rear window and the rear wheel on his side. One of his 9 mm slugs hit the tire, which blew with a misty eruption. The tail car slewed off track, curved across the road and bounced up onto the sidewalk. The front end hit a wall, bouncing the car back onto the road, trailing debris in its wake. A tire burst, and the Bentley skidded sideways, hit the sidewalk again and slammed full on into the wall. Brick crumpled and showered the front of the car, bringing it to a shuddering halt.

Both Phoenix Force cars came to a rocking stop. They piled out, guns ready, and came up on the rear of the tail car. One of the rear doors was kicked open and an armed Chinese man scrambled out. He stumbled to his knees, catching his balance as he spotted the three men approaching him. He didn't hesitate, bringing his handgun into target acquisition.

Hawkins and McCarter fired simultaneously, their combined volley kicking the man back against the side of the car. He rolled against the bodywork, arms flailing, blood beginning to stain the front of his shirt where his jacket gaped open. He dropped to the ground without a sound.

James moved closer to the car. He spotted the driver fumbling with something below the level of the front door, and was ready as the Chinese rose and leveled his weapon. The Phoenix Force Warrior didn't hesitate. He fired twice, placing his slugs in the man's chest, directly over his heart. The guy flopped back, slumping half across the passenger seat.

"This is becoming a habit," Hawkins said as he

nodded in Mei Anna's direction. "Is it going to happen every time we meet?"

She smiled. "I could say the same about you. However, I suggest we get away from here before we have to answer any awkward questions."

"Not a bad idea," McCarter said. "T.J., bring my car. I'll take Anna with me."

Hawkins nodded and headed for the damaged Rover.

McCarter took hold of the woman's arm and hurried her toward the car James was driving. James turned the vehicle and drove away from the scene, taking a number of side streets and alleys at McCarter's suggestion until they were well away from the area.

In the rear of the car the Briton studied Mei's face. She was pressed hard against the seat back, clutching the file to her chest. He knew the young woman as being competent and tough, but there was a look in her eyes that suggested she was concerned about something.

"Anna, you want to tell me what's worrying you?"

She hesitated, looking away from him for a moment, almost as if she had a guilty secret. Then her honesty took over and she lifted her head and looked McCarter in the eye.

"The day I left for the UK one of my people called and told me they were being watched. They told me they would lead their watchers away from me. I haven't been able to contact any of them since. You know what Shun Wei is like. I'm worried about my people."

"From what I remember they were pretty good at looking after themselves," McCarter said. "Anna, you can't carry it all around with you."

She smiled. "I suppose you're right. But it is hard not to worry."

They took one of the bridges and drove back into the center of London, McCarter guiding James.

"We'll go to our hotel," McCarter suggested. "If these jokers have Anna spotted, they'll probably have hers staked out."

ONCE THEY WERE safely located at the hotel, the cars parked in the basement lot, McCarter made a call to Stony Man Farm, using his cell phone and the secure satellite connection they were able to access.

"Take down this license number," he said to Barbara Price when she came on the line. "It's a UK license plate, but the Bear should be able to hack into the database. I'm guessing it'll turn out to belong to the Chinese embassy here in London."

"Any breaks yet?"

"You could say that," McCarter replied.

"Will Hal want to know?"

"He'll need to know. Whether he'll like what he hears is another matter."

"That kind of news, huh?"

"That kind."

"Be in touch when we have something."

McCarter put down the phone. He turned in time to see Mei approaching, a cup of tea in her slim hand. He took it and sat down, facing her, noticing that her hand shook a little.

"Can I tell you something?" she asked.

McCarter sensed her unease. He placed the cup on the small side table, reaching out to take her hand, pulling her down beside him on the couch.

"What is it?"

She stared around her, taking in the comfortable furnishings and the quiet that pervaded the room. When she turned back to look at McCarter, he saw the gleam of tears in her lovely eyes.

"I don't feel like chasing any more dragons," she said in a quiet voice. "I'm just so tired, David. I don't want to be, but I can't fight it any longer. Living on the run. Hiding in the shadows. Never knowing who to trust. Only seeing the bad in people and places." She stared into his eyes. "Tell me I'm being a selfish, weak woman."

"Never," McCarter told her. "I know you too well, Anna. I've seen you take on things men couldn't handle. So don't beg forgiveness when there's no need. Bloody hell, girl, if anyone deserves time off for good behavior, it's you."

"Do you know what I'd like, David? Somewhere away from everything. A nice, peaceful place. Just for a while. Until I can get myself back into shape."

"Maybe I can fix something," McCarter said. "Why don't you go and take a long soak, then use the bed. I need to have a little chat with my partners about the mission."

"Are you sure it's all right?"

"Have I ever lied to you?"

She smiled, and McCarter sensed even that was an effort. He left her running a bath and made his way to meet James and Hawkins. They were both in Hawkins's room, studying the file Mei Anna had given them.

"Where's Anna?" Hawkins asked.

McCarter told them what she had explained to him.

"Next time you see her don't make a fuss. Crazy thing is, she feels she's letting everyone down. But I'm worried about her. She's exhausted."

"I'm not surprised," James said. "That lady has pushed herself over the limit. And we owe her big time."

"I'll have a talk with base. See what they can do for her," McCarter said. He turned to the papers spread out across the table. "What have we got here?"

"Some interesting stuff," Hawkins replied.

He spread photographs and written sheets across the table, indicating items.

"This one came in from some guy named Kranski. He must have some distant connection with Anna, because he mentions Shun Wei and her meetings with a dude called Malinchek. Now Kranski must have done some traveling, because he has details of a location somewhere in Siberia. Indicates it has importance concerning Shun Wei and her Russian friends."

Hawkins searched for a particular sheet, scanning it until he was certain of his facts. He passed it to McCarter.

"What am I looking at here, T.J.?"

"I figure they're some kind of map locations," Hawkins stated. "Here and here? Longitude and latitude?"

"The boy ain't wrong," James said, peering over McCarter's shoulder. "Where the hell did this guy Kranski pick this up?"

"His report said he was in Siberia," McCarter said. "And if my geography is correct, Siberia is the closest place in Russia to bloody Alaska."

"So they have something going on in Siberia we need to see?" Hawkins asked.

"Let's give Aaron and his team a chance to check these coordinates out," McCarter said. "Have them use one of the surveillance satellites to scan the area. See what it comes up with. What do we have to lose?"

Stony Man Farm, Virginia

"ALL RIGHT, people, we have work to do," Kurtzman called.

Huntington Wethers had already opened a connection and was checking availability. His search IDed two satellites capable of a search sweep over Siberia.

"We have one coming up in a half hour. The next is two hours away."

"Give me the best bird," Kurtzman said.

"I'd go for number two. Canadian SAR satellite. It has the right orbit for our needs. We'll need something that will give us a good image in poor weather conditions. SAR can do it."

The Canadian satellite, working on C-band technology, was a versatile piece of equipment. It used a 5.6 cm wavelength that bounced an image back to the satellite sensor. The returned image was an active signal, and the SAR method showed a detailed, contoured picture. The microwave signals were able to easily penetrate mist, prevailing weather conditions and give an accurate image of the terrain below.

"I've seen images from the SAR before," Kurtzman said. "It should do what we want. We'll go for that. I'll get Hal to get us priority access, then I'll call my contact at the SAR facility. People, I want everything online for the sweep. Record every damn thing that bird gives us. No slipups. If Phoenix has to go in they'll need all the help we can give them."

Barbara Price stepped out of the Computer Room and made her way to her own office, where she picked up a phone and contacted Jack Grimaldi. She knew the Stony Man pilot was nearby. The pilot had been completing the final test runs of *Dragon Slayer,* the SOG's combat helicopter. The chopper had just undergone updates on equipment, armament and its power plants. Grimaldi had worked closely with the technicians, inputting his own considerable expertise. Since its inception, *Dragon Slayer* and Grimaldi had become almost inseparable. He was the only pilot to have flown the helicopter on missions, using the machine's awesome specifications to pull the combat teams out of trouble a number of times. He knew the aircraft inside out, and could make it do things that weren't even in the manual. With the new additions *Dragon Slayer* would be an even more powerful combat tool in the Stony Man armory. From the way things were sizing up, Grimaldi and his machine might prove indefensible on the upcoming mission.

"Hey, boss lady, is this a new way to ask me out on a date?" Grimaldi asked when he came on the line.

"Cool it, flyboy," Price said. "I'm fixing you with a date, but not the kind you dream about. This is going to be cold, a long way from home and your dates are definitely not the kind who wear dresses. Come to my office and I'll give you the details."

"On my way," Grimaldi said, and cut the connection.

Price reviewed her paperwork, shaking her head as she went through the scant information. As usual Stony Man was being handed a mission where hazy background material left the combat teams exposed and, while not exactly vulnerable, at an initial disadvantage. While the home teams only had to work on background material and dredge up what they could from data banks, the field teams were thrown to the lions, often with very little to go on, and with the possibility their enemies were armed with better knowledge on the situation. It was lucky for Stony Man that the people it sent out to face the unknown weren't only professional, but also possessed intimate knowledge of the terrorist mentality and the workings of the hard world in general. There was no denying that while Able Team and Phoenix Force depended on the data Stony Man could provide, they were on their own once they took on a mission. High-tech satellites and space imagery were all well and good, and might place them within a few feet of their target. When the chips were down and death was staring them in the face, the SOG commandos had only themselves to depend on. In the field, with bullets coming at them, there was no time to check the rule book. It became a one-on-one affair. There were no rules of engagement. The ethos was simple—*fight or die*. Barbara Price always did her best to insure her people got the best chance available.

Grimaldi tapped on her open door and sauntered in. He wore coveralls and carried a baseball cap.

"Sit down, Jack. There's a mission coming up. Actually it's already under way. You were involved when you picked up Pol in Dakota. Phoenix is moving into a second phase of the same mission. Time's coming when they'll need you and the lady. How is she?"

Grimaldi, now slumped in a seat across from Price, smiled and said, "Straining at the leash. Now I got all the new systems up and running we can't wait. Where we heading for?"

"No final details yet, but I have a feeling it might be Siberia."

"Ouch!" Grimaldi said. "That's one cold chunk of real estate. What's the deal?"

Price placed one of her files on the desk.

"In there is everything we have at present. Exactly the same data the guys saw at the briefing. Read it through and when you're ready we'll get *Dragon Slayer* geared up."

"We getting a ride out there?"

Price nodded. "I have to work on that next. Got to talk to the Air Force. See what they can do for us."

London

MCCARTER'S ROOM GREETED him with silence. He closed the door gently and crossed to the bed where Mei Anna's slim figure lay partly covered by the sheets. Her thick black hair was spread across the pillow. She was on her side, her back to him. The covers had slipped down, exposing her upper body. Mei had pulled the curtains and the room was in shadow. There was enough light for him to see the healing bruises on her back. He saw, too, the puckered, weeping bullet hole down near her waist. It was a recent wound, the edges ragged and torn, with incision cuts on either side, stitches still in place. Someone had carried out crude surgery to remove the bullet. McCarter stood in silence, unable to drag his eyes from the wound.

Not a bloody word, he thought. She never even mentioned it.

He realized now why she had looked so weary. She'd dragged herself halfway across the world to meet him and pass along the information she had gained. McCarter sat in the chair beside the bed and watched her sleep. His admiration for the courageous young woman went up the scale. Reaching a decision, he took out his cell phone and hit the speed-dial number for Stony Man. Barbara Price came on and McCarter explained quickly what he had discovered.

"I'd like to meet this Mei Anna," Price said. "She sounds like a hell of a woman."

"I can't argue that," McCarter said. "Listen, I want her taken care of. I don't give a damn how you do it, or who you have to wake up. Tell Hal to use his clout and get Anna somewhere safe where she can recover. She'll need watching, too. Those characters we clashed with here must have been warned she was in London. It could mean others are looking for her. Barbara, she deserves the best for what she brought us. If she doesn't get it, I'll start making bloody loud noises.''

"Take it easy, David. This will get my full attention. I promise. Any problems you can bawl me out personally.''

"I'll hold you to that.''

Price chuckled softly. "I believe you will, too.''

McCarter caught himself. "Sorry, Barb,'' he said. "I didn't mean to give you a hard time. If you were here, you'd understand.''

"Hey, give me some credit. I *do* understand.''

"Thanks, Barb.''

"Call you back soon. We'll sort it. Oh, by the way, you were right. That car you had me check belongs to the security section of the Chinese embassy in London. While I was on the Net I checked the news agencies. Not a word about the incident. The Chinese are keeping very low-key about it.''

"Of course they are. They aren't going to admit they tried to kill Anna because she found out they were planning something bad concerning the U.S. defense system.''

"Sneaky but not stupid?''

"You got it.''

Mei tried to be angry when she woke a little while later to learn what McCarter had done. She failed to even raise her voice. The weakness that was engulfing her body kept her strangely subdued.

"Why didn't you tell me?" the Brit asked.

"You have enough to do without worrying about me."

"That, Anna, is the worst excuse I've ever heard. Bloody hell, you could have died."

For a moment her eyes flashed with that familiar fiery spirit.

"You can't yell at me, Clancy, I'm a patient. Remember?"

"That won't cut you any slack."

A ghost of a smile crossed her pale lips. "Always the tough guy. As hard as nails and twice as sharp."

McCarter held her hand, and he felt her grip tighten. He leaned forward anxiously.

"Anna?"

"It's all right. Just a twinge."

"One question, then you're off duty for the duration."

"Tell me what I can do?"

"In the reports you gave me, there's mention of a bloke called Kranski."

"He deals in merchandise and information. We have dealt with each other a few times. Clever man. He understands the politics of the region better than anyone I know. And he doesn't like what the Chinese and Koreans have been doing with the Russians on board as allies. Kranski told me he has a bad feeling about what they've been cooking up. He was the one who told me about the Siberian base. If you need on-the-spot information, he's the one."

She asked for pen and paper, writing down numbers for McCarter. It was a cell phone number.

"His message service. He'll call you back. Trust him, David. I do."

Her words slowly trailed away, and Mei slipped back into a restless sleep. McCarter prised his hand free and left her. He met James in the corridor.

"How's she doing?"

McCarter shook his head. "Sooner she's in care the better I'll feel."

"Hey, man, she'll be okay. I spoke to Barb a few minutes ago. The arrangements have all been put in place. There's a private ambulance on its way. The clinic Anna's going to is the best. They'll look after her. They do this all the time."

MCCARTER HAD a brief moment to say goodbye before Mei was taken away by the medics from the clinic. She had been sedated, and her sleepy eyes had barely registered him as he bent to kiss her cheek. When he turned away the others were standing in a group watching.

"We'll miss her," Hawkins said on behalf of the rest of the team.

McCarter led them back into his room, glad he was in front so they couldn't see his face.

Calvin James had his laptop on the table. He was patched into Stony Man, downloading the data the cyberteam had gathered for them. Kurtzman's disembodied voice reached them through the computer's voice facility.

"The longitude and latitude gave us the position

shown on the screen map. We used a satellite scan and swept the area. This is what we came up with.''

The image changed to a digital image taken from the satellite. Kurtzman had locked on and increased the image, bringing it down to a low-level pass, and the relief sprang into focus.

''There's some kind of structure, all right. Thermal imagery shows a number of heat sources. Nothing outstanding, so I don't think you'll find a nuclear reactor ready to go critical.''

''That's a relief,'' James muttered.

''We did pick up moving images, which are probably vehicles.''

Kurtzman's pictures superimposed a pointer that tracked elements of the image for the team.

''Just remember you're in bad-weather country,'' Kurtzman said. ''I ran a weather prediction. There could be some rough changes over the next few days. Snow coming in from the northeast. Low temperatures, guys, so don't forget your thermals.''

''How accurate is the weather forecast?'' McCarter asked.

''We can't be precise here,'' Kurtzman admitted. ''Weather patterns in this region can change pretty damn fast. Look at the worst-case scenario and add fifty percent.''

''As accurate as that?'' Hawkins said. ''Nothing to worry about, then.''

McCarter connected the GPS unit he had with him. The location was downloaded into the unit and fed into the memory. The rest of Kurtzman's data was placed in the laptop's memory bank for further examination.

"Thanks for the info," McCarter said. "We may be getting back to you later."

"We'll be here," Kurtzman replied, and logged off.

James shut the laptop. He stood over it, tapping the black case.

"Cal?" Manning asked, aware that the man had something to say.

"We could be walking into one hell of a mess out there," James said. "Right now we know Shun Wei is involved. Maybe the Koreans, as well as the Chinese. And the Russians."

"So?" McCarter asked.

"What do we have on our side?" James said. "Some sketchy information Anna managed to smuggle out, and a vague contact called Kranski."

"You don't like it?"

"You have to admit it isn't a lot to go on, considering we're contemplating dropping into the middle of Siberia."

"Mmm," McCarter said. "You know what this is all about? He's been watching those cable-TV vacation shows and wants a guarantee he'll get his money back if he's disappointed."

James scowled. "How the hell do you figure things out so fast?"

"Simple," McCarter told him. "I'm just bloody good is all."

TWO HOURS LATER the Phoenix Force trio was back in the air, this time courtesy of the U.S. Air Force.

Their flight would return them to Stony Man, where the full team would pick up their equipment. Jack Grimaldi and *Dragon Slayer* would join them for the next stage, and the final flight would be in the Stony Man helicopter itself as Grimaldi made his incursion into Siberian airspace—destination Khabarovsk.

CHAPTER THREE

Siberia

Kranski had been waiting for more than an hour. He was on his fourth cup of rich, gritty coffee and had smoked six black, slender locally made cigars. The length of his wait did little to unsettle him. He had learned long ago that there was no gain in becoming agitated over something as trivial as a little lost time. All it did was affect the blood pressure. The day was unusually warm, and sitting outside the small café overlooking the town square was better than some of the things he had done in his life. So Kranski sat and waited, enjoying the tranquillity, and also young women who passed by. That alone was worth the wait.

He didn't forget for one minute the reason he was there. Above everything he was a professional, and if the job required that he remain outside the café for the rest of the day he would do so. He had a meeting arranged, and nothing would deter him from keeping it.

He leaned forward to light another cigar, catching

the brief flurry of movement on the far side of the square. He noticed it because everyone else in sight was strolling, enjoying the good weather. Drawing in the sweet smoke of the cigar he sat upright, concentrating on the distant activity. He saw instantly what was happening. The man he had come to meet was crossing the square. He wasn't alone, as he should have been. Two men were behind him, spaced so as to appear unknown to each other, but Kranski noticed their presence and recognized one of them.

Jan Petrovski, one of Malinchek's enforcers, was a grim man who saw life as a never ending struggle for existence. The other enforcer was new to Kranski. He was younger than Petrovski and hungry. It showed in his movements.

Remaining in his seat, Kranski eased open his coat, allowing him access to the 9 mm Glock in the shoulder rig. He studied the situation and decided he didn't like what he saw. The meeting was supposed to have been simple, a mere exchange of words, an unwritten contract for whatever the purchaser wanted. So why had Malinchek sent along two of his enforcers? This wasn't the first time Kranski had done business with the man.

So why the extreme precautions at this stage?

Could it be that Malinchek had found out that Kranski had been working with the Chinese woman, Mei Anna? That his negotiations with her had placed Malinchek in the broader picture? Kranski sighed. Nothing turned out as it should.

Kranski waited as his contact reached the table and

waited in awkward silence. The pair of enforcers stood some yards back.

"Janos, is there a problem?" Kranski asked, nodding in the direction of the backup men.

Janos, a lean, gaunt-faced man in his forties, gave a nervous smile. "This was not my idea," he said lamely. "There have been difficulties. Malinchek says he needs to discuss certain matters with you."

Kranski managed a smile at the delicate way his friend described the matter. "And I can guess what that is. Oh, well, I suppose he had to find out sooner or later."

"I said it before, Kranski. What you were doing was risky."

"I know. You tried to warn me off. But I believed it was right. What those people are doing is liable to cause a great deal of trouble."

"Please be careful," Janos whispered, leaning forward slightly so that he didn't have to raise his voice. "I don't like this pair. They scare me. Do what they want and let us get over this."

"And I wonder what that is?" Kranski asked as he saw Petrovski coming up quietly behind Janos.

"For you to come with us," Petrovski stated.

"I'm happy here," Kranski said. "If you have something to say, get on with it. I don't answer to you, Petrovski. Nor do I jump when Malinchek speaks. That is your privilege. If there is something you want, spit it out."

"Mr. Malinchek wants to talk with you."

Kranski smiled. "Then he is going to be disappointed. If this is all you have come to say, then I am leaving. If you wish to make an issue of it, go ahead. If not, leave me alone. This isn't the place to start trouble, but I warn you that if you try, I will resist. You know I'm always armed, Petrovski, and I am not frightened to use my weapon if threatened. But this is not a good place to stage some kind of firefight. Too many witnesses. Malinchek would not be pleased to be associated with someone who started a gunfight in a public square filled with people.''

Petrovski stepped back. He knew Kranski was right, even though he didn't like being forced to walk away. He remained outwardly calm, but fire blazed in his eyes, and Kranski was well aware that this episode had only been placed on hold.

Kranski turned his attention back to Janos. ''Give me some idea what this is all about, Janos. I don't give a damn about Petrovski, but you and I are good friends.''

''All I know is that Malinchek had visitors yesterday. I don't have any information about who they were or what they wanted with him. Malinchek has been difficult to talk to since then. He's a very nervous man.''

''It has to do with his dealings with that damn Chinese woman, the one they call Shun Wei. And the Korean.''

Janos shifted uncomfortably from one foot to the other.

''I don't really understand it myself. All I know is I was to set up this meeting and then let Petrovski take over.''

Kranski nodded. ''Don't worry, my friend. I'll see

what I can find out. *You* be careful. And, Janos, try not to turn your back on Petrovski too often, if you know what I mean.''

Janos smiled nervously. ''Unfortunately I do. He has a habit of always walking behind you. Makes it hard to know what he's up to.''

''Nothing good, my friend,'' Kranski said. ''Nothing good.''

KRANSKI RETURNED to the small, cramped hotel. It was a gloomy place, offering little apart from a bed and indifferent meals. He used it whenever he came to the area because it was anonymous and didn't attract much attention. He was known to the owner, who was somewhat like his establishment. Gloomy and indifferent. Kranski liked the indifferent part. The owner didn't take any interest in his guests as long as they paid their bills on time.

In his room he sat on the edge of the creaky bed and contemplated his options. They were scant. If Malinchek had an idea Kranski was working with Mei Anna and passing her information, then it was time to move on.

If Malinchek suspected Kranski had learned about his recent transaction, carried out on behalf of Shun Wei and the Korean, it was no surprise he was anxious to speak to him. Malinchek would be desperate to keep the deal under wraps. Despite the remoteness of the area and the poor communications, Malinchek's latest business arrangement would cause a great deal of alarm. He would need to keep it quiet, and one way of doing that would be by silencing

Kranski. It wasn't a wild assumption. Malinchek was well-known for his impulsive and violent methods.

Glancing at his watch, he was surprised to find more time had slipped by than he had realized. He quickly packed his belongings. He always traveled light, and everything he had went into one bag. He zipped it up, then checked his wallet and took out enough money to settle his bill. He placed the cash in the pocket of his long leather coat, putting his wallet back inside his coat. He also took out the Glock and checked the action. For some reason the small ritual made him feel better.

Before he left he made two calls on his cell phone. The first was to a number Mei Anna had left with him. The number was rerouted a number of times before he finally spoke to the person the woman had told him about. He found out that the man wanted to meet with him. Kranski's second call allowed him to leave a message on the distant answering machine. It was a detailed message and it took him some time.

Downstairs he paid his bill, took his change and stepped outside. He reminded himself he would have to wait more than an hour at the small station before his train arrived. At least there was a small café attached to the station where he would be able to get a drink. He noticed the moment he stepped out of the hotel that the earlier warmth had gone. The sky had clouded over and the temperature had dropped.

Kranski made for the station. He had to walk along a road that wound its way through a quiet part of the town. A light dusting of snow started. He stopped to turn up the collar of his coat, tugging at the brim of his hat. About to pick up his bag again, Kranski paused, his ears catching the muted sound of a car engine. Straightening slowly, leaving the bag where it was, Kranski turned slightly and saw a dark sedan of indiscriminate make and age moving toward him. A second vehicle appeared behind the first. This one was a later model.

While his body was still turned away Kranski slipped his right hand inside his coat and drew the Glock from the holster. He held it down against his side, in the folds of his coat, as he straightened.

The lead car accelerated, sweeping by to move ahead of Kranski. It angled across the road, blocking it. Glancing back up the road, Kranski saw the other car coming in his direction. It stopped no more than ten feet from him. One of the rear doors opened and a broad-shouldered Asian climbed out. His right hand was pushed inside his coat, and he maintained eye contact with Kranski.

Kranski recognized the next passenger to step out of the car. Tall, lithe, with long black hair sweeping her shoulders.

It was the Chinese woman he had identified previously in the information he had sent to Mei Anna.

Shun Wei.

Though a distance separated them, Kranski was able to see the cold look in her eyes. He saw the hard set of her mouth, and the moment he did Kranski knew they had come to kill him. There was no doubt in his mind. He saw the Chinese incline his head, looking beyond Kranski. He turned and saw the crew climbing out of the other car. Three of them. All armed. They started in toward him, moving with deadly purpose and raising their stubby SMGs.

If Kranski had been a religious man, he might have started to pray at that moment. He wasn't, so he raised his Glock and confronted the Chinese who had dragged his own weapon into view. There was a frozen moment, when all the players took that final microbreath, tensing for what was to come. In that moment the silence took over. It descended and held each individual in a still pose.

The first shot destroyed it all.

The bullet caught Kranski in the left shoulder, tearing at flesh and muscle. He stumbled back, sucking air in through clenched lips. His response was faster than the Chinese shooter could have imagined. As the Glock made target acquisition, Kranski stroked the trigger and put a single shot into the Chinese. The slug cored through the shooter's chest and into his heart. The man fell back, slamming into Shun Wei as he went down. She pushed him aside, clawing the autopistol from his hand and fired the moment she had Kranski in her sights.

Her shot hit him in the same shoulder, driving Kranski around in a half circle, and directly into the combined fire of the men from the first car. Kranski was knocked to his knees in a red haze, his body erupting bloody debris. A single bullet ripped through his left cheek, tearing out shards of bone and muscle. Blood filled Kranski's mouth. He choked, then spit, wrenching his torn body about as figures crowded in on him. Peering through tear-filled eyes, Kranski stared up at the tall, dark-clad figure standing over him. It was Shun Wei, scowling as she thrust her pistol at him and fired. The close-range bullet slammed Kranski to the ground. He groaned against the pain, bracing himself on his left arm and rolled on his side.

Shun Wei was bending over him, her face still bitter.

"Do you imagine I would allow you to betray me to that bitch, Mei Anna, and live?"

Kranski ignored her words, concentrating on moving his gun hand. He eased it around, knowing his time was slipping away. All he needed were a few more seconds....

Shun Wei's face registered shock as she saw the dark muzzle of the Glock line up on her. In her moment of glory at Kranski's imminent demise her concentration had wavered. Her mouth began to form a scream of rage. It was lost in the crackle of gunfire as Kranski summoned every ounce of his waning strength and fired three close shots. The 9 mm slugs tore into Shun Wei's forehead, expanding as they drove through into her skull and the brain beyond. Two burst out of the back of her head in crimson gouts. The woman arced back, arms thrown wide, her eyes wide and staring as she crashed to the hard ground, body going into spasm. Blood pooled rapidly beneath her shattered skull, catching the falling snowflakes, melting them instantly.

Kranski slumped to the wet ground, seeing the shadows of his executioners encircle him. He looked through the forest of legs to where Shun Wei's body lay trembling in her final moments. Then the combined firepower drove the life from him, bullets tearing him into bloody shreds.

The day closed down around him. As he slipped into deep shock, Kranski's world became a silent place that quickly turned dark, and he went into it without a struggle.

JANOS LEARNED about the murder of Kranski later that day. He didn't need to ask who had done it. Kranski was a marked man from the moment he refused to speak to Malinchek. Malinchek was a vicious man. He ran his organization on terror and intimidation. People followed his word if they wanted to stay alive. Kranski had known that, yet he still walked away from Malinchek's demand that he go to see him. Janos also learned that before he died Kranski had exchanged gunfire with his attackers, killing two of them, including the tall Chinese woman who had been seen around the area. She had been seen in discussion with Malinchek, obviously negotiating some kind of deal.

The moment he learned of Kranski's death, Janos got in his car and left. He didn't want to stay around while Malinchek's people were still in the area. Once he was in his car, driving along the rutted, bleak highway that trailed south across the empty Siberian landscape, Janos was able to reflect on his friend's death. He was sorry that Kranski had died. They had done business for many years, maintaining a level of trust almost unknown in their trade. Information came with many attachments. There was never anything direct with it. The buying and selling of information nurtured mistrust and betrayal, often death, and always existed on many levels. Yet Kranski and Janos managed their affairs with a quiet dignity that transcended all other considerations.

This time they had gotten themselves into an affair that swept them along, snapping at their heels, and in Kranski's case had swallowed him whole.

Janos gripped the wheel of the car, staring out through the dirt-speckled windshield, and thought ahead. Now that Kranski was gone, what did he do? He didn't trust any of the new breed. They were all too shifty for him, caught up in the world of cell phones and laptop computers. They were predators, ready to devour their own kind, as well as any outsiders. Janos thought about the money he had been salting away for the past ten years. Good enough to live on if he was careful. Enough to get him away from the machinations of the new breed. He had had enough. The cold affected him more than it had years ago. He craved warmth and a little comfort. He had a sister in Florida. She lived in a condo that overlooked the beach and had asked him to join her on a number of occasions. Why not? Maybe Kranski's dying was an omen, a warning for Janos to leave.

He reached Khabarovsk late in the evening and went directly to his cramped, chilly apartment. The moment he stepped inside and surveyed the place, he knew his earlier thoughts had been sensible. The sooner he got out the better. There was nothing left here any longer. The former Soviet Union was in a mess, with too many factions vying for power. It was fragmented, weakened by its own internal struggles, and while that went on the opportunists were reaping the benefits. Khabarovsk was a prime example. The city was a haven for corruption and double-dealing. Most businesses had pulled out, or were running on empty. Unemployment was high.

In the city the Russian architecture filled the skyline with bulbous domes and turrets. In the suburbs Chinese traders from over the border sold their cheap copies of Western goods. The old-style trading of the past had given way to shallow consumerism.

Janos made himself a quick meal. He drank some cheap, too sweet wine and decided to go to bed. Only then did he remember his answering machine. He leaned over and checked it. There were two messages. The first, surprisingly, was from his sister in Florida, asking when he was going to call her.

The second was from Kranski.

Hearing his late friend's voice came as a shock to Janos. He sat back and listened, suddenly realizing that the call had to have been made shortly before Kranski had been killed.

A greater shock followed as Kranski explained in detail what Janos should do in the event of his death. There seemed to be a finality in Kranski's tone, as if he had some kind of premonition, an indication that something was about to happen to him. Janos realized he was listening to his friend's eulogy, spoken by the man himself.

When the message ended, Janos switched off the answering machine, then erased all the messages on the tape. He knew what he had to do, and in the shadow of the events that had overtaken Kranski he had to do them immediately. There was no time to lose.

Wrapping up against the cold, Janos went down to the street and unlocked his car. He had to scrape off a thin coating of ice that had formed on the windshield. He started the car and drove out of the city, back onto the main highway, turning east and headed into the open country. A few miles from Khabarovsk lay a small village, no more than few wooden houses and a church. He drove through the darkened hamlet. Most of the houses were in darkness, their owners having already retired for the night. There was little else to do out here. There was a narrow track leading off the highway. Janos took it, dropping to a crawl. The track was rutted, and the ground under the wheels was iron hard. He felt every bump. His headlights picked out a straggling row of trees on either side of the track. They thickened as he drove on, eventually becoming a forest. The darkness out here was absolute. After about ten minutes Janos drove into a clearing. There stood a substantial wooden house built of solid timber, with a steep roof.

It was Kranski's home, his retreat from the world of deals and double-deals, his discreet seeking and supplying information. Janos had visited the place a number of times, only on strict invitation. Kranski had liked to keep his private life just that.

As Janos stopped the car and climbed out, surveying the dark bulk of the house, he realized that none of it really mattered in the end. Death had a nasty habit of bringing a man's hopes and dreams to an abrupt halt. He brought a powerful flashlight with him, switching it on as he approached the house. The single beam cut through the inky blackness. Janos saw snowflakes starting to fall around him. They crisscrossed the flashlight's beam as he approached the set of wooden steps that led to the veranda surrounding the lower section of the building.

The door he stood before was heavy, made from thick planks of smooth, hard wood. Janos moved to the side and checked out the first window. Kranski had told him he would have to break in because there were no keys available. Using the flashlight, he broke one of the small panes close to the inner catch. The falling glass seemed to make a loud noise. Reaching in, Janos opened the catch, slid the window up and climbed in. He stepped over the low sill, turning to lower the window and lock it again.

He played the beam of the flashlight across the room. From memory he knew it to be one large, open area, filled with Kranski's comfortable furniture and belongings. There was a large stone hearth where Kranski had burned logs taken from the surrounding forest. Now the hearth was cold, stacked with logs ready for lighting. Near the hearth was a large, comfortable armchair where Kranski had spent his evenings, listening to music or reading. His pleasures had been simple, undemanding. In his private life Kranski had been a solitary person, happy with his own company.

Janos was about to move when something caught his eye. He felt a chill race down his spine. In the diffused light from his flashlight he was sure he had seen a shape in Kranski's armchair. For a moment he was rooted to the spot. The moment passed and he felt foolish. What next? he thought. He'd start to believe in ghosts.

And then the shape in the chair did move. It leaned forward and spoke to Janos in English, with a British accent.

"Janos?"

The man was tall, lean, clad in dark combat clothing and he had an automatic pistol in his right hand. The weapon was held muzzle down, the man's trigger finger resting against the pistol's casing.

"I don't understand," Janos said. "Who are you? What are you doing here?"

"I could ask you the same thing," the tall man said. "Only I know. You came because Kranski left you a message on your answering machine."

"But—"

"Kranski spoke to me earlier today. We were en route to meet with him. He told me he was going to leave a message for you because you were his friend and the only man here he trusted. Tell me something. Has anything happened to Kranski since we spoke?"

"Yes. He was killed. Murdered."

"By the people he had been dealing with?"

Janos nodded. "A man named Malinchek. I spoke to Kranski this morning. I was delivering a message from Malinchek. He wanted a meeting with Kranski, but he refused to go with Malinchek's people. Looking back he probably thought they were going to kill him. So he walked away. I never saw him again, but I learned later that he had been shot to death on his way to the station. He would have been coming back here.''

"Anything else we should know?''

"Only that during the gun battle Kranski shot and killed two of his attackers. One of them was a Chinese woman.''

"Shun Wei?''

Janos move closer. "Yes. You know about this woman?''

"Oh, yes, I knew her. Had a bloody bad temper when she got upset,'' David McCarter said.

Janos sensed the presence of others in the dark room. He peered around, trying to pick out their shapes.

"Tell me what this is all about,'' he said.

"Do you have plenty of time to spare?'' a voice asked from the shadows.

Janos sighed. He was tired from the journey back to Khabarovsk. He still had to come to terms with the death of his good friend Kranski. Now this meeting in the dark with some English stranger.

"No more games,'' Janos said. He moved to sit down, ignoring the dark and what it might hold. "After what has happened today you cannot frighten me.''

"We're not here to frighten you, Janos,'' McCarter said. "We need your help. Kranski was supplying information to a friend of ours. We took over because she can't continue. Our information isn't complete. We need more so we can carry on, and Kranski was going to give it to us.''

"And now he is dead,'' Janos said. "His bequest

to me was to help you. First you must tell me one thing.''

''If I can.''

''Kranski's contact from China had previously worked with an American group. She knew their leader by a certain name.''

McCarter smiled in the darkness. Trust Mei Anna to come up with that one.

''Clancy,'' he said.

THEY GATHERED in the kitchen of Kranski's house. The shutters were all closed, allowing them to light an oil lamp. The soft yellow glow reached out to fill the corners of the room, and gave Janos a chance to see the strangers. There were five of them in total, led by the tall Englishman. All were dressed the same in dark combat suits and each was well armed. They carried H&K automatic weapons and wore holstered pistols.

''The area around here is full of people from both sides of the border,'' Janos explained. ''The Chinese come across the Amur River to bring in their counterfeit goods. They are very good at making copies of American clothes. They smuggle in other things. Drink. Cigarettes. Cases of Coca-Cola. Even the North Koreans come with their cheap coats to sell. The Japanese used to invest, but that has gone now. There is no money unless you are a gangster. They bring in the drugs.''

He paused to pour water boiled on the ancient gas stove into mugs to make instant coffee. He passed out the mugs, taking his and sitting down.

"With China so close there has been a tradition of passing information back and forth. Sometimes good, sometimes not. Once the Soviet Union broke up, the border restrictions weakened and the business increased. No one cares any longer. Kranski and I were in demand because we knew the country and where to lay our hands on certain goods. Information was Kranski's other business. For someone in this trade he was an honest man. Never cheated on his clients. He was a respected man. A few years ago Malinchek came on the scene. He's nothing but a thug, but he has power and money. Nothing is beyond his reach."

"Malinchek is the guy in bed with the Chinese and Koreans?" Manning asked.

"That is what Kranski told me. He went north with his Chinese contact and they came back with information that proved Malinchek, the Shun Wei woman and a North Korean called Yat Sen Took had meetings with a Russian group up country. I believe there was also an American involved."

"Fits what we have," McCarter said. "Janos, was the Chinese woman with Kranski called Mei Anna?"

Janos nodded. "She was very beautiful. Too pretty to be doing such work. But very brave. I met her a few times. She was consumed with stopping whatever Shun Wei was up to. Where is she now?"

"Being looked after. She was shot recently."

Janos shook his head. "A shame." He glanced at McCarter. "She had insisted on following Malinchek's group. I remember the last time I saw she looked exhausted. She was on her way back over the border into China."

"What was it Kranski asked you to help us with?"

"A package in his safe," Janos said. "I am to give it to you."

He pushed away from the table and crossed the kitchen, taking a heavy bladed knife with him. The others watched as he knelt on the floor in one corner. Janos used the thick blade of the knife to raise the lip of one of the flagstones that comprised the kitchen floor. Easing his fingers beneath the stone, he lifted it upright. A hardwood frame had supported the stone, and sunk into the ground just below was the thick door of a safe. Janos paused for a moment, searching his memory for something Kranski had told him. He bent over the combination lock and worked the sequence of numbers. McCarter crossed to stand over the man as Janos reached into the opened safe and withdrew a large manila envelope.

"This contains everything from Kranski's last trip."

McCarter took the envelope and returned to the table. He opened it and slid the contents on to the surface. There were written notes, in English, and a single white envelope with Janos's name on. McCarter handed the envelope to the man, who took it and moved away.

Reading through the notes, McCarter came across names he had heard before. Shun Wei, Malinchek and the Korean who had been mentioned. There were some new ones. One was Rick Teeler, the militia man contact who had already been identified.

McCarter's interest was sharpened when he read the main section of Kranski's report. He was unable to hold back an exclamation of shock when he reached a critical few sentences.

"Sounds serious," James said.

"You could say that," McCarter replied. "According to Mei Anna and confirmed by Kranski, Malinchek has obtained a nuclear warhead for the planned operation."

"What the hell are they going to do with a nuke?" Manning asked.

"Small yield would be enough to wipe out the Alaska radar facility and contaminate the ground for a long time," McCarter replied. "So the sooner we get to grips with this group the better."

"Time to move out?" Hawkins said.

McCarter nodded. "Let's get outside and send the call for our ride."

Janos held up the paper he had taken from the envelope.

"Kranski has left everything he had to me," he said. "Everything."

"Give you a chance to get out of this place," McCarter said. "If that's what you want."

"Oh, yes," Janos agreed. "It is. There is nothing here for me now. Only memories, and the saddest thing is to see someone living off those."

They moved through the house, making for the front door, Hawkins in the lead. He carried the signal device that would alert Jack Grimaldi and bring in *Dragon Slayer.*

Unbolting the door, Hawkins pulled it open, stepping out on to the porch, a little way ahead of the rest of the team.

He took two steps across the porch, then stopped dead in his tracks.

Anywhere else the sound would have gone unnoticed. Out here in the silence of the empty countryside even the slightest sound could be heard over a long distance. The unmistakable click of an Uzi being cocked reached Hawkins's sharp ears. The move had been made by someone too eager to engage. Maybe brought on by nervousness. Whatever the reason, it warned Hawkins they were no longer alone with Janos. Someone else was interested in Kranski's home and what it might contain.

Hawkins had already committed himself to crossing the porch and was about to negotiate the steps when he picked up the errant sound. His instinct was to turn back to try to remove himself from danger. He also knew there was no way he could outrun a bullet. So he decided, in the microsecond of time all that flashed through his mind, to keep moving forward until he was taking the first step. He kept his movements natural, resisting the urge to run, and made the move to his first step down.

At his rear the others were moving through the door. Hawkins leaned forward slightly, tensing for what he was about to do.

"We got hostiles! One to my immediate left!"

He yelled the words as he launched himself in a full-length dive off the second step, arms outstretched. As he dropped to the ground, Hawkins hunched his shoulders, twisting as best he could so that as he struck the iron-hard ground, his curving body absorbed some of the impact. He slithered on the icy ground, flinging himself in an awkward roll.

The first burst of fire ripped into the porch's main post, shredding the wood. The flash of the weapon identified the shooter, and someone behind Hawkins returned fire.

Not wanting to stay in the open and draw more fire, Hawkins rolled in the direction of the car Janos had arrived in. He dragged himself the last few feet, curling his body around the front wheel and hauling himself into a sitting position. He pulled his H&K across his chest, snapping off the safety and checking the barrel in case it had become clogged with dirt. It was clear. Hawkins heard movement out beyond the parked car and leaned forward. Peering into the darkness, he made out indistinct shapes. Heard the soft footfalls of men who had done this kind of thing before. Following on, he picked up low, whispered words in Russian.

"Welcome to the party, y'all," he murmured.

The oncoming men were obviously unaware of his presence. And when they started to fire, the muzzle-flashes caught them for an instant, frozen almost, like photographic images.

Turning the MP-5 in their direction, Hawkins fired off short bursts, altering his aim to space out the radius of his fire pattern. He heard someone curse, then someone fell hard, groaning, scrabbling around on the hard earth.

An unseen shooter fired back at him, misjudging height, and raked Janos's car with autofire. Glass burst as slugs struck the windows. Hawkins felt the car shudder as more shots drummed through the bodywork. He dropped belly down and fired from ground level, catching one target. The hit shooter gasped, pulling back with little caution this time, his fleeing figure outlined against the paler darkness of the sky. The Phoenix Force warrior hit him again, a short burst that pitched the target facedown on the ground.

Behind Hawkins, near the house, the exchange of fire had increased.

"Check the rear," McCarter instructed.

Encizo and Manning broke away, moving quickly to the kitchen. As they broke through the door, separating to either side, window glass shattered and the solid shutters were pounded by a blast from a shotgun. Someone was using an autoweapon, hitting the shutters with round after round. The hard wood withstood the assault for a while, but the relentless power of the heavy-gauge shot splintered it.

The Phoenix Force duo waited in the shadows. Only seconds had passed before the shutters were battered from their hinges. Dark shapes surged toward the window, the first scrambling up on to the sill and leaning inside.

Manning triggered his MP-5, laying a burst in the man's chest. He screamed and fell back, hindering his partners. Hoping to gain the advantage, Encizo ran forward, his own SMG up and ready. He closed in on the window and raked the area with a sustained burst that caught the other attackers as they scattered.

By this time Manning had reached the kitchen door. He slammed the bolts back and hauled the heavy door open. The big Canadian already had a fragmentation grenade in his free hand. He yanked the pin, released the lever, then tossed the bomb.

"Fire in the hole," he yelled as the projectile flew from his hand.

Both he and Encizo dropped to cover.

The grenade detonated with a hard crack, a brief flash of light breaking the shadows outside. On the fading echo of the blast a man screamed in agony, the sound shrill and short-lived.

Weapons up, Encizo and Manning breached the open kitchen door, one following the other. They fired short bursts, angling the line of fire from left to right. Reaching a wooden outbuilding they used the wall as cover. Encizo reloaded while Manning covered him. They reversed roles so that the Canadian could snap in a fresh magazine.

"See anything?" Encizo asked.

"Hard to see anything out here. Hasn't street lighting reached this part of the world yet?"

"I don't think talkies have reached here yet," the little Cuban remarked.

Manning reached into a pocket and pulled out a marker flare. He readied the flare.

"You set? Let's do it before we freeze to death."

He ignited the flare and hurled it in an overhand throw away from the outbuilding. As the orange light blossomed, illuminating the area ahead of them, Encizo spotted two crouching figures. The moment the light revealed their positions, the immobile figures opened up with their autoweapons, firing in the direction of the house. They pushed upright, retreating as they fired.

Manning leaned out from behind the outbuilding's wall and fired back. His first burst took one man in the left leg, dropping him to the ground. His partner pulled back to help him, dragging the injured man by the collar of his thick parka. Manning held back from firing again as they moved beyond accurate range.

Peering out across the illuminated area, Encizo saw three figures down on the ground. None of them were moving. He could see the results of Manning's grenade burst. Shredded clothing and flesh indicated the grenade had done what was expected.

They remained in their position in case further attacks were forthcoming.

STRAY SHOTS HIT the fuel tank of Janos's car. The spilled fuel's vapor came in contact with sparks from following shots, and the rear of vehicle quickly became engulfed in rising flames.

"Dammit to hell!" Hawkins swore. He rolled away from the car, choosing the relative safety of the darkness beyond the expanding glare of the fire.

He felt the ground slip away and rolled into a shallow dip partly filled with iced-over water. The thin ice cracked, and Hawkins gasped as the freezing water soaked through his outer clothing. He crawled out, cursing his bad luck. Pushing to his feet, he turned to check his position and heard the rustle of clothing as someone lunged at him. Hawkins spun, bringing up the H&K. He was slow. A hard object clouted him across the side of the face, driving him to his knees, the SMG sliding from his grasp. Hawkins shook his head, trying to clear the haze of pain blurring his vision. Through the mist he saw a heavy shape looming above him. The figure drove the butt of a weapon at Hawkins for the second time, grunting with the effort.

MCCARTER AND James took on the frontal attack, dropping to their knees, weapons tracking in on the indistinct shapes moving toward the house.

Janos was prone, pushed to the floor by McCarter in the first seconds of the attack. He pulled back, pressing against the door frame, hearing the savage sounds of combat around him.

The sudden surge of flames from Janos's car drove back the shadows. McCarter and James were able to see their attackers now, and they used the moment to great advantage. Between them they put down three men and pushed the others back, accurate fire taking its toll.

The attack petered out almost as quickly as it had begun. The silence that fell over the area became more pronounced as Phoenix Force realized they were alone again. The attack force had retreated, withdrawing into the darkness surrounding the house.

It was few minutes later when they all heard the distant rumble of a diesel engine. The sound reverberated for a short while, then faded as the vehicle moved away.

HAWKINS TWISTED his body to one side as he sensed the gun butt driving down at him a second time. It scraped down the side of his face, clipping the curve of his jaw. The Phoenix Force warrior kicked out, the hard toe of his boot catching his adversary on the upper thigh, pushing the man to one side. Lashing out again, Hawkins landed a hard blow to the man's groin, which drew a grunt of pain. The figure pulled back, and Hawkins used the moment to roll, getting his feet under him.

As he shoved up off the ground, Hawkins reached down and slid the knife sheathed on his thigh free from its cover. He kept it close in to his leg, rising to his full height, his move bringing him close in to his attacker. Hawkins's left hand took a grip on the man's bulky coat, using it to pull the guy in toward him, bringing the knife up in a savage arc that drove the keen blade in deep, under the ribs and up into the heart. The Phoenix Force warrior twisted the sunken blade, drawing a roar of pain from the stricken target. Warm blood seeped from the deep wound, coursing over Hawkins's hand. He ignored it, maintaining pressure on the knife until the man went slack against him. Only then did he release his grip, letting the deadweight slump to the ground.

Hawkins searched around until he located his H&K. He picked it up and turned back toward the house, skirting the burning car as he saw McCarter and James. As he joined them, Manning and Encizo came into sight.

"You okay?" McCarter asked.

Hawkins nodded. He saw Janos staring at him and realized he was still holding the knife in his right hand. They were both wet with blood.

"Janos, you want to take a look at these men to see if you recognize any of them?" McCarter asked.

Janos nodded and moved away, accompanied by Manning.

"You want to go wash up, T.J.?" James asked.

Hawkins nodded and followed him back inside the house.

"Someone meant business," Encizo commented.

"Too bloody right," McCarter said. "After reading Kranski's notes I'm not surprised. No wonder they want to keep it quiet."

Back inside the house they had a brief conference. Janos had identified a number of the dead as belonging to Malinchek's organization.

"There is something else," he added. "Two of them are military personnel."

"Former or current?" McCarter asked.

"Current as far as I know. They were up until a couple of weeks back."

"From where?" James asked.

"They were part of a group guarding a facility containing dismantled missiles, including nuclear warheads. All part of the great peace initiative. The problem is it takes forever for orders to reach here from Moscow."

"You mean there are *still* warheads lying around?" Manning asked.

Janos glanced at the big Canadian, a thin smile edging his mouth. "You have to understand the situation out here. Shock waves from the breakup of the Soviet infrastructure are still finding their way to the remoter corners of the country. This is not America. Communications have never been very sophisticated. At the height of the Communist regime the telephone system in Moscow was breaking down every week. It is even worse now. You realize how far we are from central government out here? It is almost as if we do not exist. Add to that all the infighting between those who still want to control us and the ones who desire complete autonomy. My friends, it is a mess, believe me. The army still suffers a high percentage of desertion from the ranks. Anyone who finds himself in control of some remote outpost where weapons are being stored is sitting on a possible gold mine. Illegal arms sales is big business. Talk to the right people. Show them a fistful of money and you can buy what you want. Even a nuclear warhead.''

''Wouldn't be the first time it's happened,'' Encizo said.

''Our dead soldiers out there prove it has happened again,'' Janos said. ''It is dog eat dog, and no one really cares.''

McCarter straightened. ''Well, somebody bloody well cares now.''

CHAPTER FOUR

Seattle

Fine rain drifted inland. Carl Lyons waited for Hubbard Tetrow beside the car that had brought them to the dock area. Tetrow had contacts here, and he was in conference with them. Lyons would have liked to have gone with him, but the Militia Men leader had told him to wait. It was frustrating for Lyons. A meeting with Tetrow's contacts would have been enlightening. It wasn't worth risking his cover to make any kind of fuss. Tetrow would only let "Jag" see and hear what he wanted him to. Anything else would have to wait.

Glancing across the wharf, Lyons could see the other two Militia Men who had come along for the ride. They were closer to the diner where Tetrow was having his discussion. Warner and Sutherland had been with Tetrow for a long time. They were Militia Men vets. Lyons found them a little distant since his performance back at the Shanty Bar, though they seemed to be easing up now as they got to know him better. They were typical of the kind Tetrow enjoyed dominating. Strong on muscle and dedicated to the anarchic views of the Militia Men to a frightening degree. The Able Team leader kept a sharp eye on the pair, using them to gauge the general feeling of the group. Despite having Tetrow's approval, Carl Lyons had decided to walk softly until he was sure of the others. He suspected there was a strain of malicious envy circulating among the troops due to the way he had moved into the group with the boss man's seal of merit. As an individual, Lyons couldn't have cared less how the others saw him. His concern was that nothing happened to jeopardize his cover.

Carl Lyons had no worries over his own safety as such. He was well able to protect himself. Being part of Stony Man meant he was asked to put his life on the line regularly. He had accepted a long time ago that his willingness to become part of the covert world of the SOG group meant sacrificing many of the things ordinary citizens of the U.S. took for granted. It was in their interest that he gave up his right to a *normal* life.

Stony Man's involvement in the dangerous, often life-threatening missions that came with the territory, came at a high price. The men and women of the SOG group did what they did out of sense of justice, a determination that Americans all over the country and abroad had the right not to be placed in violent, destructive situations. The complications of politics, religion, intolerance and pure, ignorant bigotry meant the burden of responsibility lay heavily on the Stony Man warriors. They would have preferred to be able to sit back and relax, free from any sudden demand on their time. But they also lived in the real world and knew for certain that somewhere out beyond the protective shield of law and military, someone would be deliberating their next destabilizing scheme.

As were Hubbard Tetrow and his bunch of zealots. In their eyes they were doing good for America, taking it upon themselves to right what they thought was a wrong created by the federal government. In their blinkered vision they would destroy and create chaos within a project designed and intended to keep the American people safe from harm, including the Militia Men. That concept seemed to have been bypassed. All Tetrow saw was a threat to freedom and democracy itself. He refused to even consider the good side of the argument, and in doing so he broke one of the laws he so strongly maintained he was defending. That being the two sides to any argument, and the consideration they both deserved in a democratic society. Hubbard Tetrow, in the classic mold of the fanatic, saw only his side of the coin. He would refuse to contemplate the fact that the other side of the argument had its merits. His was the only way, and he was prepared to move to extremes of violence to win his battle.

It was Lyons's mission to find out exactly what Tetrow had in mind and try to stop him. Now that they were in Seattle, moving closer to whatever the Militia Men were after, Lyons needed something hard. Something he could move on before they took the next step. He didn't want Tetrow carrying out any heavy action before Stony Man had been informed. Lyons wanted to call in a report, if only to bring the

Farm up to speed. He didn't have any solid pieces of information yet because the Militia Men were a close-mouthed bunch. Even when they had been at the ranch, following Jag's acceptance, none of the crew said much to him. It didn't bother Lyons at all. What did irritate him was the fact that apart from general talk the Militia Men said very little about their plans. He soon found it was their way. As a group, the Militia Men shared very little when it came to communication. Lyons couldn't figure out the reason. Maybe, he decided, it was Tetrow's way of preventing any leaks of information. If he didn't give them any more than they needed to know at the time, there was no way they could pass much on.

Lyons turned up the collar of the thick reefer jacket he wore. Cold rain had wormed its way down the back of his neck. He glanced in the direction of his fellow Militia Men. Warner and Sutherland were probably feeling as uncomfortable as he was, having to wait around in the rain.

Sutherland moved toward the diner, going up the steps and inside. He was in the place for a couple of minutes before reappearing and crossing the lot to where Lyons stood. As he neared Lyons, Sutherland reached inside his jacket and pulled out a pack of cigarettes. He fished one out and lit it, trailing smoke as he joined Lyons, leaning against the side of the car.

"Teeler wants to see you," he said.

Rick Teeler was Tetrow's second in command. In all the time Lyons had been with the Militia Men he hadn't seen the man. All he had been told was that

Teeler was away on business for the group. Now he was back, it seemed, and Jag was being summoned.

Lyons glanced at Sutherland. "He coming out here?" he asked.

Sutherland peered at him as if Lyons had suddenly grown an extra eye. He drew on the cigarette, considering Lyons's words and then broke into a slow, hoarse chuckle. Something had amused him.

"Is *he* comin' to see you?" he mimicked.

"Hub said to stay with the car. Still the man, ain't he?"

"Yeah, he's the man. But when Teeler calls, you go at the double."

"Tough guy, is he?"

"Jag, you're a funny man today. Hope for your sake Teeler is in a good mood."

"That supposed to alarm me?"

"Ask any of the boys. They'll all tell you the stories we heard about Teeler."

Lyons managed a humorless smirk. "Stories don't kill you. I like to see what a man can do. You know, Sutherland, like I did with that fuckin' FBI asshole."

Lyons pushed away from the car and crossed the lot. Warner was watching him come closer.

"He inside?" Lyons asked. "Teeler? The guy I'm supposed to be scared of apparently."

"Yeah, he's inside. Been waiting on you."

Lyons went up the steps and pushed open the diner's door. Other than the counterman the diner only held three people, Hubbard Tetrow and two Lyons didn't know. As soon as Tetrow saw Lyons, he waved him to join them.

Sliding onto the booth seat, next to one of the strangers, Lyons guessed that the man beside him, dark hair and clad in an ill-fitting dark suit, was the one Tetrow had come to see. The man seated beside Tetrow was Rick Teeler. It had to be. He had the hungry look of a true fanatic, ready to chew everything he stood against into shreds.

"Rick wanted to meet you," Tetrow said, sleeving crumbs away from the corner of his mouth.

Teeler leaned forward and took a long look at Lyons.

"I been hearing about you being a tough guy."

Lyons nodded slightly, then said, "I ain't heard a damn thing about you."

Teeler's face hardened. He glanced at Tetrow, who was grinning.

"Told you he was a sly one, Rick," Tetrow said.

"Yeah. So you did. You and me need to have a talk, Jag. I like to get to know who I'm working with."

"Anytime, Mr. Teeler. You know where I am."

"I'll make sure of that."

"Jag," Tetrow said, "this is Boris Yesinovich, one of our friends from Russia. He has the same views about the missile placement. His people feel it's going to place the same constraints on them as it does on us. His people will be working with us to deal with the problem in Alaska. A team has been training up so they'll have a damn good idea of what to expect when they go in with us."

The Russian put out a big hand and shook Lyons's.

"This time the people will make their voice be

heard. American and Russian. Perhaps we can stop this dangerous game before we all end up suffering."

"Sounds good," Lyons said.

He glanced at Tetrow. "You got anything particular in mind for me?"

Teeler nodded. "Damn right we have, friend. First thing I want is for you to make a pickup tonight. We got a consignment of equipment shipping in. You can team up with Sutherland and Warner. Three of you should be able to handle it."

"Okay. Anything else?"

"One thing at a time, boy," Teeler said. "One thing at a time."

They sat in the diner for a while longer, Lyons having to listen to the paranoid rantings coming from his three companions. The more he listened the more convinced he became they were dangerous. Clouded judgment about a government they were convinced wanted to hoodwink the entire population of America had deafened their ears to the arguments for some system of home defense.

If Tetrow had his way, the U.S. administration would simply stand back and let the rest of the world arm itself, while America became a passive bystander. If aggression was targeted against the country Tetrow's way would have her open and vulnerable, with nothing to defend herself with apart from the conventional forces. A first strike, hitting an America incapable of warding it off, could inflict horrendous casualties. Nuclear weapons also left their legacy of lingering radiation behind, deadly clouds of lethal particles drifting across the country, bringing long-term suffering to anyone they touched. The effects of such deadly poison would do more to lower the morale of a nation than any amount of swift violence. Lyons found this omission odd. Even Tetrow, despite his narrow-minded view, had to be capable of understanding the possibility of such a scenario. He was either deliberately ignoring it or he was just plain naive in his interpretation of the world and its problems. It wasn't a question Lyons had any intention of voicing in present company. Not if he wanted to stay in Tetrow's good books.

As far as Rick Teeler was concerned, Lyons realized he had a tougher problem. The second in command of the Militia Men would bear watching. Lyons had felt the tension in his voice when he had spoken. Teeler didn't like Lyons, and the Able Team commander had a feeling the man did not fully trust him, either. He was going to have to stay alert. If Teeler had misgivings about the man he knew as Jag, then he would be doing some quiet checking in the background. Teeler was the kind who wouldn't give anything away. He would smile to your face with a gun under his coat, and the minute he decided against you that gun would go off.

For the first time in his life Lyons would have welcomed the sound of Schwarz and Blancanales doing their best to annoy him. One of their prolonged bantering sessions would have gone down well right at that moment in time.

When the meeting broke up, Teeler followed close on Lyons's heels as they left the diner. Tetrow and Yesinovich walked to the waiting car and drove away, leaving Lyons alone with Teeler, Warner and Sutherland.

"Take the pickup truck," Teeler said. He handed Warner a slip of paper. "Address is there. Guy driving will have some packages for you. You'll know him. Get back here fast as you can. Jag goes with you. Let him see how organized we are."

Lyons fixed his gaze on Teeler, trying to figure whether the man was serious or trying to get a rise out of him. Teeler didn't give anything away.

"You think I'm ready for this?" Lyons asked, a trace of sarcasm in his tone.

Teeler patted his shoulder. "Well, here's where we find out, boy. Huh?"

Teeler walked away, leaving Lyons with his partners.

"Let's go," Sutherland said.

The pickup was parked at the side of the diner. Lyons opened the rear door of the crew cab and sat on the long seat. Warner drove. They sat in silence for a while, until Sutherland glanced at his watch.

"We ain't meeting the delivery until seven. Might as well go back to the motel and take a break. That okay with you, Jag?"

"Hey, I'm just the new boy. I'll go along with you guys."

Sutherland twisted around and stared at Lyons.

"Jesus, Jag, don't let Teeler get to you. He does that with everybody when they first join up."

Lyons inclined his head. "Yeah, but he's so scary, too."

Sutherland frowned until the words sank in. His

sense of humor wasn't strong. A crooked grin showed eventually.

"You are some weird son of a bitch, Jag. You know that?"

"That's what my old lady used to tell me when I was a kid," Lyons said. "Guess I still need to grow out of it."

Sutherland turned back around, shaking his head slowly. "Tell you something, buddy. Whatever you think of Teeler, just step light when he's around. He can be a mean mother. Am I right, Joe?"

"Oh, he's right, Jag. Teeler is way over on the dark side. You know what I mean? Hate to meet that bastard in a dark alley without a fuckin' Uzi in my hands."

Lyons filed the information away for future consideration.

"WALTER, OLD BUDDY," Teeler said into his cell phone, "I have a little piece of action for you tonight. Shouldn't take long. I need two or three of your boys to do a little bodywork for me. Send 'em over to meet me around six-thirty. Give me time to point out the central attraction. What? Hell, no, Walter. I don't want anybody dead. I need to check a guy out. See if he's genuine. You got the idea. No, they don't need to be too soft, either. But I need him able to walk and talk the next few days. Hell, Walter, I don't need to tell you. What is it you always tell me? You're a professional. Right? Nice talkin' to you, Walter. I'll drop the check in the mail in the morning."

BACK AT THE MOTEL Lyons lay on his bed, staring at the ceiling, trying to figure a way to get a message to Stony Man. Now that the Militia Men had moved to Seattle, he needed to pass the information back, which was a complication. One of Hubbard Tetrow's unbreakable rules denied any of his people telephone calls once they were on the road. He had paranoid imaginings that involved every man in his group. He voiced his trust in them, but overrode that with the ban on contact with anyone outside the group. There were, he told them, spies and traitors all around them. They couldn't trust anyone outside their tight-knit group of sworn Militia Men. That even extended to family and friends. The devious hand of the federal authorities often reached out to drag relations and acquaintances into its world of deceit and betrayal. A loose word, spoken to a trusted friend or loved one, might easily be reported to one of the government agencies and in the long run betray secrets.

Lyons had noticed immediately, the first time he entered his room, that there were no telephones. The TV was a pay-to-view. Not that it bothered him. It was bad enough seeing the stuff for free. Lyons was damned if he was going to pay to have his brain cells killed off one by one. When he ventured out to look for a vending machine, he checked the motel office. There was a pay phone on the wall right next to the Coke machine, but he knew he would have little opportunity to use it. The phone was in full view of the door. Anyone passing could see directly into the office. He would have to find another means to contact Stony Man.

That moment didn't arrive. Each time Lyons stepped out of his room during the afternoon, waiting for the time to ride to the pickup point with Warner and Sutherland, there always seemed to be one of the Militia Men in the motel courtyard. There was a constant stream of them moving back and forth between the rooms. From what Lyons saw they might have been short on talk, but they made up for in their capacity to consume large amounts of beer judging from the cans they permanently carried.

In the end Lyons stopped worrying about it.

THE MEET WAS on some back lot, behind a half-demolished building. It was on the fringe of the international district, close to the Chinese section. Restaurants and stores, all promising the best the Orient had to offer. The damp air was heavy with the smells of Chinese food. It drifted back and forth, pumped out by the extractor fans of the busy kitchens.

Carl Lyons sat in the rear seat of the 4×4. Warner and Sutherland were up front. They had arrived a good forty minutes before the arranged time. Sutherland turned out to be a bad waiter. He was fidgeting within a few minutes. He took out his handgun and checked it, put it away, then took it out again. His partner watched this with mounting irritation until he couldn't hold back any longer.

"Deke, for fuck's sake put the gun away and go get us some coffee."

Sutherland replaced the gun in his shoulder holster and zipped up the thick jacket he was wearing.

"You want coffee, Jag?"

Lyons nodded. "Sounds good to me."

Sutherland opened his door and climbed out. He vanished across the dark back lot.

"He always like this?" Lyons asked.

Warner half turned in his seat. "This is nothing. Which is why I sent him off. Ignore it and he gets really wound up."

"Hope he doesn't do it in a fight."

"Hey, Deke's no chicken. He'll pull his weight come the time, and don't you forget it."

Lyons raised his hands in mock surrender. "Back off, pal, I was just checking. Man likes to know he can depend on his buddies when the hammer comes down. That's all."

Warner relaxed. "I guess we're all getting a tad uptight. This deal has been a while coming. Been hard getting off the ground."

"I did my spell of waitin' to go into action," Lyons said. "Don't like the hanging around myself."

They sat in silence for a few minutes.

"We going to be in Seattle long?"

"Beats me," Warner said. "Tetrow don't tell all. He keeps feeding us little pieces when he figures we need to know."

"Why? Doesn't he trust anyone?" Lyons asked with a disarming grin on his face.

Warner grinned right back. "Maybe so. Riles me sometimes. Like we ain't as committed as he is. Christ, we all been with him through every damn thing he done. Nearly got our butts shot off when we snuck in to take a look at the radar site up Dakota way."

"I guess Hub has his reasons," Lyons said, sensing that Warner was getting too agitated. He didn't want the man to say too much and then regret it. "The guy has a lot to think about right now."

"Yeah, I guess so," Warner mumbled. "Still and all, when we hit that site we could of been took down by them fuckin' security guards. He shouldn't forget that. Maybe he'll remember when the raid goes off."

Lyons took that in but made no reply. He caught sight of Sutherland on his way back with coffee in paper cups, balanced in a cardboard tray.

"Hey, Joe, this's what we need," he said, breaking Warner's train of thought.

Sutherland climbed into the cab and passed out the coffee. It was hot and strong.

"Did anybody want food?" he asked.

No one did. They drank the coffee and waited.

The delivery arrived ten minutes behind schedule. A battered panel truck that was so ordinary even Lyons would have been hard-pressed to describe it. The truck pulled up alongside the 4×4 and a stocky, middle-aged man climbed out. He wore faded denim and cross trainers that looked only a fraction cleaner than his truck. His graying hair hung in untidy layers across his large skull. He leaned in at Warner's window.

"Coffee? You mothers look after yourselves. I ain't had a fuckin' drink since noon."

"Look, my eyes are fillin' up with tears," Warner said. "George, give me the consignment so we can go, huh? Message from Tetrow. He wants another shipment of LAWs. Couple of dozen."

George nodded. "Can do. How soon?"

"Yesterday. Know what I mean?"

"Yeah."

George glanced over Warner's shoulder, eyeing Lyons.

"New guy," Warner said. "Jag."

George nodded. "How's she going?"

"Gettin' there," Lyons replied.

They climbed out and crossed to the rear of George's truck. He dragged open the rear doors and between them Lyons and his partners carried four long wooden boxes to their vehicle and slid them inside. From the size and weight Lyons judged them to be autorifles. Next came a half-dozen smaller, heavier boxes. Ammunition. As soon as the boxes were in the 4×4, Warner closed and locked the rear door. He went across to where George was waiting and handed him a thick white envelope.

"I'll get back to you about the LAWs," George said, and ambled back to his panel truck.

Lyons watched it trundle out of the lot. He had already made a note of the license plate and committed it to memory.

"Let's go," Warner said.

He was about to drive off when his cell phone rang. He answered it and listened to the caller, then handed the phone to Lyons.

"For you. Teeler."

Lyons took the phone, wondering what the hell Teeler wanted, and somehow got the feeling it wouldn't be good.

"Jag? Let the boys haul out the delivery. You wait

there for me. I'll pick you up in a while. Something else for you and me to do. See you, pal.''

Lyons handed the phone back to Warner. ''Teeler wants me to wait here for him.''

He climbed back out of the 4×4 and slapped his hand against the door panel. Sutherland leaned out of his window.

''Hey, Jag, watch your back, buddy. Know what I mean?''

Lyons nodded and watched the 4×4 ease out of the back lot and vanish along the street, rear lights winking.

He found a place to wait, his back to a crumbling wall, watching the distant street, and wondered just what Teeler was up to. For the first time since he had joined the Militia Men he was on his own. Lyons glanced around, wondering if there was a pay phone in the area. If there was, it would likely have been vandalized. His only chance to contact Stony Man, and there wasn't much he could do about it. He couldn't risk Teeler finding him making a call. For all he knew, the man might even be watching him already, checking him out to see what he might do now he was alone.

So where the hell was the son of a bitch?

Lyons forced himself to calm down. He would need a clear head when Teeler did turn up.

Minutes passed. Very little happened on the distant street. The back lot was off the main thoroughfare. Lyons shoved his hands deep into his pockets and hunched his shoulders against the chill air.

He saw the car before he heard it. A long, low limo.

Black, with tinted windows. It sat low on its suspension, rocking as the driver turned off the street onto the uneven back lot. There were no lights showing. Lyons watched it make its way across the lot in his direction. It rolled to a stop ten feet from where he stood. It sat for a while. Lyons didn't move. He felt safer with his back to the wall.

The driver's door opened and a large man eased out and stood upright. He was broad in the shoulders and chest, but his soft gut was showing over his belt. He wore all leather, black, and even sported a pair of tinted Ray•Ban sunglasses. He wore his hair in a severe crew cut. He stared at Lyons, not speaking, then tapped large knuckles on the roof of the limo. Both rear doors opened and two more Identi-kit figures stepped out. They joined the driver, leaning against the side of the car.

"This is all very John Shaft, fellers," Lyons said conversationally, "but I'm waiting for a friend. You guys come from him?"

The driver glanced at his two companions, then back at Lyons. "What the fuck you talkin' about? Shaft was black. Do I look black to you, bubba?"

Lyons took his hands from his pockets and eased slightly forward.

"I lost this somewhere along the line," he said. "You sure you got the right guy? Like I said, I'm waitin' on somebody. If you're not the ones, then just back off 'cause I'm not in the mood for your crap."

"Friend, you got a loose mouth. You come on our territory and start shooting it off. Not nice. Time to get a lesson in manners."

Lyons groaned inwardly. This couldn't happening. It was like something out of a cheap video.

One of the trio drew a length of chain from his belt loops and wrapped a few inches around his fist, swinging the free end through the air. On a signal from the driver the three spread out and began to close in on Lyons.

The Able Team leader remained where he was, watching his potential attackers. He didn't waste time wondering what was going on, or why this bunch of idiots was intent on crippling him. That could come later. Right now his priority was dealing with the immediate threat.

He saw right away they were just local bad boys, the kind who roved the streets in groups, looking for trouble, but only if the odds were in their favor. He had dealt with plenty of them when he'd worn the uniform. Hard when their prey was weak and unable to fight back. In the back of patrol car they were sullen and silent, all the defiance fading away once they realized their backup had gone.

The one with the chain came in first, the steel links whistling as they slashed the air. The guy had that slightly unhinged gleam in his eyes that told Lyons he was on something, which made him less dangerous, but also less predictable because he wasn't in full control.

Lyons saw him tense a microsecond before he moved, signaling his intention. A soft exhalation and the guy swung the chain in at Lyons, following it close. He made a sound that was a poor imitation of Bruce Lee's trademark cry. The chain cut the air and

Lyons was able to duck under it. He felt the wind of its passing over his head, then he was powering forward, driving in fast and low. His bunched right fist smashed hard into chain man's testicles. Lyons didn't hold back, putting all his strength into the blow. It drew a screech from the chain man. Lyons continued his forward rush, shoulder slamming his target. His bulk drove the guy off his feet and almost spun him over onto his face. He hit the hard ground with a solid thump, the back of his skull impacting with a sodden crunch.

On the fringe of Lyons's vision a dark figure swept in on his left. Lyons dropped to the ground, twisting over on his back, and caught the incoming figure with a leg sweep. The guy hit the ground with force enough to drive the air from his lungs. Lyons rolled to his feet, turned and with deliberate intent drove the toe of his boot into the side of the guy's head.

Attacker number three slammed into his adversary, pushing him back, a sharp right glancing off Lyons's left cheek. The guy turned his attention elsewhere, his fists driving into the Able Team leader's ribs. Lyons took a number of bruising blows before he was able to throw his arms around the man, hugging him tight to his chest. The man, unable to get leverage now, looked up into his opponent's face and received a savage head butt that crushed his nose to bloody cartilage.

In the moment of impact, feeling the man weaken, Lyons broke his grip, pushed the guy away, then hit him with hard fists to the jaw. The blows were crushing, shattering the guy's jaw bones. He stumbled back against the side of the limo, blood streaming down his face. He made a feeble attempt at warding off Lyons's attack. He failed and went down under the brutal barrage of punches.

The former LAPD cop felt the pained ache engulfing his ribs as he bent and dragged the prone figure of his final assailant away from the limo. He slid in behind the wheel and found the key in the ignition. Lyons turned on the engine, dropped the lever into drive and spun the limo in a tight circle, taking it across the back lot and on to the street. He made a right, heading away from the area and kept driving until he hit a main highway. He drove until he spotted a fast-food outlet. He pulled into the parking area, choosing a spot in a corner and parked up. He checked the interior of the limo and after going through the glove box he found, in among all the other junk, a cell phone. He switched the phone on and found there was power.

Lyons got out of the car, leaving it open and walked away. He keyed in the Stony Man number and listened to the electronic sound of the connection being made via satellite links. It wasn't long before he was through and speaking to Barbara Price.

"Carl, are you okay?"

"Let's just say I can remember better days."

"Where are you?"

"Seattle. Arrived late yesterday. The MM have split. Some are up here, and the rest are still at the base in Liberty Flats. I think whatever they're planning is going down soon. And I get the feeling there's something here in Seattle. You want to check it out?

Can't tell you any more because I don't know. I got a name for you to check out. Boris Yesinovich. He's a Russian contact. He mentioned a team being trained up for the action in Alaska. They all figure it's going to be some party up there. Rick Teeler finally showed, Tetrow's second in command. Plays the hard guy. Tonight we had a meet with a guy who supplies the MM with weapons. His first name is George. That's all I know.''

Lyons gave Price the number of George's truck, then gave her time to list all the details.

''That's all I can give you. Everything is being played close. If I get another chance, you'll hear from me.''

''Any problems with your cover?''

''Seems to be holding. Teeler's playing at giving me a hard time. I figure he's the one to watch.''

''Carl, take care. We're all rooting for you. Especially Pol and Hermann.''

''Why? No one to piss off now I'm not around?''

''Something like that.''

''Where are they?''

''They took off for Dakota. They probably don't know there's been movement from the ranch. I'll let them know.''

''Phoenix?''

''Somewhere in Siberia. Haven't heard from them for a while.''

''I'll sign off now.''

''Okay.''

There was a click and the line went dead.

Lyons considered his next move. He was going to have to face Teeler about why he hadn't waited. But then Teeler would know. The sudden appearance of the three hardmen had been no coincidence. Teeler had sent them as some kind of test. To see if Lyons—Jag—was really as hard as he made out. Teeler would have been expecting to find Lyons laid out the ground, bruised and bloody. Maybe even crippled. It would depend on what instructions the trio had been given. When they did meet up, Teeler was going to play it close. He would be angry that his scheme hadn't worked, but the very fact Lyons had walked away might go in his favor. It would show that he wasn't going to stand by and take anything thrown at him.

Lyons looked at the cell phone. There was a temptation to keep it. So he could make contact with base when he needed to. But there was the chance it might be discovered. He figured getting rid of it was the safest option, but he didn't want anyone from the MM locating it and doing some checking on where calls might have been made to. Lyons smiled. He was getting paranoid. Or cautious. He opened the back of the phone and took out the small memory card. He dropped the phone on the ground and crushed it under his boot, kicking the shattered pieces into the trash at the side of the road. Then he snapped the card and scattered the pieces as he walked on, looking for a cab to take him back to the motel. It suddenly felt cold, and Carl Lyons found himself experiencing a moment of loneliness.

Stony Man Farm, Virginia

CARMEN DELAHUNT TOOK exactly thirty-five minutes to come up with background on the man initially identified as George.

George Simms was forty-two and twice imprisoned for theft and receiving stolen property. No convictions for violence. Simms was a fringe radical, and was suspected of passing stolen merchandise to the militia groups. He lived on the outskirts of Seattle, and while he never appeared to do much work, he managed to stay solvent.

Delahunt's digging uncovered a list of his known associates. One turned out to be a man named Jack Trenker who operated a haulage business out of Liberty Flats, North Dakota. Trenker was a known member of the Militia Men.

The moment this information came onto Delahunt's monitor she called in Barbara Price. Price scanned the information and got on the phone to Able Team, passing them the details that had come up on Jack Trenker.

"Got something for you guys to check out. Carl managed to call through. A number of the Militia Men are in Seattle. Looks like the operation has moved up a notch. The rest are still around Liberty Flats. Carl came up with a name. We checked him out and guess what—he has a contact in the Militia Men by the name of Jack Trenker. He runs a haulage company based near Liberty Flats."

"Something for us to check out," Blancanales said. "We'll go and look him over in the morning. Next time Carl calls in tell him thanks for the information.''

''Will do.''

''How did he sound?''

''Hard to say. You know Carl. He isn't the world's best at expressing his feelings.''

''I guess not,'' Blancanales said. ''Catch you later, Barb.''

South of Liberty Flats

''THERE SHE IS,'' Blancanales said, pointing across the dusty strip of highway.

Schwarz rolled the car to the far side, moving onto the rutted feeder road. He drove by the warehouse and parked on the far side of the next building along. After killing the engine, Schwarz climbed out, with Blancanales following. They skirted the rear of the far building, coming in at the rear of Trenker's place. The back lot was untidy, littered with empty packing cases and drums. There were old engine parts and a scattering of tires. Dry grass had grown up between the piles of scrap.

''Real tidy sort of guy, this Trenker,'' Schwarz said.

''You think there's anyone inside?''

Schwarz shrugged. ''No vehicle parked out front, but that doesn't mean anything. Maybe he parked inside.''

Blancanales nodded. He crouched and moved up to the corner of the warehouse and pressed against the scabby paneling. He covered his partner as Schwarz moved in, too.

There was a small access door in the rear wall, next to the larger roll-up door. When Blancanales tried the handle he found the door was locked. Undeterred, he moved to the roll-up door and saw that it wasn't fully closed. There was a two-foot gap at the bottom. Schwarz wasn't overly impressed when his partner pointed this out.

"Come on, buddy," Blancanales said, "anyone can get in through an unlocked door. This is more of a challenge."

"And undignified."

Blancanales grinned. "Since when has style ever bothered you?"

Schwarz stood by while Blancanales dropped to the ground and rolled under the door. Moments later he called Schwarz to join him. They stood side by side in the gloomy interior. There wasn't a great deal to see. As a warehouse, the place left a lot to be desired. The wide, high-roofed building was practically empty. Rows of high shelving occupied the northeast corner. Apart from a few cardboard cartons the shelves were empty. More cartons, torn open and empty, were strewed across the floor. The place hadn't seen a broom in months. At the far end of the warehouse, near the main roll-up door, stood a battered, dusty Dodge 4×4, painted a dull red-brown color. On the door they could see the legend Jack Trenker—Haulage & Storage, along with the warehouse address and telephone number. Beside the Dodge stood a sleek black Plymouth.

There was an office block in one corner of the building and Blancanales caught movement on the other side of the dusty glass.

"Trenker has a visitor," he said to Schwarz.

They drew their handguns and began to work their way down to the office. They stopped short, moving in behind the rear wall of the block. It was thin enough so they were able to pick up the tail end of the conversation.

"...and you can confirm arrival of the final consignment?"

"Said so, didn't I? Look, friend, I made my bones in this fuckin' business. If I say it'll be there, it will. Trust me."

"Do I have a choice?"

"What can I say?"

"It *must* be in place by tomorrow evening."

"Back off," Trenker snapped, his tone hardening. "I don't need anyone telling me how to run my business. You got a complaint, go see Tetrow. Only remember he'll tell you same fuckin' thing. I don't give a rat's ass who you are back in Russia. This is America. Don't push me around in my own country. The delivery will arrive here tonight. We can ship it out tomorrow and be on-site well before your deadline."

"I will come back in the morning. Perhaps by then you will be in a better mood."

"Don't count on it."

The visitor left the office, crossing to the Plymouth.

He was a stocky man, his dark hair cropped short. His square face had heavy cheeks, and there was an irregular bulge under the skin of the left one. The bone had been broken at some time and had healed awkwardly. He wore a black suit and black shirt. He moved easily, confident of his own ability to take care of himself. He climbed into the car, started the engine and swung the car around. Stopping at the roll-up door, he waited while Trenker opened it. The Plymouth rolled outside and across the yard. When the vehicle pulled onto the road outside the yard, Trenker closed the door and made his way back to the office, muttering to himself.

Edging to the window, Blancanales peered inside and saw Trenker pick up the phone. The man punched in the numbers as if he were trying to push them through the casing. He waited for a while, then slammed down the receiver when he failed to get a reply.

Schwarz had retreated to the far end of the building. By the time Blancanales reached him, Schwarz was using his cell phone.

"Run a check on this Dakota plate," he said, quoting the number from the Plymouth. "See if it means anything. Call me. Okay?"

"Trenker's delivery sounds interesting," Blancanales said.

"Maybe we should tag along and see what it's all about," Schwarz suggested.

They eased their way back to where they had entered the warehouse, then retraced their steps to the parked car. Schwarz drove back to the main highway and headed for the motel.

Schwarz's cell phone rang; Blancanales picked it up.

"He's busy driving. What have you got for us?"

Kurtzman's gruff tones boomed out of the phone.

"The license is registered to a rental company in

Minot, North Dakota, which is based at the international airport there. The vehicle was rented three days ago by a Leonid Treshenko. Apparently he's here on vacation from Europe. We're running a background check on him right now. Where does he fit in?''

"He just left a meeting with our friend Trenker. They were having words about some special delivery Trenker has to make tomorrow night. I guess we'll go along too and see what the delivery is.''

"Okay,'' Kurtzman said. "I'll get the data to you soon as.''

"We'll be back at our motel in half an hour,'' Blancanales said. "We'll use the laptop and contact you when we've arrived.''

ONCE THEY WERE BACK and in Schwarz's room, Blancanales switched on the laptop and made the connection with Stony Man. He used an instant message service to let Kurtzman know they were online.

Blancanales: Do you have anything on Treshenko?
Kurtzman: More than we expected. I logged on to immigration and downloaded his file. The background he put down on his application is a crock. Leonid Treshenko doesn't exist. Not when you go beyond what immigration checked. I ran his photograph through all the data banks we can access. His real name is Valentene Nureyev. The guy specializes in covert ops. As far as we know, he's still with the Russian security network. This joker is very good at infiltrating organizations,

getting their trust and milking them for all they've got. He's also a die-hard Communist and has been linked with similar types within the Russian military system.

Blancanales: So what's he doing cozying up with the Militia Men? We know they're tied with a Russian group with similar objectives to their own.

Kurtzman: Barb asks how do we know this Russian group is what it claims to be? Maybe they're using Militia Men for their own agenda.

Blancanales: That woman has a disturbingly suspicious mind. But she could have something. Check on any other names that come up in this Russian group. We'll talk later.

Kurtzman: Okay. Barb says good thing someone around here is on the ball!

Logging off, Blancanales leaned back in his chair, studying the text on his screen.

"Interesting point there," he said.

Schwarz nodded. "Easy way for the opposition to get at Slingshot. Make friends with a dissident group in the States and use their American know-how to get to the target. Bring in the Chinese and the Koreans because none of them would like the idea of Slingshot waiting in the wings to steal the limelight."

"Hell of an alliance there."

Schwarz shrugged. "So what's new? We set up something for our defense and the paranoid chapter starts bleating about U.S. dominance again. But no one says a damn thing about the North Koreans developing their missile systems and selling them to anyone with a pocket full of cash.''

"As far as I can see this should be an internal matter. We want to deploy missile defense within the U.S. the hell with anyone who doesn't like it.''

"Pol, the rest of the world is all peace and love now. No need to have missiles any longer.''

Blancanales curled his lip. "Yeah, and my ass is a cream doughnut.''

CHAPTER FIVE

Moscow

Nikolai Gagarin gazed from the window of his apartment and watched the slow-moving traffic pass along the bleak, snow-streaked street. The former KGB colonel didn't like the new Moscow, or the new Russia. His loyalty was still directed toward the old regime, and he felt himself lucky to be a major player in one of the influential hard-line parties that had grown out of the change. There were still many like himself, true Communists who wouldn't—couldn't— alter their ways. They saw the democratizing of Russia as a bad thing. The power and the control had gone from the masters and had been handed over to the people. The result was a nation in shambles, rolling over to play the West's games. The powerful war machine of the Soviet Union had been run down, its forces decimated, its missiles dismantled, leaving the country wide open. The government claimed the Russians still had a formidable array of weaponry, but Gagarin knew the right people to ask and they knew the truth. He learned about the desertions from the army, the soldiers slipping away because they hadn't been paid in months and were sick of the mind-numbing duties they had to perform. Old colleagues had informed about the shaky state of the air force, about the nuclear subs rotting away in the docking pens.

The dissolution was like a spreading disease, reaching out to all stratas of life. In the cities the police couldn't cope with the influx of drugs and liquor. Nor were they able to outgun the brutal gangs of criminals. The Russian Mafia, as it had been labeled, ran entire areas of the country and controlled city streets. It would never have happened in his day. The criminals would have been taken off the streets and sent to the gulags, where they would have paid the penalty of trying to threaten the state. The labor camps were gone now, their gates left wide open to creak in the bitter Siberian wind. The prisoners had been let free, allowed to return to the cities and towns where they could carry on with their illegal activities.

It was madness, but it was the new Russia. Gagarin, wise in the ways of surviving, remained silent, preferring to wait until he was in the company of like-minded men before he expressed his feelings. And all the while, silent and meticulous, those friends and colleagues were doing what they could to try to return some kind of order to the country. It was difficult now that the Soviet empire had been broken up into independent states, each responsible for its own destiny. No longer fully controlled by Moscow, the sprawling monolith had let its power drain away, leaving it weaker than before, but still with a sound heart beating. Many in government were of the old school. They were fighting the battle, quietly chipping away at the bastions of the new Russia, and making darker plans in the background.

An example was the American project to create its own antimissile shield. The plan depended on the construction of ultrapowerful radar facilities in Alaska, with other sites around the U.S. and even abroad. These radar establishments were touted by the Americans as being nothing more than purely for internal defense. Gagarin was able to study U.S. government plans for the system, known as Slingshot, courtesy of the Chinese. They had managed to steal data on the system and attempted to build a duplicate so they could control the U.S. missile-control center. Although they had gone so far down the line the replica had been destroyed by American specialists, aided by a group of Chinese opposed to Communist rule in China. After some months information surfaced, handled by a Chinese woman named Shun Wei. Previously the mistress of the Chinese colonel heading the project destroyed by the Americans, she had grandiose plans, wanting to be in full charge of the attempts to destroy the Slingshot system in Alaska. She was, however, forced to share her knowledge with both the North Koreans and the Russians. It made sense. All three nations needed the same result—the destruction of the American antimissile system. Each of the three would have been compromised if Slingshot emerged up and running. There was little trust in the words of the U.S. administration when it stated that Slingshot was to be used solely as protection for mainland America. However, neither Russia, China nor North Korea could be pacified. They all saw the system as a direct threat, placing America as the dominant power wielding nuclear strength.

Gagarin was asked to head the Russian team looking into ways of destroying the American system. He quickly came up with a solution that involved a dissident group in America that called itself the Militia Men. Gagarin studied the American phenomenon of antigovernment, isolationist groups. They almost always lived in distant rural areas, well away from the mainstream of U.S. life. They trained with weapons, forming themselves into military style organizations, and they existed on a belief in a government out to destroy them, who sent black ops groups to spy on and harass them. They believed in a coming war between the militia groups and federal forces. In their desolate hideouts they stored weapons and food, waiting for the day when they would face the government troops who wanted to deprive them of their freedom. Gagarin was amused at their naive patriotism. Their unshakable certainty that they were the true Americans and were prepared to die proving it.

It didn't take him very long to identify the Militia Men. They were already into a campaign directed at the construction of the Slingshot radar system in Alaska. The leader of the group, Hubbard Tetrow, had made it his crusade. He, and as he quoted, thousands of ordinary Americans, didn't want the antimissile system because all it would do would be to alert Russia and China and any others who stood against America to rebuild their own nuclear arsenals. The treaties and the peace initiatives would be forgotten as each nation, considering itself to be under the eye of Slingshot, threatened to start the missile race all over again. Far from telling the world that it was safe from attack, America would be inviting such attacks, because the world didn't want the U.S. to be the only major power capable of launching a vast missile program, with satellite targeting that covered the world.

Overnight Gagarin devised a way of utilizing the Militia Men. Utilizing people he had worked with before, he created the Russian militia group, developing the manifesto that would be presented to Hubbard Tetrow, along with an offer from the group to help neutralize Slingshot. Gagarin employed all his professional cunning in presenting a picture of an underground organization in conflict with its own government and desperate to halt any plans to resurrect a new missile program. His creation was a masterpiece, and Gagarin experienced a feeling that he was back in the old days, manipulating and guiding unsuspecting individuals to follow his will. With the aid of his collaborators Gagarin presented such a genuine image of a group struggling against governmental pressure that reeling in Tetrow was comparatively easy. When he had, after the first few weeks, offered physical aid and even finance, Tetrow had allowed himself to be drawn even deeper.

A rabid antiestablishment man, Teeler's response surprised even Gagarin. The ferocity of Teeler's rage against the U.S. federal authority made Gagarin realize he had chosen the right way to attack the Slingshot enterprise.

There was a carefully orchestrated set of meetings between the two groups. Gagarin's man went to the U.S., while Teeler visited Russia. It was all done without alarming anyone not involved, in either country, so that the quiet manipulation of the Militia Men continued at a steady pace. Gagarin was discreet in whom he allowed Teeler to meet. Due to the involvement of the Chinese and the North Koreans, Gagarin didn't want Teeler to be allowed to discuss too much, or begin to sense there was more to the Russian plan than he had been told. Knowing Shun Wei's feminine presence would interest the man, Gagarin arranged that she be present during one of the visits, and as he'd anticipated, the American was totally overwhelmed by her. To her credit Shun Wei simply played the game, using her beauty and sexual wiles to draw Teeler deftly into her web of deceit.

The sudden death of Shun Wei, only because she insisted on being present when the informer, Kranski, was killed, was a blessing in disguise. Her arrogant manner and desire to dominate the overall operation regarding Slingshot had been growing out of all proportion. Kranski had done them all a favor. The Chinese woman would probably have been dead within days regardless.

Niggling problems did exist, though. Kranski had been working covertly for a group dedicated to disrupting any operations the Chinese government became involved with. The very same group, led by a dissident Chinese named Mei Anna, was partly responsible for the elimination of Li Cheng and his operation. Now the same woman was interfering in the ongoing operation. Despite stringent security precautions, Mei Anna got into Siberia and gained details that might prove embarrassing to the project. She slipped away from the people pursuing her and eventually turned up in London, where she contacted someone. There was an attempt on her life while she was in London. It failed, and two of the Chinese operatives were killed.

Since then Mei Anna had vanished from sight. Gagarin assumed she was in the hands of the British or American security services and she had been taken to some isolated safehouse. He dismissed her from his thoughts after that. There was enough to do without worrying over a lone woman.

His main concern centered on the sudden appearance of the covert group who had routed the people sent to check out the late Kranski's house near Khabarovsk. The presence of the group and the resistance they offered had taken the contract group, belonging to the man called Malinchek, off guard. A number of them had died before a retreat was effected. Though it was too late to do anything now, Gagarin regretted getting involved with Feodor Malinchek. The man was little more than a street criminal. However, he was valuable because of his knowledge of the area and his control over everything contraband that moved in or out of that same area.

Gagarin was able to recruit some former military personnel, led by the forceful Vladimir Biryenko. Biryenko managed to gather a small but professional team, and they would be the ones who would lead the attack on the American radar facility in Alaska.

So, despite his misgivings, Gagarin had his group, composed of professionals and pure and simple criminals. Such, he decided, was the state of the country. In the past he would have had a full team of Mokrie Dela operatives. The KGB assassins were the cream of the Soviet terror machine, utter professionals trained in every lethal skill. Once one his most valuable assets, now they were gone, disbanded, scattered around the country, many of them beyond the age where they were of any practical use.

Unlike the American team, he thought.

Something in the style and professionalism of the new group stirred a distant memory in Gagarin's mind. He recalled coming up against a similar group some years back during his KGB days. It was a commando-style team working for the U.S. government, and Gagarin tried to establish some kind of background on it. He had failed at the time, and as events unfolded he hadn't had the opportunity to do any more about them. Had they, he wondered, come back to plague him again?

He was certain that the Americans would do everything they could to put a stop to whoever was trying to destroy their precious Slingshot project. If they had information gained from the Chinese woman, Mei Anna, they would undoubtedly use it to their advantage. The more he thought about it, Gagarin made the connection between this group and the one that had engaged Li Cheng and destroyed his island facility. He felt a little foolish when he made the connection, because it had been staring him in the face and he had almost missed it.

He remained at the window, his mind returning to the thoughts that had just intruded. The American commando team. How could he not have made the connection before? Gagarin was capable of self deprecation, though it wasn't a trait he showed in public. To himself he admitted that perhaps he was getting old. It happened to the best. The mind played tricks.

The days of the old Soviet Union had long passed, and so had time, slipping away with quiet regularity. The world had changed over time, not for the best in many instances. It was still a savage, unrelenting place. Nations still struggled for recognition, for a place in the sun, and the ones whose former glory had slipped away from them still reached out in the hope of survival. To that end they were prepared to do anything, go to any lengths to maintain their position on the map. It was ingrained in the human psyche. To be the dominant power. The top of the heap.

America was attempting just that. The policy behind the Slingshot project was a thinly disguised ploy to gain superiority in the missile stakes. Once the project became established, with the tracking and control systems in place, the missile sites would quickly follow. It was so easy for the U.S. to say the missiles were for home defense. How would anyone know the power and target distance of the missiles in the secret silos hidden around the country? With the great leaps in technology, the Americans were capable of creating projectiles that could reach halfway around the world, while in the open meetings they would condemn any other nation that admitted to building the same. Hypocrisy was self-evident in almost every statement issuing from the Americans. They had abandoned truth, using words as slippery tools to send out their messages of false hope.

But this time they would be served a kind of justice when Slingshot was toppled before it could be established, and the millions of dollars already poured into the Alaska project would be lost. The irony was the involvement of real Americans in the destruction. The disillusioned Militia Men, one of many similar groups, were tired of their own government's lies. Too many times the federal authorities had lied and cheated their own people. Pressured and bullied, their freedom on rocky ground, the Militia Men were ready to act. Before Gagarin's "militant" group had contacted them, Hubbard Tetrow was already moving down the road for confrontation. Realizing the shadow of a new cold war and arms race was about to fall across the land, Tetrow had taken his followers into the front line. They were already forming their plan, ready to fight for their very lives. Now, with the cooperation of Gagarin's group, the campaign was moving inexorably toward zero hour.

Tetrow had a contact within the federal government, and this individual had provided valuable information. He was able to access construction plans for the Alaska radar facility, and using those plans Gagarin's group had constructed a mock-up. His team was using it to train, allowing them to refine their actual strike on the real site. They would get one chance. There would be no rerun. No second strike. Once the teams stepped into the light, the Americans would react quickly. The site would suddenly become inaccessible. Even the American President would find it difficult to get near. One thing about the Americans. They might be lax sometimes, perhaps through a feeling of superiority, sure that no one could ever strike them. The moment they were caught off guard, the steel shutters went up and the security shield went into overdrive. So any operation against Slingshot needed to be foolproof. It had to go perfectly on the day. A phrase Gagarin had heard somewhere before came into his mind: failure was not an option.

Gagarin's attention was drawn to the sound of his telephone. He crossed to the desk and snatched the instrument from its receiver. The voice came through sharp and clear on the satellite link system.

"They are here," Malinchek said. "I believe they are looking for the camp."

Gagarin was silent for a moment, frustrated at the way Malinchek seemed incapable of dealing with anything requiring a degree of intelligent thought.

"Are they close?"

"Close enough for us to worry."

"Then deal with them," Gagarin said. "I want them dead. Get a team out from the camp and find them. Kill them. If they are dead, the threat ceases. And this time send your best men. I need Biryenko at the facility."

"We should be able to send the strike team to Alaska soon," Malinchek informed him.

"How soon is soon?"

"Two days."

"Too risky. If this American team is close and it manages to get inside the facility, our timetable could be compromised. Get Biryenko to the phone. I need to speak with him.''

"He is here.''

Moments later the deep tones of Vladimir Biryenko came on the line.

"What do you need me to do, Comrade Gagarin?''

"It is possible that an American incursion team is close by. They will be coming to look at what we've been doing. They must not be allowed to interfere with you and your team. The risk is too great. Leave as soon as is possible. Load up with everything you need, take the helicopter and get away from the compound. You will need to find somewhere near the coastline. Set up a base, establish radio communication with me and then wait for my signal for you to go in. Is that perfectly clear?''

"Of course.''

"Vladimir, this is for your ears only. Do you understand? For you and *your* men.''

"Understood.''

"Put Malinchek back on the line and go about your business.''

"I am here,'' Malinchek snapped when he took the phone back.

"Don't sulk, Feodor, it doesn't suit you. Do what I ask and everything will be fine.''

"If you say so, Nikolai.''

"Use the radar. You might be able to pinpoint where they have landed. I am guessing they will have flown in from Alaska and put down some distance from the facility so as not to be spotted. That gives you the advantage. They do not know the country.

You do. Use that to track them. Harass them. Keep them away from the place for as long as possible. That will give you time to strengthen the defenses if they do get through.''

''Very well,'' Malinchek said.

''Keep me up-to-date with matters,'' Gagarin stated. ''If you have problems, contact me immediately.''

He cut the connection and sat down. More problems. But nothing they couldn't handle with a little foresight. Malinchek, despite his excellence when it came to acquiring matériel and information, wasn't a military tactician. When it came to conflict, he simply resorted to his bullying technique. That was of no use when he might be up against a superb paramilitary force such as the American team.

Gagarin hoped fervently that the Americans were the ones he had previously encountered. Perhaps this time he might be able to reverse the outcome and remove them from the scene permanently. It would be something good he could take into his retirement, he thought wryly.

CHAPTER SIX

Siberian Peninsula

The ground underfoot was hard, any vegetation frosted and stiff from the low temperature. Expelled breath hung in pale wreaths, and air drawn into lungs was sharp.

"And I thought Chicago could be cold," Calvin James muttered.

His words were the first thing to be spoken for a long time. The extremes of the Russian climate seemed to have achieved something other situations had failed to do—blunt the edge of the team's usual banter. Even the casual McCarter, the mainstay of their verbal output, was keeping his mouth closed. As far as the group was concerned, that was even more scary than anything else.

They were all feeling the cold despite the layers of protective clothing they wore. The constant wind, though not fierce, had a keen edge to it. It sought out any minuscule gap in their clothing, and when it penetrated the effect was felt instantly. It was easy to understand why the old Soviet Union had used the desolate Siberian area to establish its labor camps. Escape from any of the camps simply took the hapless escapee from one living hell to another. Ill clad and most probably on the verge of starvation, the fugitive would have little chance of survival.

As they traveled, McCarter constantly checked the GPS readout, making sure they were maintaining their correct line of travel. The featureless landscape was bereft of any significant landmarks, and the Briton knew they would have been in trouble without the help of the satellite fix.

In early afternoon they took a short break, sheltering in the only handy spot, a natural dip in the land that allowed them a slight escape from the wind.

"Hey, David, how much farther?" Encizo asked.

"Two, maybe three hours," McCarter said. "Unless the weather changes and slows us down."

"Bet you're glad you asked now," Manning commented as Encizo curled his lip.

"Sure, I'm over the moon."

"Be cold up there, too," Hawkins observed.

Encizo glowered at him, shrugging deeper into his heavy parka.

"Think of somewhere warm," James suggested. "In your mind. Imagine a sandy beach in Cuba."

"I'd rather imagine you guys running around out here in your underwear," Encizo said.

McCarter glanced at him. "That make you feel warmer?"

"No. But it makes me happy thinking of you jokers freezing off your butts."

"Some people get like that in extreme temperatures,'' McCarter said. ''They just lose all sense of proportion and get downright grumpy.''

''You think *this* is grumpy?'' Encizo asked.

When they emerged from their cover they noticed the wind had increased in power. It slapped at their clothing, rattling anything loose, and in the process of skittering across the landscape it picked up loose, powdery snow and flung it around like pale sand. The iced granules stung the exposed skin of their faces, and by a perverse whim the team found it was walking directly into the wind.

Within the next twenty minutes the wind force increased dramatically, snow started to fall, covering them with a brittle layer of freezing flakes.

McCarter ordered them to close up, making certain that each man could see the one ahead. He was aware how easy it would be to lose contact with one another simply by stepping out of line and being swallowed by the swirling mist of snow. The wind, changing direction every so often, battered them from all sides. There wasn't a thing they could do except keep moving. When McCarter stopped, the others stopped, waiting patiently until he signaled for them to move on again. The only reason he did stop was to take another look at the GPS unit, locating their position and moving them back on track if they had veered away for any reason.

Hunched over, clutching their weapons tight against their chests, Phoenix Force maintained its pace until McCarter called another halt. This time he called them around him.

''Looks like something ahead,'' he told them. ''I

don't think it's the base. Could just be a rock formation. It might give us some shelter.''

"Maybe it's a Kentucky Fried Chicken outlet," Hawkins suggested.

"You and your damn stomach," Manning said.

"I'm a growin' boy."

McCarter tapped James and Encizo on the shoulder. "You two flank me. Keep in sight of each other. Gary, you and Starvin' Marvin bring up the rear. You watch all of us.''

They stepped forward, moving with extreme caution as the dark shape emerged from the white swirl ahead. Ten feet from the object they were still unable to make out what it was. McCarter hefted his MP-5, checking the action, then walked a little ahead of the others until he was almost touching the object. They all picked up his burst of laughter.

"It's a bloody hut!''

Shuffling through the snow, they gathered around McCarter, who was thumping his gloved fist against the rough timber of what was obviously a wall.

They checked out the size and shape, moving around the hut and picking out windows, and eventually a door. Encizo put his boot against it and shoved it open. The door swung back on creaking hinges made from hard leather. He pushed his H&K ahead of him as he peered inside. The interior was gloomy, the shadows relieved by pale shafts of light penetrating gaps in the timber structure. Sensing one of the others behind him Encizo ventured inside, glad to be out of the wind.

It was no more than a large hut, a wide single room

with a low roofline. The interior walls were composed of rough, untreated logs, the bark still in place. The floor was nothing more than hard-packed earth. In the center, directly beneath a deliberately constructed smoke vent, was a fire pit ringed by flat stones. A stack of cut timber had been stacked in one corner.

The team piled inside and Hawkins, the last man in, pulled the door shut. A coiled leather loop designed to slip over a peg on the wall secured the door.

Knowing that they might have to move out quickly and their time could be limited, they broke out their supplies. Hawkins and James managed to get a small fire going, and they used some of their water to boil over the flames. Under normal circumstances they might have debated the risk of lighting and fire, creating smoke that might be spotted by a potential enemy. With the windswept snow still billowing outside, the chances of escaping smoke being seen were slender. Even so, as soon as the water had boiled, enabling them to make strong coffee, the fire was extinguished.

"Now, this is cozy," McCarter said, sipping his coffee. The brew was hot, but the resultant coffee was far from being a connoisseur's choice.

As soon as they had all finished their drinks, the utensils were cleaned and packed away.

While the rest of the group took a break, Encizo stood the first watch, his parka pulled tight around his body and head while he patrolled the exterior. The Cuban had volunteered on the grounds that first out got it over with. His dislike of the cold prompted him to take the first stretch.

Resigned to his stint, Encizo gave his full attention, aware that if any threat appeared he was the group's lookout, and if he slacked in his duty the others would suffer the consequences.

The first ten minutes passed without incident. Encizo found that his observations were confined to the near distance, due to the ever changing pattern of the drifting, swirling snow. The fragmented curtains of flakes made it hard to distinguish between genuine sightings and simply a phantom shape created by the falling snow. Encizo gave up trying to peer too hard because it blurred his vision. He moved away from the hut, but not so far that he was unable to see it behind him. Keeping contact with the hut was important. If he lost that, he could easily wander away from the vicinity and become disoriented. He would only have needed to take a wrong step, lose his sense of direction and contact with the hut could be gone in seconds.

A number of times Encizo paused, checking out something he felt certain was more than just snow shadows. After convincing himself he was seeing things, he continued his circuitous route around the hut, watching more than listening because the constant wind noise drowned sounds quickly.

But not enough to totally fool him.

The brief sound bite reached his ears, and Encizo knew this time it was real. He continued his patrol, in case someone was watching, and maintained his motion without a break. His senses were highly tuned now. He *had* heard something—the fading chug of an engine. The clunky beat of a big diesel. Maybe a truck? Encizo corrected himself. It was more likely to be something designed for the area. The answer came suddenly—Snow Cats, tracked vehicles designed for the kind of terrain around them.

He considered his impression, convinced he hadn't been wrong. The sound, as fleeting as it had been, had cut through the wind noise, its beat different from the softer one created by the wind itself. Snow Cats meant human presence. And if there was one individual out there, how many more could there be?

Encizo turned back in the direction of the hut, keeping his movements calm and unhurried. If he was being watched, he didn't want to alert anyone and cause them to do something before he warned the others. He paused at the door, kicking snow from his boots before he pushed the door open and stepped inside.

Manning glanced up at the Cuban's entrance.

"Shortest watch I ever saw," he said.

Encizo dragged the hood of the parka from his head.

"We could be having visitors," he said. "I heard the sound of a Snow Cat cutting out. They probably decided to stop so the noise wouldn't reach us, but the wind must have carried it."

McCarter pushed to his feet, his H&K in his hands. He didn't even stop to consider Encizo might be wrong. He trusted every man in the team, knowing that they, like himself, survived by relying on instinctive reactions to situations. Instincts honed to a razor edge by constant exposure to field conditions and combat awareness. There was no book ever written that could instill that kind of gut reaction in a fighting man. It had to be learned via the battlefield, through numerous conflicts and actual hand-to-hand combat. McCarter accepted Encizo's pronouncement with his usual calm.

"Let's go, ladies. Got to look our best if someone is calling. Cal, you and T.J. take the back wall. I'll stay up front with Gary."

"What about me?" Encizo asked.

"I figure you've caused enough trouble already," Manning said in mock-serious tones. "Can't send you outside for five minutes without you upsetting the neighbors."

They had no more time to debate the issue.

There was a low whoosh of sound, increasing with each second, then the dull thump of a mortar detonating. It was short of being a direct hit, but there was enough force in the explosion to blow a section of the front wall inward, filling the hut with flying shards of wood. Smoke billowed in through the gap, dragging in swirls of snow, and behind the cloud of smoke came moving figures, bulky in dark parkas and combat gear. They were all carrying AK-74s, and each weapon was in the firing position.

In response to some unheard command the armed intruders opened fire, raking the front wall with a steady volley. The shots that failed to penetrate the gap thudded against the weakened front wall, filling the air with their murderous sound.

"Find your targets. Individual fire," McCarter yelled.

He could have saved his breath. The men of Phoenix Force knew the drill by heart.

"One coming in to your right," Manning said quietly.

McCarter brought his MP-5 online, picking up the dark shape emerging from the snow mist. The attacker was clad in cold-weather gear and carried a Kalashnikov AK-74. He was pushing hard through the drifting snow, slipping on the hard, icy footing. It hampered his movements, made them less than sure. The man was trying for the solid wall of the hut, hoping to hang there until his partners joined him. He failed to reach his objective. McCarter pulled the trigger and caught him with a short burst that stopped his forward movement. The man paused in midstride, then toppled sideways, first to his knees, then facedown on the hard snow. His weapon spilled from his hands, unfired and forgotten.

Gary Manning, turning back from warning McCarter, picked up additional movement as more armed men emerged suddenly from the snow mist. The first gunner opened fire the moment he saw Manning at the window, his AK crackling with a hard, vicious sound. His forward movement reduced the accuracy of his shots, the burst harmlessly hammering the windowsill above Manning's head. The big Canadian drew back, leveling his MP-5, and laid a burst into chest of his attacker. The man fell back with a short, stunned cry, crashing to the ground with a heavy thump. Swiveling at the hip, Manning fired at the second man to emerge and saw his burst catch the man in the side of the head, blowing away flesh and bone.

Immersed in the sudden agony of his wound, the man stumbled to his knees, weapon forgotten as he slid into his personal world of horror, hands clutched to the raw gap where part of his face had been.

Calvin James and T. J. Hawkins found themselves under a concentrated attack as at least four armed men rushed their side of the hut. All four carried AKs, and they were firing as they came. The wall of the hut recoiled under the attack, the savage volley filling the air with shredded bark and wood splinters. The Phoenix Force pair ducked below the level of the sill, feeling the wood splinters dropping on them from above.

''Man, this is heavy,'' James muttered.

''Not as heavy as this,'' Hawkins said, hefting one of his fragmentation grenades. He pulled the pin, released the lever, then held the activated grenade, counting off deliberately. He didn't lob it through the window until the last moment. There was no time for the attackers to avoid the projectile. It exploded before it hit the ground, filling the air with its hard flash and smoke, spewing metal shards in all directions. The four men were blown off their feet, bodies torn and bloody. Two died instantly. The third lay semi-conscious from his wounds, while the survivor, who had escaped with a few facial gashes, dropped to the ground, his autorifle held ready.

James poked his head slowly above the windowsill, saw the waiting man with the AK and dropped back a split second before the man fired. The black Phoenix Force warrior felt something gouge the side of his face and felt blood stream down his cheek.

"Son of a bitch," James muttered, wiping his hand across his bloody cheek. "Son of a bitch!"

"There you go, stickin' your head where it's not wanted," Hawkins chided.

He moved to the far side of the window, raising himself so he could see without actually exposing himself to anyone outside. As he angled his head to one side, Hawkins saw movement and focused on the wounded attacker. The man was crouched low, closing in on the window. He had almost reached it when Hawkins leaned forward slightly, angled the muzzle of his H&K forward and down. He triggered a burst that took the attacker in the upper chest and throat, tearing into flesh and severing a main artery in the man's neck. The attacker fell back and lay shuddering on the cold ground as he bled to death.

Above the gunfire came the *whoosh* of another mortar. It exploded on contact with the roof, blowing a gaping hole and showering the defenders with debris. The floor of the hut became littered with splintered chunks of smoldering wood. A third mortar whistled in, falling short and exploding with a sharp crack some ten feet from the front of the hut. The detonation had the effect of pushing back the attackers, and in the delay before they moved forward again, McCarter seized the moment.

"Let's go, mates. Move out before they hit us again."

He didn't need to issue the command a second time. While he and Manning stayed at the front, laying down a constant line of fire in the direction of the dazed attackers, the rest of the team ducked out through the side window and moved to the rear of the hut. Seeing the others were clear, McCarter and Manning tossed a pair of smoke grenades out the front window. The moment the thick plumes of smoke began to rise, mingling with the swirling snow, the two Phoenix Force warriors moved to the window and went through themselves. They joined up with the others.

"I think the wisest move at the moment would be a bloody hasty retreat," McCarter suggested. He jerked a thumb in the direction of the hut's rear, and Phoenix Force moved out. They pushed forward quickly, wanting to achieve as much distance as they could between themselves and their attackers before it was discovered that they were no longer in the hut.

The snow mist swallowed them quickly. Hawkins took the lead, with McCarter close behind checking the GPS unit. James brought up the rear, while Manning and Encizo kept an eye on their right and left flanks.

The constant wind acted as a buffer, muffling the sound of Phoenix Force's passing. The other side of the coin was that *they* were unable to hear how close the attacking force was. McCarter, never one to dwell on what couldn't be controlled, simply kept them moving. With the GPS fix he was able to swing them in a wide arc, bringing the team more or less back on track after an hour's travel. He also decided to call a time-out, giving the team a brief rest.

The snow was still falling and the wind had lost none of its bite. They moved in close to a bluff, easing around it to try to get out of the wind. They succeeded only partially. The wind still tugged at their clothing.

McCarter put Hawkins on guard duty, watching him scale the side of the bluff and stretch out on the crest.

"What the hell was that all about?" James asked, referring to the unexpected attack. "How did they know where we were?"

"Good question," McCarter said. "Pity I don't have answers."

"They probably expected some kind of attack after we tangled with them earlier," James said. "It wouldn't take that much guesswork to figure out we'd probably pick up information from Kranski and Anna. So they stayed alert."

"Well, great for them," McCarter said. "Let's concentrate on getting ourselves in the bloody clear. Our chums back there are going to be on our tails once this storm blows itself out. So the best thing we can do is keep moving and make sure we don't get caught napping a second time."

While they took their brief rest, each man checked his gear and weapons. On the move in poor conditions didn't allow the luxury of relaxation. If they found themselves in another confrontation, they would need to know they could use weapons at a moment's notice. They replaced used magazines, inspected the functions of their individual weapons, then carried out similar inspections of packs and ancillary gear. By the time they had completed this, McCarter was ready to move. He called Hawkins back down to join them, gave him the opportunity to check his gear, then issued the order to move out.

"How we doing?" Manning asked as they readied themselves.

McCarter had just completed another check of the GPS unit.

"According to this, we need to swing slightly west. That should bring us back in the right direction. Depending on the weather, I reckon another hour or so. But don't hold me to that, mate, because this miserable place could stop us in our tracks if it has a mind to. Bloody hell, Gary, I thought Canada could be cold. This place beats it hands down without trying."

"Never thought I'd hear you admit to that." Manning grinned.

"I'll deny it later," McCarter replied. "I'm on safe ground. Nobody heard but you and me."

"I heard you," Calvin James said from somewhere nearby.

"So did I, boss," Hawkins called.

"How long have you buggers been listening in to my private conversations?" McCarter asked.

"How far back do you want to go?" James asked.

"Right!" McCarter said. "Nobody gets time off tonight. Forget any trips into town, getting drunk and chasing loose women."

There was silence for a moment until Encizo muttered, "So what's new about that?"

JACK GRIMALDI, sitting in comfort inside the sealed cabin of *Dragon Slayer,* watched the swirling snowfall and admitted to being a little guilty. His time might have been spent simply waiting for the team to call him in. It sometimes got a little boring, his inactivity chafing at his natural exuberance. In the end he couldn't complain too much. The others were out in the cold, battling the inclement weather and hostile environment. He was cocooned in a warm cabin, with reasonable amenities, so he stopped feeling sorry for himself.

Grimaldi checked the time. The team had been gone for almost five hours. In that time he hadn't heard a word from them. Radio silence was paramount until he got the call to action. Until then he stayed silent and simply waited.

He finished the mug of coffee and screwed the top back on the thermos. Pushing upright, he started a systems check, making sure that the combat helicopter was in full readiness if he received the signal to head out. He didn't anticipate any problems. *Dragon Slayer*'s updated specifications included a computerized self-diagnostic program that would immediately flag any malfunctions in the machine.

The aircraft had been fitted with equipment that wasn't yet available to the military in some cases. Prototype weapons, tracking and surveillance, improved engine performance. The Stony Man combat chopper was a flyer's dream, and Jack Grimaldi was the pilot who got the opportunity to push her through her paces. He had been with *Dragon Slayer* since its original conception. During the design stages, Grimaldi had been there, offering sound advice and original ideas. He had test-flown the aircraft, helped strip her down after and check out the stress and strain put on the machine. From that, over a period of time, the sleek helicopter had emerged. Only when Jack Grimaldi gave the word was *Dragon Slayer* commissioned and handed over to Stony Man. Refinements were made after each mission, each one increasing the capabilities of the helicopter, and still Grimaldi kept pushing her to the limit. He took nothing at face value, nor were any of his requests made casually. Out in the field, when he found himself on the knife edge, with the lives of the combat teams depending on him and *Dragon Slayer,* Grimaldi wanted no breakdowns, no malfunctions that might cause him to be minutes late—which could easily mean being too late—when he was making a pickup run.

So he sat inside his cabin, watching the readout on the monitor screen that informed him all systems were fine. He settled back, idly scanning the spread of instrumentation on the curved console in front of him. A winking light caught his eye. Grimaldi sat up, stroking a couple of keys.

A screen lit up, showing thermal images. The source was one of the latest instruments fitted to the helicopter—a proximity sensor. It sent out thermal waves in a spread pattern surrounding the helicopter, relaying the results back as the moving shapes on Grimaldi's monitor screen.

He could make out the shapes as a number of men closing in on *Dragon Slayer.* Armed men. And they hadn't come to welcome him to Russian soil.

"Damn!" Grimaldi muttered.

He keyed buttons and activated the helicopter's external security shield. All the hatches were locked down. At the touch of another button the chopper's outer skin was given an electrical charge that would knock down anyone who touched it. It was something but not enough, Grimaldi knew. *Dragon Slayer* was seriously lethal to any attacker but not fully impregnable. She might withstand a bullet, but a LAW rocket would make a hole. Grimaldi's survival depended on the intentions of his visitors. If they only wanted the helicopter, they weren't about to do anything to damage it. On the other hand their orders might be to take *Dragon Slayer* out of the game altogether.

Grimaldi unholstered his Beretta and cocked it. He lay the 9 mm pistol on the seat beside him and took his Uzi from its clip on the bulkhead.

Briefly he considered firing up the engines and getting the hell out. He dropped the idea just as quickly. If these people had come looking for a helicopter, they would have brought along armament capable of disabling it. There was no point aggravating an already difficult situation, Grimaldi decided.

He sat back and waited. Sooner or later they were going to let him know what they wanted. He watched the monitor and saw the group split apart. Now he had armed men on either side.

An amplified voice penetrated the bulkhead. The speaker spoke English with a Russian accent. His words were distorted slightly by the amplified microphone he was using, but they were clear enough for Grimaldi to understand them.

"You are surrounded. If you try to take off, we will use missiles to destroy you. We will also use missiles if you do not surrender in the next thirty minutes. It is your choice, American. Personally, I do not care if you die along with your machine. Your time starts now.''

Thirty minutes. Grimaldi glanced at his watch. Long enough to have another mug of coffee, he decided. Not a casual thought. Once he stepped outside the helicopter he was going to be subjected to the extreme weather. There was no telling where he would be taken. That was if they left him alive. If they did, he had a chance of escape. Maybe a chance to get back to *Dragon Slayer*. In the meantime he needed to survive, and getting some hot liquid inside him would help him resist for a while. After that he was going to have to make it on his wits.

He poured the coffee and while he drank Grimaldi keyed in code sequences known only to himself that would, at the touch of a single button, shut down *Dragon Slayer* and put her in a standby mode. To anyone not familiar with the machine she would appear to be completely shut down. Nothing would function. There wouldn't be a single indicator lit. It would be like putting the aircraft in suspended animation. The only way the chopper could be activated would be by the keying of a text-number sequence. Until that happened the helicopter would be nothing more than inert metal and cold circuitry.

The lockdown sequence would also activate deep-planted devices installed to deter anyone trying to remove any of the aircraft's equipment. The attempted removal would trigger small charges that would simply burn out the equipment.

Once he had the sequences set, Grimaldi refilled his mug and sat back, waiting out the last few minutes. He had to try to keep *Dragon Slayer* whole because Phoenix Force was still out there, not knowing what had happened to him. When they needed him, they would activate the homing device they carried, and Grimaldi would be expected to bring them out. He couldn't risk doing anything that might result in the helicopter being damaged. Somehow he had to keep it in one piece, himself alive and his would-be captors out of his hair.

Grimaldi emptied his coffee mug, then checked his watch. Time was almost up. He glanced at his weapons. No way he could take those with him.

"Be back soon," he said, more to convince himself.

Grimaldi deactivated the electrical body charge and tapped in the lockdown sequence. The program would activate in sixty seconds. The Stony Man pilot freed his hatch. It swung open with a hiss, and he felt cold air reach inside. He swung his legs outside, dragging his heavy parka with him. The moment he appeared, a number of armed men, muffled in heavy clothing, advanced on him. Pulling on the parka, Grimaldi nudged the hatch and it swung to, clicking shut with a solid thump.

"We need the hatch open," one of the men said, pushing past Grimaldi.

He was confronted with a smooth, unbroken surface. There were no external handles to break *Dragon Slayer*'s sleek profile. The man stared at the fine line that marked the outline of the hatch.

"Open it," he demanded, jerking Grimaldi around to face him.

Grimaldi stared into the Russian's bearded face. "No," he said.

The Russian held Grimaldi's gaze, his expression showing his surprise at the American's defiance.

"You know I can have you killed simply by raising my hand?"

"So what does that tell me?" Grimaldi asked him.

"It should tell you I am not a person to be treated lightly."

"And if you kill me you'll never get inside," Grimaldi said. "This machine is locked down until I say different. You kill me, and there's no way you get inside, pal."

The man turned away and snapped out a command in Russian that sent his group around *Dragon Slayer*, checking every inch of the fuselage. Grimaldi used the time to zip up his parka and make sure he was well protected from the cold. He had already decided that the weather wasn't the only source of low temperatures. His captors were decidedly cold. After a few minutes the group—Grimaldi counted four of them—gathered around the leader again, and a hurried conversation took place.

"Our orders are to keep you here until we are told otherwise," the man informed Grimaldi. "Be warned, American, that I will not hesitate to do whatever is necessary to get what I want."

"Looks like we're all in for a long wait, then," Grimaldi said. "What do we do? Stand here and freeze, or what?"

The Russian scowled. He snapped out something, and one of his men turned and disappeared into the snow mist. Long minutes later Grimaldi heard a low rumble, and a truck emerged from the snow, a heavy, ex-military truck with a canvas body. It had tracks at the rear and rolled across the bumpy ground at a few miles per hour, coming to a jerky halt twenty feet from the helicopter.

"We can sit inside," the Russian said. He was about to move Grimaldi toward the truck when he paused, a faint smile lingering around his mouth. He raised his arm and called in two of his men. He spoke to them and they handed their weapons to their partners before advancing on Grimaldi and commencing a thorough body search.

"We have to be careful," the Russian explained.

You do that, Grimaldi thought. You be very careful, pal, because my time's coming.

With the search over Grimaldi was hustled to the truck and made to climb inside. There were rough wooden benches running the length of the body. Grimaldi sat down. The Russians climbed in, as well, sitting so that the pilot was hemmed in on both sides. The Russian in charge sat directly across from him.

"You and your friends were very foolish to come here," he said. "They won't succeed. Nothing is going to stop us. We will wait here in case any of them manage to escape and return. But I do not think that will happen."

"You always talk so much?" Grimaldi asked.

The Russian grinned. "I can afford to be generous. For now. Later perhaps not so much when I want you to tell me how to get inside your helicopter. It looks to be a very intriguing machine. Like something out of a movie. I think it would be a valuable addition to our armory. So that is something for you to think about. Just remember that not to tell me will be a big mistake.''

Grimaldi leaned back and stared at the smiling Russian.

The mistake is yours, Ivan, he thought. You made it when you didn't kill me right off. Bet your ass I don't make the same one when my turn comes.

LATE AFTERNOON. The weather had eased. The snow had lightened, though the wind still swirled it about. Visibility was better, though it deteriorated as the light began to fade.

"Christ, what a bloody horrible country," Mc-Carter muttered. "Cold, icy, and it gets dark in the middle of the day."

They had moved out a couple of hours earlier, and keeping their profile low had managed to avoid being picked up by the force that had attacked them at the hut.

"Where the bloody hell are they?" McCarter had asked more than once as the team moved in single file across the barren landscape.

McCarter didn't like unexplained occurrences. He would have been happier to see their attackers following them. The fact that they seemed to have vanished from the scene altogether unsettled him.

"Maybe they headed back to base," James suggested. "Then again they could be waiting for us over the next hill."

McCarter glanced at him. "What next hill?"

"Bound to be one around somewhere."

"I go for them making it back to base to consolidate all their people in one place. A stronger defense," Manning suggested.

"They know where we're heading," Encizo said. "It makes sense, David."

"That's the part I don't like," McCarter replied. "I know it makes sense. It just means we end up with a lot more people to deal with."

Dusk was starting to slide in around them. Shadows lengthened. The temperature dropped by a few more degrees.

McCarter checked the GPS unit. The others gathered around as he made his announcement.

"We should be coming up on the target soon. If they know we're coming, they're not going to be showing much light so the last piece is down to us."

In the end they located the target without much additional effort. James's hill turned out to be more of a gentle rise in the land and as they reached the summit they were able to make out the compound on the far side. They crouched below the summit and checked out the base below. It was surrounded by a barbed wire fence, which was supported on thick poles sunk in the hard ground. Inside the compound itself were three long wooden barracks-style buildings. Smoke rose from the tin chimney stacks of two of the buildings. In the last gleaming of daylight armed figures could be seen patrolling outside the perimeter fence.

In the center of the compound was an unusual structure that appeared to be built from concrete. The ground around it had been provided with a short length of roadway, with security gates and high wire fencing.

McCarter studied the object for a while, his mind going back to the Stony Man briefing, and he suddenly made the connection.

"It's the bloody radar facility," he said. "So that's what this is all about."

"They're building one?" Manning asked.

McCarter shook his head. "Not for what you think," he said. "This is being built so they can work out a strike plan. Once they have that down pat, they'll go for the real thing in Alaska."

"This is for dummy runs?" Hawkins said.

"That's the idea."

"No wonder they sent those storm troopers to chase us off," James said.

"I still get an uncomfortable feeling about them," McCarter said. "Like they're going to pop up any minute."

"If they were going to take us on, why wait until now?" Encizo asked. "They're back. Behind that wire."

"There's one way to find out," McCarter said.

They grouped together, discussing the options for an assault on the compound.

"We don't know how many of them there are,"

Hawkins pointed out. "Something we need to think about."

"This boy is getting so smart he'll become dangerous soon," James muttered.

Hawkins grinned. "You old-timers need the sharpness of youth to keep you on your toes."

"So how about the young buck getting out there and doing a recce?" McCarter suggested.

"Okay, boss," Hawkins said.

He checked his gear, making sure he wasn't wearing anything that might rattle and give away his presence, then made certain his weapons were fully loaded and operational.

"Hey, you want me to come along for backup?" Encizo asked.

Hawkins nodded and the pair slipped away, merging with the lengthening shadows.

CHAPTER SEVEN

Siberia

The falling darkness covered their movements, easing their approach. Regardless of the conditions, Hawkins and Encizo closed in on the compound with extreme caution. Moving in close to assess the strength of an enemy wasn't an easy task. The intention was to count numbers without being detected, so that their main force had some idea of the odds they were up against. A casual move could easily lead to their discovery and that in turn would put the rest of their people in jeopardy.

It took them at least thirty minutes before they were close enough to be able to take a detailed look at the potential threat. The two armed guards patrolling outside the wire trudged a regular pattern. The Phoenix Force duo monitored it for a couple of circuits, calculating how long they would have once the guards had passed to get in closer to the wire. Once they had crossed the guards' path, they crawled the last few yards and worked their way right up to the barrier.

From where they lay on the iron-hard, snowy ground they could see right into the compound. Powerful floodlights on tall poles lit up the inner area. The first thing Encizo saw were two of the Snow Cats. They were parked alongside one of the long barracks buildings. Some way off from these was a Soviet Hind helicopter. It was painted in military drab but there were no markings on it to suggest it was still an operational machine. On a closer look Encizo could see the sections where the military markings had been painted over. The paint was a shade brighter than the rest. He took another look at the Snow Cats. They were in the same color and also had sections where the original markings had been painted over.

Hawkins caught his attention by nudging him. He pointed to a group of men crossing the compound. They were moving in the direction of the radar mock-up and were in agitated discussion about something. One of them, clad in dark clothing, seemed to be doing most of the talking. Unlike the others he hadn't pulled up the hood of his parka, and Hawkins could make out his thick black hair and broad, angular features.

"Chinese. Maybe Korean," he said.

Encizo nodded. "Every time we come across anyone involved in this, the Chinese are there."

"Figure it out, Rafe. The Chinese and the Koreans have a big stake in this. Putting Slingshot out of action would be something they'd love. No American defense shield leaves the country wide open to anyone who might want to make a first strike."

"In this time of global peace and harmony?"

"In your dreams, bro," Hawkins said. "I may be green, but I'm not simple. The day this crazy world turns into one big peace camp I will have been dead and buried a long time."

The Asian was nodding vigorously, concentrating his discussion with a large, powerfully built man. This one seemed to be in charge. After some minutes the group broke up. A number of them crossed to the Hind and began to work around it, while the rest, including the Asian, went back to one of the occupied barracks buildings.

"You get the feeling something is about to happen?" Hawkins said.

Encizo nodded.

"Time we got back and let the others know."

As with their journey in, Hawkins and Encizo used the same procedure. It took patience and skill that was only acquired through actual combat experience. No amount of reading the manuals and making dummy runs could be substituted for the real thing. Training was simply that. A practice, with the knowledge that if a soldier blew it, the worst he got was a severe lecture from the instructor. In the field when a person made a mistake, it usually meant a burst from an enemy weapon or a knife between the ribs. Those kinds of penalties tended to sharpen the senses and increase the care taken.

"Miss us?" Hawkins asked as he and Encizo slid back in among the waiting team members.

"You been somewhere?" James asked. "Jeez, we never noticed."

"Okay, okay," McCarter said. He was relieved to see his two friends back with them, unharmed. "Was the trip worth it?"

Hawkins and Encizo related what they had witnessed in detail. The fact about a possible move by the group inside the compound was an important factor.

"Damn," McCarter said. "They could be heading for their rendezvous with the Militia Men. Looks like we're going to have to go in now."

"Just give the word, David," Manning said. "Anything is better than sitting here freezing."

"Got to agree with that," the Briton replied. "All right. Priorities. The nuke is our main target. We need to get our hands on that. If we don't achieve anything else, that has to be prevented from being taken into Alaska. Secondary targets any computer setup they might have. Same directive as we had when we breached Li Cheng's facility. Equipment destroyed, any disks or related information confiscated."

"Rafe and I know the sentry patterns on the outside," Hawkins said. "We'll deal with them."

McCarter nodded. "Quietly. We need as much advantage as we can get."

They all ran a weapons check, making sure nothing had seized due to the cold. Once that was done, Encizo and Hawkins took the lead and Phoenix Force moved out. Time was running out, and the operation had to be engaged now that there was a chance the strike team could soon be leaving for Alaska.

NO ONE HAD SAID a word for some considerable time. The atmosphere in the truck had become tense. It was down to the fact that a message had come through on the radio that the local force had clashed with the intruders. The locals had suffered a number of casualties before the intruders escaped under cover of the weather.

Grimaldi could tell he wasn't the most popular person inside the truck at that moment.

"Does this mean we're not friends anymore?" he asked.

The bearded Russian rounded on him, anger bright in his eyes.

"You want to die now?"

"You still want to see inside my chopper?" Grimaldi countered. He was getting tired of sitting back, helpless, when his buddies might be needing him. Sooner or later Grimaldi was going to have to force the issue. Reckless or not he had to do something. If Phoenix Force had encountered the enemy force, his teammates might need him for pickup any time. Sitting helpless in the back of a truck, Grimaldi wasn't going to be much help. He needed to get back to *Dragon Slayer*. He began to check out the truck's interior. There wasn't much he could see that would give him any advantage.

The canvas flap at the rear was raised and a face

peered in. The newcomer began to speak in Russian, directing his words at the bearded leader of the group. The leader nodded and called out instructions to his men. Two of them got up and moved to the front of the truck, where they raised the top of a compartment section and began to lift out metal containers. Grimaldi recognized them as fuel cans. They had a flame symbol on the side, the universal symbol for inflammable liquids. The cans were set near the tailgate, which was lowered. The man who had asked for them to be lifted down took one and vanished into the gloom.

Grimaldi watched this with interest. They were fueling up for the return journey. He smelled gasoline as the helpers in the truck loosened the tops on the other cans. One of them jumped down and hauled one of the containers onto his shoulder. Grimaldi heard him calling to the driver.

The Stony Man pilot watched the movement inside the truck. He only had one man sitting next to him now, the others all helping to move the gas cans down the truck. The bearded leader, still across from Grimaldi, had his vision blocked each time someone passed him with a can.

The operation wasn't going to last long, Grimaldi knew. His chance, probably his only chance, had to be taken now.

One of the men hauling a container stepped close to where Grimaldi sat. The Stony Man pilot leaned back, moving his hands as if protecting himself. He quickly turned, making a grab for the autorifle resting across the lap of the man beside him. Grimaldi whacked the weapon across its former owner's head, knocking the man off the edge of the seat. His finger slipped across the trigger as he arced the weapon around and fired into the body of the guy carrying the can. As the man stumbled, groaning from the impact of the 5.45 mm slug, he dropped the can and it rolled along the floor of the truck. Raising his leg, Grimaldi slammed his foot against the shot man's hip and shoved him aside. The bearded leader had started to rise from his seat, grabbing for his own weapon, but as his injured companion fell the muzzle of Grimaldi's AK-74 lined up on him. The weapon crackled sharply as the pilot triggered a trio of shots into the man. The Russian fell back, his chest cleaved by the hollowpoint slugs.

Sliding along the seat, Grimaldi turned the weapon on its former owner and put two fast shots through his upper chest, spinning him off the seat. The man crashed to the floor of the truck, screaming in pain. Grimaldi sensed movement close by and turned, seeing the guy who had been at the far end of the truck lunging at him, using the container he carried as a battering ram. The heavy can caught the pilot in the chest, driving him back against the canvas side of the truck. He felt the material sag, and for a second he was sure it was going to tear and pitch him to the ground outside. The canvas was tough and held his weight, giving Grimaldi time to react to the attack. The guy holding the heavy container realized he had restricted himself, and tried to remedy it by dropping the can and going for his holstered autopistol. Grimaldi cut him no slack. Still leaning into the canvas sheet, he turned the AK-74 on the man and fired off a long volley. The bullets took the Russian in his lower torso, piercing his flesh and organs and blowing out the back in a bloody spray.

A gun fired from the tailgate of the truck, the slug burning through Grimaldi's parka and searing his side. The pain triggered a solid response from Grimaldi. He rolled from the canvas to the floor of the truck, dropping to his knees and firing from that position. His burst hit the shooter in the chest and tossed him over the tailgate. Grimaldi followed him, taking a reckless dive from the back of the truck. He landed on his feet, stumbling on contact with the hard ground. Recovering quickly, he turned and faced the first of the two men as they came around the rear of the vehicle. He had the slight advantage of knowing which direction his opposition was coming from. He took out the first guy with a single shot to the head, then moved down the side of the truck and positioned himself midway along its length. On his knees Grimaldi peered under the vehicle, trying to see the last man. He caught a brief flurry of movement as the guy ran toward the front of the truck. He lost him, but the slam of a door told Grimaldi the guy had climbed back into the cab. The growl of the powerful engine broke the silence. The driver stepped on the gas pedal, grinding the gears as he yanked hard on the stick. The vehicle lurched forward, the metal tracks kicking up dirt and snow as the driver made his bid for freedom.

Grimaldi didn't try for the cab in case the driver had a weapon in his hand. He moved to the rear, where the fuel cans were rolling back and forth across the floor. He raised the AK and pumped shot after shot at the cans and the metal body of the truck. The vehicle was starting to pull clear when one of his random shots caused a spark that ignited the gas vapor from the leaking cans. The burst of flame caught the pilot by surprise. The gasoline ignited with a terrifying thump, expanding within seconds. The rear of the truck became a ball of fire that searched out more fuel to feed on. A second blast lifted the rear of the vehicle off the ground, the flame engulfing the whole of the half track. There had to have been some ammunition stored on the truck. It began to spit and crackle, sending gushes of incandescent flame in all directions. The truck rolled on for a few yards, jerked, then came to a dead stop. Grimaldi eased around so he could see the cab. It was hidden by flames, and there was no movement.

Grimaldi turned and walked to where *Dragon Slayer* stood. The combat chopper was covered in a smooth layer of white snow. He bent under the fuselage and reached inside the off-side landing wheel housing, his fingers locating the small touch pad recessed there. He pressed the pad and heard the soft hiss as the cabin hatch unsealed. By the time he stepped out from under the fuselage, the hatch was open. He leaned inside and knocked off the fail-safe facility. If he hadn't activated that within thirty seconds, the aircraft would have shut herself down again automatically.

Climbing inside, Grimaldi took off his parka and dumped it on the floor behind his seat. He slid into the body-form seat, closed the hatch and entered his own code sequence into the small keyboard near his left hand. *Dragon Slayer* came to life, the control banks lighting up and the powerful engines beginning their warm-up sequence.

He activated the homing signal. The readout screen showed that one of the devices had been activated. He checked the monitor, the visual told him the signal had been operational for almost three hours.

"Son of a bitch!"

He fed the signal into the computer and let it work out the source of the pulse. While that was going on, Grimaldi teased the engines to full power, feeling the machine come to life around him. He snapped into his harness, put on his helmet and plugged himself into the helicopter's communications facility.

The readout told him the chopper was ready for liftoff. Grimaldi took her straight up, using the screen display to show him where he was as much as he did his own eyes. The visibility wasn't the best. Snow had started to fall again, and with the currents created by *Dragon Slayer*'s rotors he was flying into a white fog. Undeterred, Grimaldi checked the computer. He saw that the analysis of the homing signal had been completed. The monitor was displaying the optimum course setting. He keyed in his acceptance, and the information was sent to the navigation grid. Grimaldi felt the chopper alter course as it responded to the autocourse command. The readout was displayed on the visor of his helmet, so he only needed to raise his eyes to check it.

Course was set. Grimaldi ran a weapons check and the report flashed on his monitor. *Dragon Slayer* was up and running, armed and closing in on her destination.

All Grimaldi had to concern himself with was whether he got there in time.

CHAPTER EIGHT

Siberia

Encizo slid his Gerber knife from the sheath strapped to his thigh. He pressed flat to the ground as he spotted the guard moving his way, and kept the man in his sight. The guard was moving slowly, stamping his feet every few steps to increase the circulation. There was a reluctance in the way he moved, as if he didn't really want to be where he was. More than once he turned his head to look through the fence at the light showing from the barracks hut, thinking about the comfort of a warm fire, no doubt, a hot drink. Anything, Encizo knew, had to be better than patrolling the icy perimeter of the camp.

Flattening himself against the ground, the little Cuban counted off the seconds as the guard approached and moved past. He flexed his fingers as he removed his glove, closing them around the handle of the knife. As the moment came, he pushed all thoughts aside, concentrating on what he had to do. No misgivings or doubts. Encizo rose out of the shadows, coming up behind the unsuspecting guard. His left hand reached up to clamp over the man's mouth, shutting off his ability to call out and also to yank his head back. In the same instant his knife hand brought the keen blade across the taut, exposed throat. A single deep cut from left to right severed arteries in a moment. The stricken guard struggled, body stiffening in response to what had happened. His exertions only increased the blood flow from the massive wound, and Encizo followed the man as he sank to his knees, keeping him pulled tight against his own body. He held his position until the trembling body became still, then lowered the man to the cold earth and took the AK-74 that had fallen to the ground. He slung the weapon over his shoulder, stood and began to pace out the dead guard's path.

As Encizo took the place of the man he had silenced, T. J. Hawkins eased the body of the second guard close up to the fence, followed Encizo's pattern and walked the line.

McCARTER PICKED UP Encizo's brief signal on his transceiver.

"Okay."

The Briton turned to James and Manning, giving them the nod. They moved forward, closing the distance between themselves and the barbed wire fence surrounding the compound. They covered the last twenty feet flat on the ground, crawling until they were at the base of the fence.

"Check the wire," McCarter ordered. "See if it has any kind of detection. I don't think there will be, but let's make sure."

Manning wriggled back to check the first of the support posts. It was a thick wooden pole, with strips of shriveled bark still clinging to it. The strands of barbed wire were stapled to the pole. There was no kind of insulation to suggest the wire was electrified or connected to an alarm. Manning rechecked, going over the section again to make certain he hadn't missed anything. Satisfied, he returned to where the others had made their inspections and had also reached the same conclusion.

"This has to go down quickly," McCarter said. "We go in and hit these buggers hard. No time for fancy strategy."

They studied the interior of the compound, picking out the three guards around the Hind, watching the crew preparing the big helicopter for flight.

"As they always say in the best B movies," McCarter said, "time to rock and roll."

Manning took a compact pair of wire cutters from one of his zip pockets. The others held the wire as he cut through, then pulled back the severed ends, creating a gap through which the team entered the compound. Staying low and moving quickly, Phoenix Force crossed the first patch of open ground, taking cover behind a stack of metal drums that were stored away from any of the barracks buildings and the Hind. They crouched in the shadow of the drums, taking time to recce the compound in front of them.

Each man went through a final weapons check, insuring they were fully loaded. This was for SMGs as well as handguns. Each man still carried a selection of fragmentation and stun grenades. Encizo and Hawkins still had the AKs they had taken from the perimeter guards. They slung their H&Ks by their slings, preferring to use the Kalashnikovs first to conserve their own ammunition.

"Rafe, you and T.J. take the right flank," McCarter said. "See if you can work your way around to the far side of the chopper pad. Keep your eyes open for any guards on the far side. I'd like to kick this off with us all in place, but if the brown stuff hits the whirly blades, go for it. I'd rather you shot first if it comes to it. Don't hold back if you're up against it, and that's an order. Five came in, and I want the same number going out."

Encizo and Hawkins eased away from cover and vanished in the darkness beyond the throw of the light from the area of activity.

McCarter led Manning and James in the opposite direction. He wanted to be able to bring the helicopter under fire from two positions, catching the enemy in the middle. It sounded good in his head, and if everything went as it should...

McCarter led his team toward the closest of the barracks, hoping to use the building as cover, enabling them to move to a close position. It might have worked if a four-wheel-drive Toyota hadn't swept into view from around the hidden, far side of the barracks hut. A passenger operated a powerful spotlight, and he started to make wide sweeps, illuminating the area between the fuel stack and the hut.

McCarter, James and Manning were held in the glare for fleeting seconds. The Toyota driver jammed on the brakes, bringing the vehicle to a rocking halt.

The beam from the spotlight wavered, jerking away from Phoenix Force briefly. But it was long enough for them to separate, go to ground and start shooting. Manning caught the spotlight with his second burst. Glass blew away in shards, and the spotlight died with a hot crackle. Thinking fast, the driver hit the headlight switch and twin beams lanced through the darkness.

On one knee McCarter raised his MP-5 and raked the windshield, sending shattered glass into the faces of the driver and passenger. The driver kicked open his door and left the vehicle in a clumsy dive that ended with him bouncing awkwardly on the hard ground. He struggled to his feet, yanking an autopistol from his belt, and he aimed in the general direction of the intruders. He began to fire random shots, all aimed at the ground. Bullets chewed at the hard earth, chipping at stone.

Manning, half-crouched, leveled his H&K and took steady aim, his finger stroking the trigger as he fired off a short burst. The 9 mm slugs caught the driver in the side of the body, chest high. They cored through flesh and inflicted telling damage to the target's lungs. He toppled over, making a strangled sound and hit the ground facedown, arms waving in protest.

With the pressure off for a few moments, James and McCarter turned their attention to the second man as he struggled out of the vehicle, hauling an AK-74 with him. James triggered his weapon and stitched the guy from groin to chest, the stream of 9 mm slugs cutting a bloody path over the man's body. He took an awkward backward step, shuddering under the impact before he collided with the body of the Toyota and fell hard.

"Let's bloody move it!" McCarter yelled, waving his team forward.

They skirted the 4×4 and made for the wall of the barracks hut, flattening against it as they heard the rush of booted feet across the hard earth. A number of dark figures came into view around the end of the hut, only to be met by the concentrated firepower of the Phoenix Force trio. The newcomers were shot to pieces, dark specks flying from their twisting bodies as they were knocked off their feet.

"Bugger the finesse," McCarter growled, plucking a fragmentation grenade from his harness as he advanced to the corner of the hut. He peered around it and spotted a milling group some distance away. The Briton pulled the pin on the grenade and tossed the bomb with unerring accuracy at the group. He ducked back behind the wall a split second before the grenade exploded, the blast briefly lighting the compound. The explosion was followed by a burst of screams and yells. Men were driven to the ground or scattered in every direction.

"Go, now," McCarter said, and followed his two partners as they broke cover and moved toward the center of the compound.

They fired as they moved, using more grenades as they pushed deeper into the conflict.

RAFAEL ENCIZO and T. J. Hawkins had barely reached the far side of the compound when they heard the shooting start. To avoid detection they had kept to the perimeter fence, where shadows covered their advance. Going that way also meant it took longer and they were caught off guard when the first shots were fired.

"Sounds like David's impatience got the better of him," Encizo said.

"Diplomacy isn't one of his strong points," Hawkins remarked.

"It isn't going to do us any good, either," Encizo said sharply.

Hawkins glanced up and saw the trio of armed men coming into view from behind a stack of building materials. The two groups came almost face-to-face.

Already moving forward, Encizo kept his stride and slammed his shoulder into the closest guy. The impact drove the man off balance, more than ready to accept the solid whack across his jaw from Encizo's Kalashnikov. The guy went down, dazed but still able to react as he threw both arms around his attacker's left thigh and tried to drag the Cuban down with him.

"*Son of a bitch!*" Encizo yelled. He slammed the AK-74 against the back of the guy's skull, knocking him flat on the ground.

Hawkins had witnessed Encizo's collision with the first of the opposition. He was a number of steps behind his partner, and the only way open to him was to use his weapon. The barrel of the raised AK-74 tracked in on target. Hawkins fired on full-auto, the hard crack of the weapon jarring in his hands. The volley caught the two Russians in midstride, cutting them down in a bloody moment of pain and confusion. They went down without a chance to even cry out.

Hawkins and Encizo ran on, zigzagging as they moved across the open compound. Their way was less hazardous as the majority of the defenders appeared to be concentrating their efforts around the Hind. The bulky ex-Soviet war machine was plainly a priority. Figures were busy at the helicopter itself, readying it for flight.

They reached the radar facility mock-up, crossing the short stretch of road leading to the twenty-foot concrete structure. Even in the short time they were near the construction, the Phoenix Force pair was able to see the care that had been taken to make the mock-up as realistic as possible.

As they paused beside a checkpoint booth, assessing the way ahead, Hawkins cast a final glance at the concrete structure.

"Rafe, they really meant it," he said. "These guys are no beginners."

Encizo nodded, his attention drawn by a sudden increase in gunfire.

"I think that's for us," he said.

They broke cover and ran in a wide semicircle, bringing themselves in toward the Hind from the side away from the main gun battle. Their appearance didn't go unheeded. Several armed figures turned away from the firefight and fanned out as they approached the Phoenix warriors.

"*Shit!*" Hawkins muttered.

As bullets winged in at them, Hawkins and Encizo hit the ground, teeth clenched against the solid impact. There was no option except to return fire, the opposition moving in quickly, weapons on continuous fire.

Hawkins felt the ground vibrate close to him as 5.45 mm slugs hammered the frozen earth. He felt hard chips pepper his clothing. The closeness of the shots drew an automatic response, and Hawkins cradled his Kalashnikov, concentrating his fire on one target. His first burst took the guy in the left thigh, dropping him to his knees, the gunner cursing wildly in the instant before Hawkins adjusted his aim and put a short burst into his chest. Before the target hit the ground, Hawkins moved on to his second target, aiming and firing coolly. He ignored the shots striking the ground around him, eased back on the trigger and placed a tight group of shots into his man. The guy flew backward, arms thrown wide as bloody gouts burst from his chest.

The time elements ran almost parallel for Hawkins and Encizo. The Cuban took on his adversaries at the moment Hawkins triggered his first shots. There were three men angling in Encizo's direction, on the move, weapons jerking as they ran. The movement took away some of the accuracy they might have retained if they had stayed still. It was their loss and the Cuban's gain. Down on the ground, with the AK-74 snug to his cheek, Encizo aimed and fired, the only definite movement being the swiveling of the muzzle as he ranged from target to target. It was precision firing, almost too easy.

Three times he fired, his short, accurate bursts puncturing flesh and splintering bone. His targets tumbled, crashing to the ground, and were still kicking out the remnants of their lives when Encizo and Hawkins hurried by.

VLADIMIR BIRYENKO PUSHED his small group of specialists beyond the fighting, toward the idling Hind. His was a single objective—to get his people on board the machine and away from the compound. Their work here was done. The training that had filled their days over the past weeks, going over and over the planned assault on the American radar facility— all that was fixed in their minds. They could carry out the strike in their sleep. It would all have been useless if they failed to get away from the compound now that the American commando group had breached the place, taking out Malinchek's ill-trained hardmen with ease. The same was happening inside the compound. Malinchek and his mercenary thugs were good for providing information, equipment and bullying tactics. As combat specialists, they were laughable. On the other hand their sacrifice would allow Biryenko and his team to move on to the next phase of the operation. Once clear of the facility, they would fly to a spot close to the coast, where the flight to Alaska would take only a short time. Once they were on American soil, close to the radar facility, the team would go in on foot, meet up with the Militia Men under Hubbard Tetrow's command and carry out the strike.

The Militia Men had provided much useful information and planning for the operation. They would open up the assault, unaware that the Russian team was bringing in the nuclear device that would lay waste to a large section of the Alaskan coastline. The irradiated earth would be useless, preventing the Americans from using it for their secretive purposes again. The blast would anger the American people, who would be convinced their government had been building some kind of nuclear installation, and the "accident" would show the carelessness of the federal authorities, its disregard of public safety in its desperation to construct the missile facility. There would be a lot of mileage in the incident. If it was handled correctly, it would discredit the U.S. government, and Gagarin would make certain that the blame was laid on the Americans. One way or another the antimissile program would be made to look reckless and of little use in the protection of America.

Aware of the importance of the mission, Biryenko drove his men with total disregard for anything else. Let Malinchek and his men deal with the American team. Not that there was much doubt as to the outcome. Malinchek wouldn't win, but that didn't matter. As long as they held the Americans back so that Biryenko could get his people off the ground, that would be satisfactory.

"Come on you old women. Haven't I taught you to run faster than this? Get your fat asses onto that helicopter. You don't want to miss this one-way ride to hell, do you?"

MCCARTER HAD SPOTTED the small group making a break for the Hind, and he knew it was the strike team. The Russians were closer to the chopper than

Phoenix Force. Added to their frustration was the barrier formed by Malinchek's men. They weren't seasoned combat veterans, but the resistance they offered was enough to delay Phoenix Force from getting to the people they really needed to stop.

And McCarter was already experiencing the sinking feeling that they weren't going to get there in time.

CHAPTER NINE

Siberia

Biryenko reached the Hind ahead of his team. He yelled at the pilot, instructing the man to power up the helicopter to liftoff capacity.

"Come on, you lazy bastards," Biryenko screamed at his men. "You want to live forever?"

The team raced in the direction of the Hind, heads lowered to avoid the stinging bite of the icy particles whirling around in the rotor wash. As they reached the access hatch, Biryenko reached out to grab hold of their clothing, practically throwing them inside.

The moment the first pair was inside, they took up positions at the open hatch, turning their AKs on the American commando team, laying down a hail of bullets that scattered them, leaving them to deal with the remainder of Malinchek's hired thugs.

Biryenko dragged the last man into the Hind, and the pilot, who had been watching, increased the power. The Hind shuddered, lifting sluggishly until the pilot trimmed the controls and brought the massive machine online. Biryenko's team composed more men than the usual complement carried in the Hind. Their combined weight held the gunship back as it rose from the ground, but under the skilled hands of the pilot it overcame the weight difference, rose a few feet, then surged forward, away from the heart of the battle. It skimmed the perimeter fence and was swallowed by the darkness and the falling snow. Altitude was gained quickly once the compound vanished behind them.

Biryenko headed to the cockpit via the cabin access and leaned in to speak to the pilot.

"Gagarin said they were good, but not good enough to stop us, Pieter," he said.

The pilot nodded. "Let them freeze out there while we make fools of the Militia Men."

"That won't be difficult. Those idiots are so blinded by their grievances with the American government they will follow us like lambs to the slaughter."

Biryenko and the pilot spent some time going over the course, checking the charts. They worked out that the flight would take about four hours. When they reached the chosen spot, the Hind would be covered with camouflage netting and they would sit out the time until they received the call from the Militia Men that they were in position and ready to join up with the Russians.

Once his business with the pilot was complete, Biryenko moved back to the rear of the Hind and sat next to the North Korean, Yat Sen Took. Biryenko's team had settled themselves on the center benches, or on the floor, grumbling at the lack of space. The Korean, hunched against the bulkhead, glanced around as Biryenko joined him.

"Is everything to your satisfaction?" Biryenko asked.

Took turned his expressionless gaze on the Russian. As always the Korean gave little away.

"If I say yes, it implies I am happy with second-best. Conversely, if I say no you look on me as a person who is difficult to please. So how should I answer?"

Biryenko burst into laughter, shaking his head at the Korean's reply.

"I have been to North Korea twice," he said. "Both times I looked around and thought what a miserable place it was. With an attitude like yours I'm not surprised. Are they all like you, Took? I asked a simple question, and you turned it into a philosophical debate."

"We live in a complicated world," Took said. "It places a great burden on each of us."

"No. You are wrong," Biryenko said. "Life is not complicated. People make it difficult because they talk a lot of foolishness. I see a problem and I deal with it. I don't sit around for days analyzing it or myself. I've read Freud, Jung and Nietzsche. They made careers out of talking a lot of crap. It's the same with all those Oriental dreamers. Believe me, Took, life *is* as simple as a bullet coming out of a gun barrel. It gets you or it doesn't. You cannot get much simpler than that."

Took pursed his thin lips, considering his words before he spoke.

"The device is ready. When we reach the site, I will activate it and set the timing device. When the time has elapsed, the device will detonate. Is that *simple* enough for you, Comrade Biryenko?"

Biryenko stood up, still smiling. "Brilliant. That was all I wanted to know," he said. "That was not difficult, was it?"

He turned and rejoined his team.

"Friendly, isn't he?" Bering asked. The young ex-soldier was broad and blond, with a baby face that belied his combat skills. "Is that because all they eat is boiled rice and fried rat?"

"*Fried rat?*" Biryenko said. "That's only on Sunday. The rest of the week it's just rice."

Bering shook his head. "I didn't know that. The result of a poor education."

"I'll cry in a minute," someone said from behind Bering. "Hey, Vladimir, when do we get to fight the Americans?"

"Stop worrying. The time will come."

"The sooner the better."

THE HIND LIFTING OFF was a bleak sight. David McCarter watched the bulk of the big machine fade out of sight.

"Damn and bugger it!"

His anger manifested itself in renewed aggression as he turned his H&K on the defenders of the compound. They were already starting to fall back, still putting up resistance, but with a lessening in intensity. They were headed for one of the barracks, a thin line covering the others as they moved inside. Windows were broken as the defenders shoved the barrels through the glass so they could maintain a defensive attitude while remaining under cover.

Sheltering behind one of the Snow cats, Phoenix Force took time to reload its weapons before carrying the fight to the enemy.

"Any grenades left?" Manning asked.

The grenades were collected. There were five fragmentation and two stun.

The big Canadian took a couple of them and worked his way around the Snow Cat. From his new position he was able to see the side of the barracks hut and specifically one of the closest windows. He considered the distance, deciding that he needed to get closer. He glanced over his shoulder and saw that James and Encizo were crouched behind him. They saw the window and realized what Manning intended.

"You need covering fire?" James asked.

"If I get close enough, I can lob a couple of these through that window."

"You got it," Encizo said.

James and the Cuban positioned themselves so they had a clear shot at the window. Manning stripped off his slung H&K and made sure his handgun was secure in its holster before he moved slightly ahead of his partners.

"Do it," James said.

He and Encizo opened fire, riddling the window with concentrated fire. The head and shoulders of the man using the window as a firing position drew back quickly as bullets chewed and splintered the wood around the window frame.

Once the figure pulled back, Manning took off. He made a direct run for the window, taking a final rolling leap over the last few yards. He slithered across the icy ground, coming to rest beneath the window. Manning pushed to his feet, back hard against the wooden side of the hut. He pulled the pins on the grenades and let the levers spring free, then counted deliberately, holding the grenades until the last few seconds before turning and hurling them in through the window. The moment he had thrown the projectiles the big Canadian hit the ground, arms clasped around his head.

The grenades blew with twin crackles of sound, lighting up the interior of the barracks hut. Smoke and debris blew out the window above Manning's prone position, showering the outside with smoking fragments. Even as the smoke was still curling out the window, McCarter and Hawkins took a dead run for the door to the hut.

McCarter was yards away when the door was flung open and a figure staggered out, clothes smoking and in tatters. Blood seeped through the ruin of a mangled arm and shoulder. The man, clutching a stubby Uzi, raised the weapon as he saw McCarter. The Briton triggered his MP-5, putting a burst into the guy that spun him off the step and down to the ground. Stepping over the body, the Phoenix Force leader went up the steps and into the barrack hut, breaking to the right as he entered, then dropping to one knee to reduce his target size.

A bulb on the end of a cord swung back and forth. McCarter could see a number of figures down on the floor. Some moved, while others were forever stilled. As Hawkins came into the hut, his MP-5 sweeping the area, a figure rose up from behind an overturned table, feverishly working the cocking bolt on his AK-74. Hawkins caught him with a fast burst, knocking the man backward, the Kalashnikov flying from nerveless fingers.

There was little more resistance. The grenades had taken out the bulk of the men inside the hut. Those still alive were in no fit state to fight any longer. As soon as Phoenix Force was back together, they rounded up the living and disarmed them. James tended to the wounded, doing what he could for them. After a hesitant start one of the Russians showed James where the first-aid kit was.

McCarter assigned his team to carry out various tasks.

"Gary, go check communications and put what they have out of action. I don't want any messages going out about our being here."

"You got it," Manning said.

"Rafe, collect all the weapons and extra ammunition. Dump it somewhere. T.J., I want food and water collected. Put it in one of the other huts for these people. When we leave, they stay locked inside. Once we're gone, they look out for themselves."

McCarter moved to a quiet corner of the hut and took out the powerful signal transmitter Grimaldi had given him. He activated the signal and placed the device on one of the windowsills, out of sight of any watching eyes. Once the pilot had received the signal, he would come in and pick them up.

A while later McCarter was standing beside James. The team's medic had finished tending the injured and was packing away his gear. One of the Russians sat watching McCarter, an undisguised look of contempt in his eyes. The Briton put up with the man's glare for as long as he could.

"Something troubling you?" he asked finally.

The Russian glanced around at his own men, then back at McCarter.

"You believe that winning here will stop us?"

"Stop *us?*" McCarter said. "All I see is a sorry bunch of losers. The deal's over for you blokes. If I were you, I'd start thinking how I was going to get through the next few days."

"You know who I am?" the Russian said.

"I suppose you'll tell me anyway."

"An important man in this territory. I have influence. Money. You would do well do listen to me. I am Feodor Malinchek."

McCarter moved to confront the man.

"I've heard the name. Not that it does much for me. Little blokes with big ideas leave me cold. Put me right. Wasn't it your half-wits we sent packing at Kranski's house? You had him killed, too."

"Then you will see you should not trifle with me. Others have tried and suffered." He thought for a moment. "Like that interfering Chinese agent who worked with Kranski."

"You knew her?"

Malinchek leaned forward. "Not so intimately as I would have wished. Or so that I would refrain from shooting her. I hope the bitch suffered."

"She still is," McCarter said very calmly, and the gentleness in his tone alerted the rest of Phoenix Force.

"Not dead? My aim must have been off. Pity that."

"I'm surprised you missed," McCarter said. "Seeing as she had her back to you at the time."

The Russian shrugged. "What is that saying? Oh yes, you always get what's coming to you. That little slant-eyed bitch did."

Manning reached McCarter's side and placed a firm hand on the Heckler & Koch the Briton was gripping. He could see the white patches showing on McCarter's knuckles.

"No, David," the Canadian said. "Not this way."

McCarter turned to look at him. The expression in his eyes was frightening to see. He didn't say a word, but looked down at Manning's restraining hand, then back at his friend.

"Just take the bloody thing," he said, allowing Manning to remove the weapon from his hands.

Malinchek was watching this with a puzzled expression on his face. He was still trying to figure out what was going on when McCarter stepped in front of him.

"Any street thug can shoot a woman in the back," McCarter said. "That doesn't take guts."

"You believe I care what you think?"

"I hoped you'd say that." McCarter stood with his hands at his sides. "Go ahead, Mr. Big, show *me* how tough you are. Take your shot. Hit me if you can."

Malinchek hesitated, frowning, uncertain what

McCarter was up to. He glanced around the hut. Even his own men were watching with interest.

"Something wrong, Malinchek? The odds not in your favor? Maybe I should turn around. Show you my back. Would that suit you better?"

Malinchek's rising anger showed in the flush that colored his face. He was clenching and unclenching his hands, trying to hold back.

"I will not...."

"I figured that," McCarter said with a slow smile. "Man of importance, my arse. All I see is a cheap gangster full of wind."

Malinchek yelled something unintelligible. He lunged at McCarter, lashing out with a clenched fist that the Briton avoided easily as he leaned to one side. The Russian's punch drew him forward, close in to McCarter. The Briton slammed a hard left into Malinchek's stomach, knocking the breath from his lungs, and as the Russian sagged forward McCarter hauled off and slammed a powerful right to his jaw. The blow hit with a meaty sound, the force spinning Malinchek off his feet. He crashed to the floor of the hut with a hard thump, bouncing, his face hitting the boards. The Russian lay still, blood gushing from his nose and mouth. His jaw sagged at an awkward angle where McCarter's blow had dislocated it.

"Bloody hell, that hurt," McCarter groaned, shaking his right fist. The flesh had been skinned from knuckles.

"Don't expect any sympathy from me," Manning said as he handed back McCarter's MP-5. "If you were only going to hit him, I would have let you keep the damn gun.''

McCarter looked at the Canadian. ''You were right to take it, mate. I would probably have shot the bastard.''

''You finished?'' Encizo asked, staring down at Malinchck. ''You're too soft. One punch wasn't enough.''

''Rafe, I'm getting sentimental in my old age.''

Encizo grinned.

''By the way, I checked out the third hut,'' Manning said. ''It didn't seem to be in use until I had a look inside. They had radar set up, satellite communication. Pretty sophisticated. The radar dish was out back on a retractable mast. It could explain why they were waiting for us. They could have tracked *Dragon Slayer* flying in, maybe got a fix on where we were starting from.''

''You pulled the plug, I suppose?'' McCarter asked.

''Yeah. When I checked the rest of the hut, I found their computer room. We should go take a look before we leave.''

The prisoners were taken to the hut that had been prepared for them. The wooden weather shutters on the outside were swung into place and secured. The food, water and medical supplies, along with blankets, had been placed in the hut. Once the prisoners were inside, the door was closed and secured on the outside.

Phoenix Force made its way through the still falling snow to the hut that contained the computers, radar and radio equipment. The place had the look of having been evacuated in a hurry. Someone had dumped a pile of papers in a metal wastebasket and set light to them. All that was left was a layer of black ash.

"Check it out," McCarter said.

"Hey, the radio is working okay," Hawkins commented. He sat at the desk and started to check frequencies. It didn't take him long to locate *Dragon Slayer*.

"Hey, flyboy, where are you?"

Grimaldi's voice came through. "I'm closing in on your location. Should be there in about forty minutes. You guys okay?"

McCarter picked up a headset. "We're fine now. Objective neutralized. Get here fast, mate, we need to move out."

"Would have been available earlier but I had a slight distraction. Unfriendly locals if you get my drift."

"They're all bloody unfriendly around here, chum."

"See you soon. Over and out."

"T.J., keep monitoring that thing."

"You got it, boss."

"David, this bunch didn't go in for any frills. They were living on basics," Manning said. "Just enough to get by on."

James was opening drawers and pulling out the contents.

"Hey," he called. "Look here."

He had found a roll of paper that had been pushed to the back of a drawer and overlooked. He spread it out across a desktop for examination. The diagram printed on the large sheet showed the radar facility that had been created outside. It detailed sizes and dimensions, thickness of concrete walls and the depth that the main shaft would go underground. James pointed to the logo at the bottom of the paper. It was the imprint of the U.S. Department of Defense. "Somebody gave them this."

"Curtis?" Manning asked.

"Seems the likely candidate."

McCarter crossed to where Hawkins sat at the radio.

"Something on your mind, boss?"

"This thing works via satellite, right?"

"Yeah."

"Can you patch me through to Stony Man?"

Hawkins nodded. "Sure thing."

He adjusted the digital tuner, scanning the range for the satellite uplink. Once he had the connection, Hawkins used the attached keyboard to tap in the security code that switched the outgoing transmission to the Stony Man secure feed. He established contact with the Computer Room.

"Ice Wolf calling Stony Base," Hawkins said. "You read me?"

Aaron Kurtzman's voice came through the speaker.

"You got time to make personal calls?"

"You still got the coordinates for this place?" McCarter asked.

"Yeah, why?"

"We need you to do check on a chopper that flew

out of here a while ago. My guess is it's heading for the Bering Strait, maybe over into Alaska.''

''Give me a minute,'' Kurtzman said. ''I need to check when the satellite's going to be online again.''

Stony Man Farm, Virginia

''AKIRA, I WANT the satellite schedule. First choice the SAR.''

''Coming up.''

Akira Tokaido tapped in the information and the screen filled with data. He isolated one stream and focused in on it, running down the time schedules.

''She'll be online in forty minutes.''

''Okay. I want a fast window as soon as. Get ready for it. Key in the coordinates we used to pinpoint the Siberian facility last time. Phoenix need us to track an outgoing helicopter to see if we can find out where it's heading.''

''Is that possible?'' Tokaido asked. ''I mean, it's a big piece of land out there and lousy weather conditions.''

''We have to give it our best shot. We won't have all that much time, so we'll have to be ready.''

Kurtzman reached for the phone. He was going to have to call his contact at the SAR facility again and ask for a second favor. The way things were going, his credit line would soon be empty.

On the other side of the room Barbara Price lifted her head as she picked up on Kurtzman's conversation. She returned to her work briefly, checking off the final items on her list, then stood. Pausing, she stretched, easing her stiff spine, and made her way over to Kurtzman's station.

"Phoenix still on?"

Kurtzman shook his head. "They'll contact again in a while. We decided it was best to stay off-line until we had something to talk about. Somebody might pick up their transmission. They're on Russian soil illegally remember."

Price nodded, smiling indulgently. "There are times, Aaron, when you sound like a damn lawyer."

Kurtzman handed a sheet of printed data. "This came through. Phoenix found construction plans for the radar facility, and they're marked U.S. Department of Defense. The suggestion is Paul Curtis needs taking into custody ASAP."

"Okay, I'll go talk to Hal."

AT THE APPOINTED TIME the SAR satellite responded to the signals it was receiving. The orbiting object changed its angle, directing its electronic eyes toward the distant spot on Earth where it would focus in. As the data was absorbed and transformed into active commands, the satellite swung into position. With cold precision it locked on to its minuscule target and followed the designated course set for it by Aaron Kurtzman. Despite the prevailing weather conditions in the Siberian location, the satellite's signals penetrated and began to send back the images to the Stony Man monitors.

"COMING THROUGH," Tokaido announced.

He had already set his computer to lock and record

every item of information beaming back from the SAR. He watched the images on his monitor. The Russian facility came on first, the image the same as the one they had stored earlier, the same three main buildings and the radar facility mock-up. There were fewer figures moving around on the site this time.

''Recording online,'' Tokaido advised Kurtzman.

He had no desire to get chewed out by forgetting to record the incoming data. His boss was a good man to work for, but he could also be hell on wheels if things went wrong.

Once the satellite was set, Kurtzman used it to follow the probable course it would have taken to reach the coast, bearing in mind the inclement weather. The SAR's microwave signals were able to see through the falling snow and give a clear enough image. He carried out a long-range sweep, hoping he might pick up something. Nothing. He got shots of the Siberian terrain but nothing else. He settled back in his seat and moved on, extending his range of search, veering to either side of the direct line to the coast. Again nothing. Kurtzman avoided checking the time. He was aware of it slipping away, shortening the possibility of picking anything up before the natural orbit took away the SAR. Kurtzman couldn't wait until the satellite was available again. There was no second chance this time around.

He was becoming aware of his window starting to close. Sharpness started to deteriorate. The image was on the slide. Kurtzman remained calm, keying in a constant stream of commands. He made the satellite do exactly what he wanted, and on the edge of its sweep he picked up what he was looking for.

The feedback by now was distinctly lacking in quality. Kurtzman reached in close to pluck what he could from the blurring image. He had what he wanted. Pictures. Heat sources courtesy of the thermal imagery. The distant helicopter was almost at the coast, flying low and making good time despite the bad weather. Kurtzman registered the coordinates and relinquished command of the satellite. His release allowed the SAR to return to its standard orbit.

"Tell me we got everything," Kurtzman demanded.

Tokaido swung his chair around, holding up both hands, thumbs raised. "We got it all."

Siberia

DRAGON SLAYER touched down just under an hour later. The snow was falling heavier, driven by a chill wind that drove against exposed flesh. Phoenix Force boarded the combat helicopter, breathing a collective sigh of relief when the hatch clamped shut. McCarter settled into the seat opposite Grimaldi.

"One small item to attend to," McCarter said as the aircraft lifted off.

He guided Grimaldi to the center of the compound where the radar facility mock-up stood. There was no need to elaborate further. Grimaldi turned the combat helicopter and activated his weapons system, selecting a Sidewinder missile. A touch of the firing button sent the missile on its way. A flash was followed by a muffled explosion as the Sidewinder demolished the mock-up and the base where it stood.

"Nice shot, Jack," McCarter commented. "Would have been red faces all around if you'd missed that."

As an added safeguard McCarter had Grimaldi repeat the procedure on the third hut, where the radar and computer equipment had been found.

"So, where to now?" Grimaldi asked.

"We're going hunting, Jack, my lad, looking for an ex-Soviet Hind."

"You going to give me a clue which way to go?"

"You want it easy," McCarter said. He handed over a sheet of paper on which Hawkins had written the coordinates relating to the Russian Hind's course.

Grimaldi scanned the information.

McCarter slapped him on the shoulder. "It says east, my lad, toward the coast and the Bering Strait."

CHAPTER TEN

Seattle

Rick Teeler burst into Lyons's motel room without knocking.

"Make yourself at home," Lyons said.

He was stretched out on the bed, reading a copy of a gun digest, a can of beer in one hand. Behind Teeler, Lyons saw the bulky figure of Hubbard Tetrow. The Militia Men leader closed the door and moved to one side.

"Well?" Teeler demanded. "I turn up and you ain't there. You forgot my orders?"

"I was there," Lyons said. "Until a bunch of local lard asses came by and decided I was invading their turf. I disagreed and we settled it kind of aggressively."

Tetrow crossed to stand beside the bed as Lyons swung his feet to the floor and stood.

"Looks like you caught one," he said, looking at the bruise on Lyons's cheek.

Lyons pulled up his sweat shirt to show the bruises over his ribs. "And some," he said.

"Any broken?" Tetrow asked.

"Sore is all. I had worse in jail."

"So what happened to the other guys?" Teeler asked.

"The three stooges? They'll be hurting a lot longer than I will. I was easy on them. Killing them would have got the local cops interested. Could have interfered with our business. We wouldn't want that, would we, Rick?"

Teeler held his ground. His expression didn't change a fraction.

"Hell, no," he said.

"Glad you're all right, Jag," Tetrow said. "You take it easy, huh? Rick, you were wondering if Jag could cut it. I guess we all know now, don't we."

Teeler turned to smile coolly at Lyons. "Yeah, now we know."

Lyons reached down to the ice bucket on the bedside table. He picked out a couple of cans.

"Beer, anyone?" he asked.

AFTER A NIGHT'S sleep Lyons felt stiff, but otherwise he was able to move around. He took a long shower, dressed and met the others in the diner across the street from the motel. He joined Warner and Sutherland at their table and ordered breakfast and coffee.

"We heard what happened," Warner said. "You okay?"

Lyons nodded.

"Weird, or what?" Sutherland said. "Teeler gets you to wait on your own and next minute you get jumped."

Lyons only smiled as he picked up his coffee mug.

"You figure Teeler sent them, don't you?" Warner said.

"I *know* he sent them."

"How do you know?"

Lyons glanced at Sutherland. "I got the power," he said evenly.

Sutherland stared him out for a while, then smiled. "Shit," he said. "That's no fuckin' answer."

"It was no question."

"I guess not," Sutherland admitted.

"We said watch your back," Warner said.

"That you did."

They spent some time eating their breakfast. Lyons could see that others from the group were also in the diner. He spotted Teeler and Tetrow at the far end, deep in conversation. At one point Teeler looked up and caught Lyons's gaze. It was Teeler who finally looked away.

"So, did I miss anything last night?" Lyons asked.

Sutherland chuckled. "Did you miss anything? Jesus, compared to you we had a crap night."

"I think this deal is ready to go down," Warner said. "Tetrow was giving out the word for everyone to be ready to move. Something's going to happen tonight, way I see it. Maybe we get the chance to kick some federal fuckin' ass. Make the bastards sit up and listen."

Lyons nodded. "About time."

Moments later Tetrow approached the table. "Finish up and meet in my room soon as." He turned and left, Teeler on his heels.

"Here we go," Sutherland crowed.

"OUT THERE in the bay," Teeler said, "the two barges anchored on their own."

They were parked on a headland overlooking the water. Following Teeler's finger, Lyons made out the shape of the oceangoing barges. Long and low in the water due to the cargo they were carrying, the diesel-powered barges rested on the calm surface. Lights showed aft in the crew quarters.

"All they have is a skeleton crew," Teeler said. "Three men to each vessel. Regular crew doesn't come on board until next week. They'll spend another five days getting the barges ready to sail before they head out for Alaska."

From the rear seat Sutherland said, "Only they won't be making that trip this time."

"What do they have on board?" Lyons asked.

"Final construction materials for the facility. One of them has special crated cargo," Teeler explained. "Electronics so installation can go ahead as soon as they finish building."

"How we going to do it?" Warner asked.

"Hub had a delivery yesterday. It's waiting for us in a lockup. The high-explosive devices will send those barges to the bottom. The special cargo will have its own separate package so the gear gets trashed, as well."

"When?" Sutherland asked.

"Tonight," Teeler said. "We go tonight. We take out the barges. The others back in Dakota hit the radar facility there. And we head out for Alaska to meet up with the Russians for the final phase."

"Sounds a lot to keep on track," Lyons said.

"All in the planning, Jag."

"Any reason we're out here looking at the boats?" Sutherland asked.

"Man needs to recognize his target," Teeler said. "You boys hit the jackpot. We're the ones who get to sink the barges."

Carl Lyons had the feeling things were going from bad to worse.

"Once we get back to the motel we stay together," Teeler said. "No reflection on anyone, but we can't risk any leaks about what we're about to do."

He was staring directly at Lyons as he spoke.

"Right, Jag?"

"Wouldn't have it any other way."

THEY ROWED OUT to the barges in a large rubber dinghy. It was fitted with a powerful outboard, but that was only for emergencies. The outward journey had to be made in silence. Each man wore a black coverall and woolen cap. Hands and faces were blacked out. They carried 9 mm Beretta pistols fitted with suppressors. In addition each man had a sheathed knife on his belt. In the dingy with them were three large, solid packs containing the prearmed explosive charges. All they had to do was place them where necessary and set the timers.

They had set out from a dark inlet south of the wharves and rowed out in silence. The calm water was dappled by the fine rain falling across the area, which helped to cover their presence. It took fifteen minutes for them to reach the pair of barges.

They checked for movement on the vessels, using night-vision goggles that possessed enhanced magnification. The poor weather had kept the skeleton crew inside the cabins.

Teeler sent Sutherland over the stern rail, then passed him the tie rope to secure the dinghy. Between them they passed up the explosive devices, then followed until the four of them were crouched in the shadow of the superstructure.

"Anyone shows and gets in our way, you know what to do," Teeler said. "I don't need any fuckups on this. I don't have time for any of these people making themselves heroes."

"We going to do it, or sit here getting wet?" Lyons asked.

Teeler stared at him. "We're set. Hey, Jag, you're with me."

"Why didn't I see that coming?"

Sutherland and Warner took their package and moved out. They had to cross to the second barge, leaving Teeler and Lyons with two packages.

"Let's go, tough guy," Teeler said, picking up one of the explosive packs.

Lyons slung the other package from his shoulder by the webbing strap provided and followed Teeler along the rain-slick deck. They reached a hatch and Teeler eased it open. Lyons followed him down a metal companionway that took them to the cargo area. Another hatch let them move into the actual hold where the barge's cargo was stored. Even though the water outside was calm, Lyons could feel a slight swell moving the deck under his feet. He followed

Teeler until the man halted, placing his package on the deck. Lyons did the same with his.

They were surrounded by stacks of building materials—steel work, prefabricated sections for buildings. The cargo ran the length of the hold and stood about ten feet high.

"If we place one of the packs here, she'll punch a damn great hole in the hull," Teeler said. "This thing will go down fast."

He moved on until he came to a section that held a large sealed container.

"This is the special cargo. According to our information, this is real high tech. Something to do with the guidance system. It has to be installed at this stage of the construction 'cause it's sealed up inside the center core of the unit." Teeler patted the side of the container. "Won't really matter when we take out the site, but this is all about gestures. Makin' the fuckin' government hurt when they find the whole damn project is dead and buried."

"You think this is going to stop them?" Lyons asked. "A couple of barges and a chunk of hardware? All they'll do is start again."

Teeler turned, anger darkening his face.

"You want to know something, Jag? You are beginning to piss me off. Hub figures you're some kind of wonder boy. Just the kind of recruit he needs for the Militia Men. What the hell you got on him? Pictures of him and naked boys?"

"I know you're paranoid, Teeler, but I didn't figure you were stupid, as well."

Lyons had intended to anger the man. He was running out of time and he needed to do something about Teeler. What he hadn't expected was the wild reaction he got.

Teeler pulled his gun and leveled it. Lyons saw the move and ducked in under Teeler's gun hand, jerking a hard elbow into Teeler's ribs. The man gasped, twisted and swung his gun at Lyons's head. The barrel of the weapon scraped along the Able Team leader's skull, tearing the skin. Throwing up both his hands, Lyons caught Teeler's arm and swung the man in a half circle that ended when Teeler slammed face first into the large container.

There was a moment when Teeler seemed to have lost it, but then he shoved a foot against the container and pushed hard, the momentum taking him and Lyons backward across the deck. They crashed against a stack of steel girders, Teeler turning so he was facing Lyons. He lashed out with he gun again, opening a bloody gash in Lyons's cheek that began to stream blood. The blow dazed him and he had to force himself to ignore the pain, grappling with Teeler as the Militia Men leader struck out again with his gun.

Lyons took the blows on his raised arms, gathering himself for the moment when he was able to drive forward, closing on Teeler. As they came together, Lyons rammed his knee into his adversary's groin, wrenching a subdued groan from the man. Dropping his head, Lyons leaned in, then whacked the back of his skull up beneath Teeler's jaw. The force of the blow snapped the man's teeth together hard. His trigger finger jerked back and the Beretta went off with a suppressed chug. The 9 mm bullet bounced off steel and whined into the darkness. Still a little groggy from Teeler's pistol-whipping, Lyons fought back without pause. The full extent of his backed-up frustration exploded in a wild response to the hurt he felt. He hammered blows into Teeler's side until the man wriggled sideways to escape the punishment.

Briefly clear, Lyons reached for the knife at his side and dragged it clear of the sheath. He brought it up and around in a slash that cut deep into the flesh of his opponent's left arm above the elbow. Teeler backpedaled wildly, lost his footing and fell. Lyons was on him instantly. He slammed his foot down on Teeler's gun hand, crushing it against the ridged deck plate. Teeler howled, struggling to free himself, but all he did was strip flesh from the back of his hand. Increasing the pressure on Teeler's hand, Lyons saw the man's fingers loosen their grip. He reached down and pried the gun away, tossing it into the shadows. Switching his knife to his free hand, Lyons took out his own Beretta and held it on Teeler. He stepped away from the man.

"Up," Lyons snapped. "In your words no heroes tonight."

Teeler stood up slowly. His mouth was bloody, and he sleeved it away. His eyes were hot with rage.

"I knew it. Damn Tetrow. Got himself taken in by a fuckin' Fed."

"What makes you think I'm a Fed?"

"You're no damn militia man."

"You got that right, Teeler. I couldn't get myself dumb enough so I had to fake it. Now, let's get out of here before your two buddies come back."

"We never left," a voice whispered close behind Lyons.

He recognized it as Warner's a fraction of a second before something hard and brutal slammed across the back of his skull. Lyons pitched facedown on the deck. Somebody kicked him hard in the side, turning him over on his back. Lyons saw the foot raise again. He tried to avoid what was coming but failed. The sole of the boot slammed against the side of his head. Pain flared, only briefly, and then the night and the darkness overtook him as Lyons passed out.

CHAPTER ELEVEN

North Dakota

Trenker headed north. He was in a battered panel truck driving at a steady clip. Rosario Blancanales and Gadgets Schwarz followed without lights, keeping at a safe distance. The road they were traveling had little traffic so they had no difficulty keeping Trenker in sight. While Schwarz drove, Blancanales studied a map he had spread out on his knees. He was also talking to Stony Man on his cell phone.

"The only place he can be going is the secondary radar installation site in North Dakota," Blancanales said. "It fits the plan these assholes have conjured up."

"Excuse me, Pol, but is that a technical term?" Barbara Price asked.

"What? 'Plan' or 'assholes'? If it's the latter, then yes, it's a technical field term."

"Okay, I give in."

"Look, the guy picked up a shipment of AT-4s. No doubt. We were close enough to recognize them when he did the transfer. You don't handle those things if you're going on a raccoon hunt.''

"We'll get the details on the site. Hal needs to talk to the President.''

"Let's hope he hasn't decided to slip off to Camp David for the weekend,'' Blancanales muttered.

"I heard that,'' Brognola said over the other line. "I'm on it, Pol.''

"Hey. You heard anything from Carl?''

"Not since his previous call. But we figured out what they might be up to in Seattle. We found out there are a couple of barges anchored in the bay, waiting for final instructions to head on up to Alaska. They're carrying construction materials for the radar site up there. One of them has a special cargo, as well. Electronic equipment for the facility. Very expensive equipment.''

"You think the Militia Men might go for that, too?''

"The more damage they do, the harder it's going to be for the project to be completed by the set date.''

"Crazy bastards,'' Blancanales said.

Brognola spoke to someone in the background, then said, "Pol, I have to go talk to the Man. Get back to you soon.''

Stony Man Farm, Virginia

BROGNOLA TOOK the phone Huntington Wethers handed him.

"Thank you for calling back, sir. We need to know the exact location of the North Dakota facility for the

Slingshot radar site. Two of my men are following one of the Militia Men, and our feeling is that's where he's headed.... No, sir, but the man has a consignment of AT-4 rocket launchers in his truck.... I'd say that, sir. We heard from Phoenix Force a little while ago. They took out the facility in Siberia where the mock-up was. Unfortunately, the strike team got away from them. According to Phoenix Force, they're most likely making a run for the coast and the Bering Strait.... No, sir, they're on their tail. I'll keep you informed, sir.''

Brognola put down the phone. He crossed to Kurtzman's desk.

"Transmission will be coming through shortly, providing the location of the North Dakota site for Slingshot. I need you to get a satellite on it fast."

"We might have to tread on some toes to get access," Kurtzman pointed out.

"If it needs doing, we'll worry about it later. Right now I want that scan. Able is going in with only two men. We don't know what they might find. I'd like to give them some advantage, Aaron."

Kurtzman nodded. "You'll get it."

Before he had time to turn around, his cyberteam was busy at work, logging on to every available satellite to see which one could give them what they needed.

North Dakota

"OKAY, BARB, we'll wait for your call," Blancanales said, then cut the phone.

"Well?" his partner asked after a reasonable silence.

"They're on it. Soon as they have the details, Barb will call."

"Sounds reasonable to me," Schwarz said.

A few miles farther on Trenker turned off the main highway and picked up a two-lane road that wound up into sparsely wooded hills. He drove with the confidence of someone who knew where he was going. Schwarz let the car fall back to a greater distance.

"Nothing on this damn map," Blancanales grumbled.

"What do you expect? A picture of the radar site?"

"Be helpful."

"The Bear might come up with something useful."

"Better be quick. Any time now we could drive right into the middle of the Militia Men rally."

Stony Man Farm, Virginia

"HERE SHE COMES," Huntington Wethers said.

He had returned to duty in time to access the satellite close enough to allow surveillance of the Slingshot site. Using the coordinates transmitted via a presidential aide, Stony Man began a low-level scan of the area and was able to isolate the site and its surrounding terrain.

"The site is there," Wethers pointed out.

They saw a blurred outline moving across the monitor screen as one of the security guards made his rounds, showing up as a heat source. Wethers zoomed out, using the digital imagery to show a larger picture of the immediate area. He had to pull out even farther before they saw anything more.

"There," Tokaido said, jabbing a finger at the screen. "Vehicles."

"Here we go," Wethers said.

He manipulated the satellite camera and focused on the indistinct shapes the younger man had spotted. Closing in, he sharpened the image and they found themselves looking at a cluster of parked vehicles in among heavy foliage. Moving figures denoted people. They counted six.

"Get through to Able," Brognola said. "Hunt, can you work out the position of that group?"

Wethers nodded. Using the original coordinates, he overlaid a map of the area and pinpointed the spot where the waiting vehicles and people were.

The information was relayed to Blancanales.

"What about Trenker?" he asked. "He show up yet?"

"Nothing yet," Kurtzman said. "Hunt's going to take a wider view. Check out that stretch of road."

A moving shape showed on the monitor. Wethers tracked back and shortly picked up a second vehicle following the first.

"Hey, I got them both."

Kurtzman relayed the information through to Blancanales.

"Great. Ask Hunt how many fingers I'm holding up," he said.

"Hold it, guys," Wethers said. "He's turning off the road. Looks like a narrow track. Tell them it's about a half mile ahead of them. To the right. And about a mile from the waiting vehicles.''

North Dakota

''WE SEE IT,'' Blancanales said.

Schwarz slowed the car as he made the turn onto the dirt track.

''Easy now,'' Blancanales cautioned.

The car rocked over the uneven surface of the track, which led between thickets and rising banks. Driving without lights would have been difficult if it hadn't been for a bright moon. The pale light at least allowed them some vision. Schwarz guided the car over loose dirt and stones, staring through the dusty windshield with an expression of expectation on his face.

They had covered almost three-quarters of a mile when Blancanales suddenly said, ''Let's hope they don't have any pointmen out there.''

THE SHARP CRACK of an autoweapon shattered the silence. Bullets thumped against the body of the car. One of the rear passenger windows imploded, glass blowing across the seats. More shots erupted from the shadows. A tire burst and the front corner of the car sank.

Blancanales scrambled out of the vehicle and into cover against the roots of a tree, hugging his MP-5 to his chest. He still had the cell phone in one hand, and he could hear a voice coming from it. That would be Kurtzman. Blancanales shoved the phone into a pocket and closed the zip. He pressed hard against the tree, flicked off the MP-5's safety and waited until the hidden shooter opened up again. The brief muzzle-flash gave away the shooter's position. Blancanales leaned out and returned fire, letting go with a short burst that forced the shooter back under cover. Blancanales fired again, then gathered himself and pushed to his feet, making a run for a low bank several yards in front of him. He was still a few yards away when the shooter triggered another burst. The slugs chewed at the ground in Blancanales' wake, kicking up dirt and leaves. He gained the last few almost on his knees, coming to rest in the cover of the bank with a jolting thud.

On the other side of the car Schwarz remained where he was, his MP-5 held snug against his shoulder. He had already spotted the shooter's position, picked up when the guy returned Blancanales's burst. There was a short lull, then Blancanales fired again, raking the shooter's position with a burst.

The shooter was unable to resist taking up the challenge. He dropped a few rounds into Blancanales's position, and in that action he exposed himself to Schwarz. Already in firing position, Schwarz turned the muzzle of the MP-5 and triggered a single shot that hit the target midchest. The shooter tumbled backward, making a great deal of noise as he went down.

Somewhere ahead the brake lights on Trenker's panel truck came on as he slithered to a stop. His door burst open and the man scrambled out, dragging an M-16 with him. He ran toward the rear of the vehicle, raising the rifle. He was yelling over his shoulder, alerting the waiting Militia Men.

"This isn't the plan," Blancanales said, joining Schwarz.

"Tell me about it," Schwarz said. "It's going to get busy around here anytime."

"You want to back off?"

"Funny guy."

"We need Trenker's panel truck. If those AT-4s get to the Militia Men, we could still have a problem."

They moved forward, pausing at the front of their bullet-riddled car. The thin moonlight showed them Trenker's panel trunk and someone moving in its shadow.

"I'll take this side," Blancanales said. "You want to cut around to the right?"

Schwarz nodded and they parted company, picking up the pace as they closed in on Trenker's position. Both Able Team warriors were conscious that the waiting Militia Men had to have heard the shooting, and even Trenker's warning yell.

Blancanales found he was close to the truck. He kept in the shadows as much as possible. Trenker would be nervous now, wondering what was going on and when he would be the next in the firing line. Down on one knee Blancanales studied the outline of the panel truck. He peered into the gloom, searching for movement, and was rewarded as Trenker eased into view. The man was clutching his M-16, moving the muzzle back and forth in sharp arcs. Any little sound seemed to spook him.

Dammit, Blancanales said to himself, he's going to start firing!

The M-16 opened up, single shots, directed at Schwarz's position. Blancanales couldn't be sure whether Trenker had actually spotted his partner or was firing from panic. It didn't really matter which. Schwarz might still stop a bullet.

He stepped out into the open, his MP-5 settling on Trenker. Blancanales fired, the burst catching the militia man in the chest. Trenker half turned, hitting the side of the truck, then dropping facedown. When Blancanales reached him, the man was still moving, harsh gasps coming from his lips as he died.

"Over here," Blancanales called. "Trenker's out of it."

Schwarz emerged from the brush on the far side of the track. He was rubbing the upper part of his left arm.

"You okay?" his partner asked.

"That son of a bitch nearly hit me," Schwarz grumbled. "Ducked out of the way and got tangled in some damn thorny bush."

Blancanales checked the rear door of the panel truck. It was locked.

"Go get the keys," he said.

When Schwarz returned, Blancanales unlocked the rear door and yanked it open. The bed of the truck held a number of familiar military boxes—LAW rocket launchers. There were also a number of M-16s and a couple of ammunition boxes.

"Where the hell do these numb nuts keep getting

hold of this stuff?'' Schwarz asked angrily. ''Is the Army holding garage sales, or what?''

''Right now I don't give a damn,'' Blancanales said.

''Yeah? Well, I know someone who does.''

They both heard the sound of an engine. It was close, someone stepping on the gas as he moved in low gear along the bumpy track. The vehicle came into sight about two hundred yards away, sweeping around a bend in the track. It was an open Jeep, swaying under the load of a half dozen armed men in camou gear.

''Rock-and-a-hard-place time,'' Blancanales muttered.

Two of the passengers in the rear of the Jeep jumped from the vehicle and were running ahead. A spotlight was turned on, the bright beam of light sweeping back and forth, pausing when it rested on Trenker's prone form. The Jeep came to a squealing halt.

''Back off from the truck,'' someone yelled. ''Do it now!''

Blancanales glanced at his partner. ''You want to tell them?''

Leaning his MP-5 against the rear of the panel truck, Blancanales reached inside and opened one of the boxes. He lifted out a LAW, Quickly pulling out the extensions. With the weapon armed he placed it over his right shoulder and stepped out from behind the truck, lining up the launcher on the Jeep.

''Justice Department,'' Schwarz called out. ''I'll

say this once. Get out of the Jeep. Throw down your weapons. Do it now.''

"Go to hell! We don't recognize federal demands.''

A number of autoweapons opened up.

In the second before the LAW burned its way from the tube, Blancanales heard Schwarz mutter, ''Recognize this!''

The missile hit the front of the Jeep. The explosion lifted the front wheels off the ground, tipping the yelling Militia Men from the vehicle. A burst of flame and smoke obscured the Jeep and its occupants from view.

Schwarz tossed aside the exhausted LAW casing and snatched up his MP-5. He ducked back behind the cover of the panel truck, glancing at Blancanales.

"Very diplomatic," Blancanales said.

"The hell with diplomacy," Schwarz snapped. ''These guys want to play grown-up games, that's fine by me.''

The rattle of autofire showed that some of the Militia Men were still in a fighting mood. Bullets raked the steel of the truck's body, rocking it on its suspension. The sound of hard boots on the ground told the men of Able Team that they weren't alone.

Blancanales took the left side of the truck, Schwarz the right. They crouched, lowering their target size, and eased out from behind cover.

The Jeep was nose down on the ground, the front suspension having vanished in the explosion. Flames were starting to creep back along the underside of the Jeep from a fractured fuel line. There was one man sprawled halfway across the hood, arms dangling in front of him. Smoke rose from his charred clothing. Another was down on the ground, sagging back against the side of the crippled Jeep. His arms were clutched across his body, hugging himself. Schwarz could see that the side of his face was bloody and raw.

Schwarz was faced with two Militia Men, just level with the front of the panel truck. They were firing as they ran, their aim high, where they expected to see an upright figure. By the time they took stock of Schwarz's crouching stance it was too late. He raked them both with an extended burst from his MP-5, ripping them apart with 9 mm slugs. They went down hard, punctured and bleeding.

On the opposite side of the truck Blancanales faced down a single militia man, his burst of 9 mm fire catching the man in the legs. The guy fell, screaming in pain as his legs were shattered by the volley. His head crashed against the rim of a wheel and he flopped over on his back, bleeding heavily from his gunshot wounds and the deep gash in his skull.

Moving to the front of the panel truck, Blancanales met Schwarz and together they checked out the area. There didn't seem to be any further movement around or near the Jeep. The trickle of flame under the vehicle had grown to engulf most of its rear section, and flames were starting to rise up into the passenger area.

A sudden stir of movement caught their attention. An unsteady figure rose from where he had been lying across the rear seat, pushing upright, then rolling over the side to drop to the ground. His clothing was scorched and blackened. The man lurched upright, turning to face the Able Team duo. His face was lacerated down the right side. His right arm hung at his side, glistening with blood and he seemed to be missing sections of his hand.

Blancanales recognized him instantly. It was the Russian they had first seen talking to Trenker. The man they now knew as Valentene Nureyev.

He gripped a pistol in his left hand. He moved forward a few steps.

"Get rid of the weapon, Nureyev," Blancanales called out.

"If I do, you will not have an excuse to shoot me."

"Cut the crap, Nureyev, we're not in the mood to play games," Schwarz said. "Right now I don't need an excuse to put you down."

Beside Nureyev there was a burst of flame as fuel ignited. The heat forced the Russian away from the Jeep and as he moved to the edge of the light cast by the blaze, Nureyev swept his pistol up into the firing position, his finger catching the trigger a fraction too quickly. The bullet sailed over the heads of the Able Team warriors.

Schwarz triggered his MP-5, taking time to line up on his target. He laid in the remainder of his magazine, the burst tearing into the Russian's torso and chest cavity and dumping him to the ground in a bloody, twitching heap.

"Dumb move," Schwarz said. "I did tell him."

They moved forward to check out the Militia Men. Two were still alive. Blancanales put through a call to Stony Man, advising them of the situation and arranged for a cleanup detail to be organized.

"You think there are any more around?" Price asked.

"Right now we don't know. Sooner we get some backup in here the better."

"Leave it with me, guys."

"Any more from Carl?"

"Nothing. But Phoenix is following up team they expect to go for the facility in Alaska."

"Barb, we need to be there, too. Have a word with Hal. This thing needs wrapping. If this end is shut down, Gadgets and I need to be with the others. And not next week, Barb."

Stony Man Farm, Virginia

CARMEN DELAHUNT SWUNG around in her chair as Barbara Price entered the room.

"Update, Barb. The backup team has arrived at the site. They checked out the vehicles the Militia Men traveled in. They found details on the radar site, information about the security personnel, construction crew. There were enough weapons in the vehicles to start a small war. Right now we're getting details on the AT-4s Able Team found in Trenker's panel truck. Lucky for us they were still in the original cases. That means the military markings were still available."

Price nodded. "That means they're traceable. That might give the military something to go on."

"Able Team has been taken by helicopter to an Air Force base. There's a plane waiting to fly them to Alaska. Equipment will be supplied by the Air Force."

Brognola had trailed behind Price. He was holding up a sheet of paper. The big Fed looked weary enough to fall into a deep sleep right there and then.

"Now the bad news," he said. "I just had confirmation from Seattle that the two barges anchored in the bay were sunk late last night. Simultaneous blasts blew holes in the hulls and they went down. There were only skeleton crews on board each barge. They all got out except one man, who was caught in the undertow and drowned. Seattle police divers are investigating now. The Navy is sending in some of their people, too."

"What about Paul Curtis?" Wethers asked. "Has he been picked up yet?"

"Son of a bitch is dead," Brognola growled. "Police went to his apartment and the guy decided to shoot it out. Wounded two cops before he was shot down. FBI have moved in now and are going through his stuff."

Silence descended for a moment. Kurtzman ended it by banging his fist on the edge of his desk.

"Come on, people, we don't quit just because of a couple of setbacks. Able stopped the attack on the Dakota site. Phoenix is tracking the team from Russia. Let's back them up!"

CHAPTER TWELVE

Siberia

The moment the Hind touched down, the team slid open the door and dragged out the camouflage sheets. Struggling against the bitter wind and the icy snow, they covered the bulky helicopter, tying down the sheets to the undercarriage struts. With the task completed the team ducked beneath the covers and back inside the Hind.

Biryenko was on the radio talking to Gagarin.

"We'll wait now until we get word from Yesinovich that the Militia Men are in position," the team leader said.

"Good. I spoke to Boris earlier. They have left Seattle. However, there have been developments. An undercover operative was discovered in the Militia Men ranks. He attempted to stop the destruction of the construction barges. He failed and is now in the hands of the Militia Men."

"Who is he?"

"That has not been discovered yet. I'm betting on

him belonging to part of the organization who sent the American team after you. If that's so, he may be able to furnish us with vital information."

"These Americans are not as stupid as they are made out to be," Biryenko said.

"Vladimir, I have been telling our people that for years. They insist on clinging to some ancient theory that the U.S. is naive and not smart enough to mount anything serious in the way of covert operations. From my experience the Americans can be as underhanded as anyone. And when it comes to combat teams, they are not to be treated with anything but respect."

"How is this going to affect the rest of the operation?"

"We carry on. Allow Tetrow and his collection of patriots to create the diversion that should allow you and your team to get inside the facility and plant your bomb. After that, my friend, leave the Americans to fight among themselves. They will stop soon enough when our package detonates in their faces."

"Very well," Biryenko said. "My only concern are these Americans following us. They could be a nuisance if they locate us."

Gagarin sighed. "I understand, Vladimir, and I wish I had the power to reinforce your team. Unfortunately, we do not have the time. However, there is something I can try. No guarantees. But I will do my best."

"We will get ready to move on your command."

"I will try not to disappoint you."

THE TRACKING SIGNAL had been getting fainter. Grimaldi did what he could to enhance the image on his monitor.

"Weather's closing in, guys," he said. "I'm staying on our heading, but I'm losing the signal."

McCarter slipped into the seat beside Grimaldi. "Any ideas, Jack?"

"Could be weather conditions interfering with the signal. I don't believe we're losing it because the lady isn't functioning. This gear was given triple checks day before I took off, and everything was fine."

"Then we stay with what we've got. We could try Stony Man. See if they can run a satellite sweep again."

"Coming up," Grimaldi said.

He connected with Stony Man and brought Kurtzman online. McCarter explained their problem.

"Right now I don't have access to anything capable of penetrating that bad weather. It'll be an hour before I can bring anything online. How bad is your signal?"

"Getting fainter all the time," Grimaldi said.

"Listen, is it possible they landed somewhere and covered the helicopter?" Kurtzman asked. "That would deflect the signal, muffle it if they've taken cover and shut down their power source."

Grimaldi nodded at McCarter. "He could have something. Bad enough with this weather distorting everything. Maybe that's what they've done. Decided to sit out the storm, or wait until they get a signal to go in."

McCarter stared out through the canopy. Snow swirled by as *Dragon Slayer* flew on through the darkness. The combat chopper was flying on auto, following the course Grimaldi had logged in at the start. The electronics allowed the craft to judge locations and ground changes, course and height alterations being made and adjusted continuously.

In the cabin section behind Grimaldi's control deck the rest of Phoenix Force had already selected and checked out weapons. They had geared up with extra ammunition and grenades, taking whatever they needed from the storage lockers.

Now they were taking time to rest, using the flight to relax as much as they could before they were plunged back into action. They had eaten and drunk from the rations on board. Nothing fancy but enough to satisfy the needs of their bodies. With that out of the way they settled back in the body-form seats and slept.

"Hey, David, they have the right idea," Grimaldi said. "You should, too."

"Somebody has to keep *you* awake," the Briton said.

"Me? I'm fine. Pilots don't sleep."

"Excuse me, but that is bollocks," McCarter said. "Hasn't exactly been a vacation for you, mate."

Grimaldi had reluctantly told Phoenix Force what had happened to him, his time in the hands of his captors and his eventual escape. As far as the Stony Man pilot was concerned, it was just part of his daily routine. In that respect he was just like the rest of the team. Unless pressed to explain, he would pass over some stressful incident and carry on as normal. It would never occur to him that what he might have done would be considered exceptional by other people. In Grimaldi's eye the hard parts came with the job and he saw no reason to talk about them as something special.

THE MILITIA MEN had taken chartered flights from Seattle to Anchorage, picking up the second leg of the trip to Nome after an overnight stay. The internal flight was with a small charter company that took them to an independent airfield that catered mainly to the oil and construction business. As far as the operator knew, that was exactly what Tetrow's group was doing. The cases they shipped in with them were marked as belonging to the American Oil Survey Company. They were on an exploratory survey into a possible new oil field. The booking agent was happy enough. Tetrow, acting as the project supervisor, had paid up front in cash for the flight, which was good enough for the struggling charter company.

Once established, the Militia Men checked out the local rental companies and hired a trio of sturdy all-terrain vehicles that were large enough to accommodate the group and their survey equipment. They stayed long enough to obtain fuel, with extra cans strapped to the 4×4s. Food, water and other supplies were purchased, and in the late morning the day after they arrived, Tetrow led the Militia Men out of Nome and followed the highway north. Later they cut slightly east in the direction of Council, but took off cross-country once they had skirted the town.

The advantage for the Militia Men was the scarcity of traffic on the highway, and once they left the main highway behind they found themselves driving across a featureless, chill landscape with nothing of comfort to show. There was still snow about, lying across the land in long white drifts. The radio in Tetrow's vehicle offered a regular weather update—more snow was forecast. Already a keen wind could be felt slapping against the sides of the vehicle.

Hubbard Tetrow shared a vehicle with Rick Teeler, who was doing the driving. Behind them sat Warner and Sutherland, and between the pair was Carl Lyons.

Lyons was secured by plastic cuffs around his wrists and feet. Since being dragged off the barge in Seattle and returned to the Militia Men motel, Lyons had said very little. He was aware his position was tenuous. Aggravating the Militia Men wasn't a wise option, so he remained dumb. Back at the motel he had come very close to dying. Teeler had wanted to kill him right off and had even got as far as placing a gun muzzle against the side of Lyons's head. Only the intervention of Hubbard Tetrow had stopped him.

"Think straight, Rick," Tetrow said. "We need him alive until we can find out what he knows. Christ, we don't even know who he works for."

"Give it any fuckin' title you want, Hub, he's still a Fed. He works for the government. We don't need to know his badge number or his pension plan."

"Rick, be mad as hell with me. I screwed up big time. I believed this mother. Let him in. He knows about us. Before he dies I need to know where he comes from and who else knows what we're doing."

Teeler eased back, a crooked grin on his face.

"Maybe we'll find out when we get to Alaska.

What if he's already tipped off his people and they're waiting for us? Think about that, Hub. The minute we make our play, the spotlights go on and we're surrounded by the fuckin' law.''

''I been thinkin' about that ever since you called and told me what happened. But I ain't for quitting, Rick. We've gone too far, made too many commitments. If we back off now, we lose. Christ, this country didn't get where it is by people backin' off when the dice started rolling. You want to crawl back to home like some chickenshit one-day wonder? You forgot the people who helped us get this far? They believe we're right. We know we are. If we don't try to shut down this damn missile deal we're lettin' the government do what they want with this country, and we all know what that means.''

Tetrow had turned to stare at Lyons, his face flushed with anger. The militia leader had shook his head, then with a speed that belied his bulk he had backhanded Lyons across the side of the face.

''For what it's worth, Jag, or whatever your damn name is, I got to hand it to you. Made a fool out of me. Had me believe you were one of us. You were good, boy, I'll give you that. Sitting there all cool and smiling. Listening to our talk. Doing your damnedest to find out what we'd got planned. You want to know? Okay, you can come with us, see just what we're going to do. Maybe by then I'll be getting around to Rick's way of thinking and we'll bury you under that fuckin' missile base.''

Lyons recalled that conversation now as he leaned back in his seat. He remembered, too, the journey from Seattle, his hands bound and under close escort when they boarded the charter aircraft. Being cargo planes, there had been little scrutiny by the flight crew, who had its job to do. Lyons had been walked on to the aircraft, with a gun muzzle in his ribs, knowing that if he offered any resistance he would die.

He resigned himself to accepting his position for the time being. As long as he was surrounded by the group, his chance for escape was reduced. He needed to be patient, to wait for the right moment—if it came. As long as he remained alive, there was always a chance.

The flights were long so Lyons had plenty of time to reflect on the sudden change in events. His infiltration into the Militia Men had turned sour, and now he was their captive. From undercover to hostage. He'd known from the moment he accepted the assignment that there were few guarantees. Once he walked in and presented himself as Jag, with his own agenda and showing sympathy for the Militia Men and their cause, he was on his own. That condition didn't worry Carl Lyons. He still maintained the trait in his character that allowed him to detach from the team and go out on his own. Self-sufficiency had been part of his makeup as long as he could remember. It was something he believed in passionately and right now it was the only thing he could depend on.

LYONS WATCHED the Alaskan landscape slip by as the three-vehicle convoy pushed deeper into the country. His mind was busy, creating and dismissing ways he might escape his current situation. In part it was a way of keeping himself alert, active mentally. It would have been easy to just let himself wallow in self-pity, to drift into a state where he accepted what had happened and went with the flow. That wasn't Carl Lyons. He didn't look back; what had happened was in the past. Nothing related to that now. It was over. He had to look to the future. To the time when he got his chance, and the moment anything showed itself Lyons would go for it. His only regret was not having had the chance to pass any more back to Stony Man. He just hoped they *had* followed through the small amount he had given them.

Up front Tetrow leaned across and showed something on the map to Teeler, who nodded.

"Enjoying the trip, Jag?" Tetrow asked over his shoulder.

"Always wanted to visit Alaska," Lyons said. "Makes all the difference having you boys along."

"Only difference is you have a one-way ticket," Teeler said.

Beside Lyons, Warner chuckled. "He's right, Jag. You ain't goin' home."

Lyons turned to stare at the man. He didn't say a word. His eyes said it all.

"What you starin' at?" Warner asked. "I swear, Hub. This asshole gives me the creeps. Let me pop him now."

"Relax, Joe. He can't do a damn thing. Hog-tied and all," Teeler said.

"Still gets on my nerves," Warner complained.

"Forget him," Tetrow snapped. "We got other

things to think about. Joe, unpack that radio we brought along.''

Warner reached over into the rear of the 4×4 and dragged a pack from the equipment they had loaded. He moved to the extreme edge of the wide seat and opened the pack, exposing a satellite-uplink radio communications setup. He took out the retractable dish and connected it to the transmitter.

''We need to stop,'' Warner said.

Teeler braked and the 4×4 rolled to a halt. Warner opened his door and climbed out, bringing the satellite dish with him. He fanned out the mesh dish and stood it on the roof of the vehicle. Leaning back inside, he switched on the set and set the digital tuner to the frequency Tetrow gave him. The other vehicles drew up close. Boris Yesinovich climbed out and crossed to join them, pulling the hood of his parka around his face.

''Have you made contact?'' he asked.

Warner glanced up. ''Just getting there.''

The satellite dish arced on its base, tilting skyward as it searched for the elusive frequency.

''This is a cold place,'' Yesinovich said as Tetrow appeared.

''Hell, Boris, we're not that far from the damn Arctic Circle up here. What do you expect? Palm trees?''

''It is still cold,'' the Russian grumbled.

''It'll warm up when we hit that radar base,'' Warner said.

Yesinovich only smiled. Warner thought it was an odd expression, as if the Russian knew something but wasn't about to say. He didn't realize just how close to the truth he was.

If only they really did know, Yesinovich thought. By the time they do it will be too late.

Warner uttered a sudden exclamation and gave the thumbs-up to Tetrow.

"They're on," he said.

"You talk to them, Boris," Tetrow suggested.

Yesinovich took the handset and slipped earphones in place.

"Is that you, Biryenko?" he said in Russian.

"Yes. Give me an update."

"We are en route to the rendezvous. According to calculations, we should arrive just after dark. You have the location?"

"Of course."

"How are things with you?"

"That depends how you define good and bad. We had problems at the compound, but we left on board the helicopter with everything intact. However, there may be an American team following us."

"Are they close?"

"Hard to say. The weather is bad here. We made a landing some hours back, concealed ourselves and have been waiting for your call."

"Then begin your departure procedure."

"I look forward to seeing you soon," Biryenko said.

Yesinovich smiled as he looked across at Tetrow.

"They will be making the final part of their flight

soon, across the Bering Strait to meet us at the rendezvous point."

"Damn me, boys, I do believe this is coming together," Tetrow said.

CHAPTER THIRTEEN

Stony Man Farm, Virginia

Akira Tokaido yawned, stretching his lean form as he glanced at the time and saw how long he had been on watch. He was tired to the point where he couldn't even be bothered to listen to any more music on his disk player. He flexed his shoulders, glancing round the Computer Room. He was sharing duty with Carmen Delahunt. Even Kurtzman had taken a break. They were all waiting for the next satellite sweep to come up, and waiting was the worst part, especially knowing that somewhere out there Phoenix Force needed an update.

"We have to get back to Hal about having our own satellite," he said to Delahunt. "The guys could lose out with all this waiting around."

"You don't have to convince me," Delahunt replied. "Only I don't chair the appropriations committee."

"Stony Man is the President's baby. He could do something if he wanted. It wouldn't be the first time."

"The President can't fire up a satellite just like that.

Too many people involved. Remember we're supposed to be so off the books nobody knows about us. What do you expect him to do? Launch it from the White House lawn?''

Tokaido grinned. ''Hey, wouldn't that be something cool?''

''And what would be cool?'' Kurtzman asked as he rolled his wheelchair back into the room, Barbara Price close behind him.

''We were discussing the pros and cons of getting the President to okay our own satellite,'' Delahunt said. ''Akira isn't too happy about the loss we have to put up with begging time from other agency birds.''

''We miss something one day,'' Tokaido said, ''some of our guys are going to get hurt. Or worse.''

Kurtzman poured himself a mug of coffee.

''You don't have to remind me,'' he said. ''I'm having this discussion with Hal all the time. Problem is he understands our frustration because he has them himself. And he keeps bringing it up with the President. The Man has it on the back burner until he can figure out a way of getting it up and running without having to explain it to the oversight committee.''

The image on Tokaido's monitor changed, a warning signal telling him the satellite was coming online. He tapped in the acceptance code and quickly put in the command that would alter the course of the satellite, bringing it back for a sweep of the area where *Dragon Slayer* was operating. His quick fingers rapped in the sequence, and the clearing image on screen returned Stony Man to the Siberian wastes.

"I got them," Tokaido said.

Kurtzman opened his screen and took the same image.

Watching the monitor over Tokaido's shoulder, Price cleared her mind of the grid-reference pattern and the digital readouts, concentrating on the moving blip that was *Dragon Slayer*. Tokaido hadn't chosen to go to real-image yet, preferring the digital display until he had all his coordinates sorted. As was customary, he carried out a peripheral scan, taking in a wide area on all points of the compass. This allowed a fifty-mile view in all directions around the helicopter.

"What's that?" Price asked.

"Yeah, I see it," Tokaido said.

Kurtzman had picked up the new blip, as well.

"Coming in fast," he said, "from the southwest."

"Checking configuration," Tokaido stated, channeling the computer memory banks to lock on to the image and establish identity.

Delahunt opened a channel and raised *Dragon Slayer,* speaking to Grimaldi.

"We picked up a blip on the satellite scan," she said. "Something coming in fast behind you."

"How bloody fast?" McCarter asked.

Tokaido muttered under his breath as data flashed on the screen. He keyed his mike so he could talk to *Dragon Slayer.*

"About as fast as a Russian MG-29, guys. From my calculations she's on an intercept course and will be in range in four minutes."

Aboard Dragon Slayer

"NO IN-FLIGHT MOVIE, just a real-life MG-29," Grimaldi said calmly. "Sorry, guys, time to strap yourselves in. The ride could get a little rough from here."

"What does this bloke have?" McCarter asked. "Remind me, Jack."

"Oh, 30 mm cannon, a selection of rockets, heat seekers. All designed to do nasty things to us."

"That's comforting to know," McCarter said.

"But there are things he doesn't have," Grimaldi said.

"Convince me."

"He can't do this," Grimaldi said, easing the stick and taking *Dragon Slayer* in a swift descent that brought them to near ground level.

With the combat helicopter motionless, Grimaldi activated his radar and ran a scan of the sky behind and above them.

"There's our boy," he said, pointing at the moving blip on the monitor.

Gentle touches to his control panel brought *Dragon Slayer*'s weapons systems online: a 30 mm chain gun capable of delivering over 600 rounds per minute, a batch of free-flight HE rockets, twenty Hellfire missiles and three Stinger air-to-air missiles for self-defense. With the weapons primed and ready for use Grimaldi activated his helmet array, the monitor screen's image now transposed on his visor. It gave him an instant image of the radar and targeting schematic without having to look down at the screen.

From this display Grimaldi could decide his defensive-offensive action.

Leaning forward, the pilot tapped a command into his onboard computer. When he received the acknowledgment response, he keyed a single button. There was a slight movement from *Dragon Slayer* that Grimaldi corrected.

"Just dropped the extra fuel pods," he informed everyone. "They were almost empty. Loss of weight gives us better maneuverability and an increase in speed. We're on the standard tanks now."

The helicopter hung in the still falling snow, her matte black, sleek configuration offering a low-profile image for any incoming hostile carrying out a search. The powerful engines, running on silent mode, barely whispered and any sound was pulled away by the chill Siberian wind.

"Somebody really has it in for us," McCarter said, "if they're calling out the Russian air force."

"I don't suppose we could conjure up an entry visa between us," Grimaldi said. "You figure they have a point somewhere along the line?"

"Jack, you're just splitting hairs," the Briton said dryly.

The MiG swept in low and fast, loosing off a missile that overshot and exploded ahead of *Dragon Slayer*. The dark shape of the thundering jet flashed by, pulling up quickly and beginning its return run.

"Why didn't he use a heat seeker?" McCarter asked.

Grimaldi shrugged. "Maybe he doesn't have any."

He concentrated on the image of the MiG as it

gained height above and behind them, then curved down in a long swoop. The pilot was riding the fence tops, taking the jet as low as he dared in the poor visibility. Grimaldi gave the pilot credit for having the balls to carry out such a maneuver. With a machine like the MiG underneath him, the Russian was pushing it to the limit. It would be so easy for him to lose it in such adverse weather.

Using his own innate skill and judgment Grimaldi calculated the time the Russian would fire his second missile. He held, knowing he could easily misjudge, then stepped up the power and took *Dragon Slayer* to the right and up, his feather light touch bringing an instant response as the helicopter's turboboost cut in. The sleek aircraft made a curving turn that flattened Phoenix Force against the backs of their seats. *Dragon Slayer* completed its full turn and was already dropping back when the MiG's missile exploded.

Now Grimaldi was behind the jet and he locked on and loosed off a Hellfire missile. The missile grabbed on to the MiG's heat trace. It swooped and veered, clinging to the MiG's jet exhaust, homing in with deadly accuracy. The Russian pilot, obviously aware that he had been tagged, threw his aircraft about in an effort to lose the deadly missile. The Hellfire stayed on its tail, the in-built targeting mechanism keeping it directly on a collision course with the MiG. The distance closed rapidly, and the Hellfire struck.

The MiG vanished in a ball of incandescent fire. It blossomed, filling the air with a rain of debris and then was gone as it fell into the surrounding darkness.

Stony Man Farm, Virginia

"I SAW IT but I don't believe it!"

"We all saw it," Kurtzman said, "so believe it."

Akira Tokaido pushed away from his station and stood.

"Jack just put down a MiG fighter from *Dragon Slayer*. What is that guy—the Terminator?"

"No," Price said, "just the best flyer I've ever known. Now, let's get back to what we should be doing. Helping Phoenix find that Russian helicopter."

"If they have the damn thing covered, the snowfall is going to blend it into the landscape," Kurtzman said. "Damned if we'll pick her out in that."

"Only way we'll pick anything up is by thermal imagery," Tokaido said. "The problem is, even body heat is going to be masked by the covering and snow."

"Let's enhance the thermal imaging to its limit, see if we can get *anything*," Kurtzman said.

Tokaido overlaid the last position they had on the Hind. The recorded data flashed up on the screen, and he used the coordinates as the commencement point for the new scan. Tapping in commands, he had the computer lay in an extrapolated course for the Hind. Once that had been fixed, he brought in the thermal imaging. He narrowed the imaging scan, keeping it to the plotted course and let it run.

"Needle in a haystack springs to mind," Price said. She was standing at Kurtzman's workstation, watching his monitor.

"Don't I know it," Kurtzman said. "What else do

we have right now? Not a damn thing. Times are, Barb, all we can do is gamble. Look at this place. Full of the best money can buy. We have satellites up there carrying the most sophisticated equipment there is. And right now none of it means squat. If we can't pick up any heat traces, there isn't a thing we can do for Phoenix until that chopper makes a move.''

"And we don't know how long that might be," Price said, carrying through Kurtzman's thoughts. "If *Dragon Slayer* hangs around too long, the Russians might send in another MiG. As good as he is, Jack can't take them all on."

"I rest my case," Kurtzman said. "Akira, get the lead out. We need a result."

"And I thought slavery had been abolished," Tokaido said.

"Not on my team, it hasn't," Kurtzman boomed, a grin on his face that Tokaido couldn't see.

The readouts flickered as data streams changed, altered before their eyes. Tokaido's fingers flashed back and forth across the keyboard as he attempted to coax a higher response from the satellite and its on-board equipment.

Huntington Wethers entered the Computer Room. Moments later Hal Brognola joined them, popping a couple of antacid tablets into his mouth to settle his grumbling stomach. He sensed the mood so didn't make any comment. He simply stood at the back of the room, merely nodding to Price as she turned to acknowledge his presence.

Brognola knew the problem. Phoenix Force was hanging fire, staying in the hot zone of Siberia as long as possible, hoping that Stony Man might be able to locate the Hind.

"Something's showing," Tokaido said almost ten minutes later. "Slight heat sources. There. See them?"

"Damn right, I do," Kurtzman said. "Get *Dragon Slayer* on the line fast."

As the connection was made, Tokaido checked the coordinates and held them on the screen. His attention had also been drawn to something else, and he tapped into another readout, groaning softly as his initial fear was confirmed.

"Bad weather moving in fast from northeast," he called. "Heavy bank of snow. Wind level rising, too. It's going to be with the team in the next thirty minutes."

Aboard Dragon Slayer

"OKAY, IT'S THROUGH," Grimaldi said.

He had just received the coordinates for the heat source Stony Man had sent them. The pilot immediately entered the data and locked it in. He pulled up the area grid and the computer identified the position, indicating it with a highlighted area on the monitor's screen chart.

"It'll take us about an hour," he told Stony Man.

Tokaido's voice broke through. "Listen, guys, I just picked up a satellite-generated weather update. This is no guessing forecast. There's one hell of a snowstorm coming your way. It'll hit you in less than half an hour, and it looks like a bad one. Wind velocity is rising, as well. Sorry not to have something better for you.''

McCarter activated his mike. ''Don't worry, mate, we'll get you later.''

''Thanks for the input,'' Grimaldi said. ''Let's see what we can do with it. Talk to you later. Over and out.''

Pushing *Dragon Slayer* forward Grimaldi brought the coordinates into play and felt the electronic lock take over. The sleek machine altered course, settled and responded as the Stony Man pilot upped the power. Once the course had been established, Grimaldi was able to check out the on-screen data. The point Stony Man had given them showed as a faintly pulsing green dot.

Checking his other readouts, Grimaldi saw that the wind velocity was indeed rising. Peering through the canopy, he was confronted with an increase in the swirl of snow. White flakes clung to the canopy, heavy and wet, but freezing within moments of hitting the tinted Plexiglas. Grimaldi switched on the wipers, which struggled to keep the screen clear.

''Praise the Lord for radar guidance,'' Grimaldi said.

''Hang on, chums,'' McCarter called over his shoulder, ''we're in the hands of the machines.''

''Oh, great,'' Calvin James said. ''Did he really need to tell us that?''

''You mean you'd rather be in the hands of Jack against a tiny microchip?'' Hawkins asked.

''Look at it this way,'' James said. ''If we're going to crash while the chip is driving, how will I know?

With Jack behind the controls, all I have to do is see his face go white and listen to him yell in panic. At least then I get a warning."

Hawkins grinned. "Man, as long as I got you along, I know everything is going to be upbeat."

"That's what I'm here for."

Up front McCarter nudged Grimaldi.

"Jack, the bloody thing is moving."

Grimaldi glanced at the display, watching as the green dot altered position, only slightly. Its size increased, as well.

"They're on the move," he said. He made contact with Stony Man to confirm what they had sighted and received a positive acknowledgment. They had seen the same thing.

"Step on the gas, my man," McCarter said. "Time to get serious."

"GET THE DAMN SHEETS away from the helicopter," Biryenko yelled. "We don't want them getting dragged up by the rotors."

Cursing and stumbling, their faces stinging from the wind-driven snow, the members of Biryenko's team hauled the thick canvas sheets off the Hind. They were hindered by the frozen snow that had layered the sheets, turning hard in the low temperature. It made the task difficult. Some of them had gone outside without their gloves and were suffering frozen fingers and raw hands. The driven snow penetrated any gap in their clothing. The wind dragged at them, slowing their movements as they fought to overcome its power. By the time they had the heavy sheets on the ground and at a safe distance from the Hind, they were all exhausted.

Biryenko ordered the pilot to fire up the twin turbine engines. The sequence was slow, the power plants groaning due to the low temperature, but Biryenko had badgered the mechanics to overhaul the engines while the Hind was at rest at the compound. He had made them go over the systems time and time again, ignoring their grumbles. He and his team would be putting their lives at stake once they committed to the helicopter. He had seen disasters many times before when poorly maintained machines faltered in the heat of battle, or even on takeoff. He had no intention of that happening to him and his team.

The engines caught and began to turn the rotors. The pilot coaxed more power as the engines warmed up, his touch sure and steady on the controls. The roar of the turbines increased, the Hind vibrating until the correct pitch evened out the beat of the engines.

Moving back to the main cabin, Biryenko made sure all his men were back inside before he ordered the door closed and secured. His men sank onto the benches lining the center of the cabin, grumbling at the cold and the hard work they had done. Even Bering, usually cheerful, looked sour.

"Cheer up, boys," Biryenko said.

"Easy for you to say," Bering answered. "You haven't been out there freezing your balls off."

"Of course not," Biryenko said. "It's one of the privileges of command. But I was with you in spirit. Right?"

"Yes, of course you were," Bering said, unconvinced.

The Hind gave a ponderous lurch, almost tipping everyone from their seats, then swung as the wind caught it. After a few moments the pilot righted the massive helicopter. He increased power and the Hind lifted off, plunging into the stormy darkness.

"We are going to America," Biryenko said. "Please have your passports ready for immigration."

The pilot called over the intercom for Biryenko.

"What is it?" Biryenko asked.

"Gagarin for you."

Biryenko took the call as the pilot switched it through.

"What is your status?" Gagarin asked.

"We are en route for the meeting point in difficult flying conditions. The weather is very bad. Heavy snow and strong wind."

"Vladimir, I have bad news. The American team is still active. My plan to have them removed failed. I thought you should know."

"We are no worse off than before then. I appreciate your efforts, but we will deal with them if the occasion arises. At least the weather conditions will be the same for them. It doesn't matter how smart they are. Not even the Americans can control the weather."

"I suppose not. Good luck. Contact me when you have news."

"I will. Over and out."

Biryenko switched back to the pilot.

"Don't take the wrong turning, Pieter, I have no

desire to end my days discussing the finer points of Marxism with a bunch of penguins.''

Biryenko made his way back to the main cabin and dropped onto the seat beside Bering.

"The Americans are still with us," he said.

Bering inclined his head. "This could turn out to be an interesting excursion. Either way it doesn't sound as if it will be boring."

"Bering, you are crazy."

"Of course. I wouldn't have signed up to work alongside you if I were sane. Would I?"

Biryenko glanced along the cabin and watched the Korean making final adjustments to his nuclear device. He shook his head.

We are all mad, he thought. We have to be.

CHAPTER FOURTEEN

Alaska

"How close are you?" Barbara Price asked.

"About thirty minutes' flight from the immediate area," Rosario Blancanales said. "Local weather forecast says there's snow due any time."

"We'll try and pick up a satellite scan," Price said. "*Dragon Slayer* has already been caught up in the bad weather on the Russian side. Give you all the backup we can."

"Thanks," Blancanales said, and switched off his cell phone connection. He adjusted his headset so he was back in contact with Schwarz and the pilot of the helicopter.

Schwarz glanced at his partner. "What do they say?"

"Bad weather on its way. They'll try and get a satellite scan to keep us informed."

"Just great," Schwarz said.

"What else can they do? Just remember to smile in case they take pictures. Don't want them to think we aren't enjoying this."

Schwarz closed the zip of his thick parka.

"Not enjoy freezing my butt off in the far north? Only thing missing is a dogsled and somebody yelling mush."

"Day isn't over yet," Blancanales reminded him.

Up front the pilot, a young state trooper called Boone, spoke into his throat mike.

"You guys sure you're from the Justice Department?" he asked. "Don't sound like it to me."

Blancanales listened on his headset. "Sure, we are. You never heard Justice Department agents make jokes before?"

"I never met any of you guys before."

"So?"

"I expected you to be real serious."

"We are," Schwarz said. "Wait until somebody starts shooting at us. We get really serious then."

"Jesus," the trooper said. "There might be shooting?"

"That bother you?"

"Damn right it does."

"Scares the shit out of me," Blancanales said.

"You guys worry me. My captain said when he was asked to give you assistance it would be real educational to see you operate."

"Did he really say that?" Schwarz asked.

"Yeah."

Schwarz leaned across to Blancanales. "Somebody should have a word with the captain."

"I heard that."

Blancanales reached out and tapped the young trooper on the shoulder.

"Take it easy, Boone. You got to learn to take life as it comes."

"If it interests you, I can see tire tracks down there," Boone said. He swung the helicopter in the direction he had indicated, dropping to a height where Blancanales and Schwarz could clearly see the tire tracks.

"Heavy tread," Boone commented. "Look like off-road vehicles. Three of them."

"What's in that direction?" Schwarz asked.

"Nothing much," Boone answered. "Pretty barren country out that way. I guess that's why they chose to build that government installation out here."

"Some secret," Blancanales said.

Boone chuckled. "Place like this you can't do much without people knowing about it. What with all that construction stuff being moved out and the crews. Thing is when it's built the military will have it closed off so no one can get near. There'll be armed patrols and all that stuff. Not that I need to tell you. I mean, come on, guys, get real."

"We'll have to do that some time soon," Blancanales said. "Get real."

"So you figure these three off-road trucks are what we're looking for?" Boone asked.

"I'm sure they are," Blancanales said. "You want to follow those tracks, Boone, see where they lead us?"

"Sure. Be a good idea if I gain some altitude. I mean, so we don't let them know we're around."

"If this damn storm hits, we won't be able to see where we are," Schwarz said, peering at the sky ahead of them. It was already showing that unnatural brightness that often preceded a storm. The scrappy clouds were already being dispersed by the increase in wind movement.

"Yeah," Boone said, "they come in pretty quick hereabouts. One minute nothing, next thing you're in the middle of a snowstorm. Easy to get lost if you don't understand the country."

He took the helicopter on a steady climb, keeping on a course that held them to the line of tire tracks. Blancanales and Schwarz peered through the Plexiglas windows and followed the trail themselves.

"Pol."

"What?"

"You figure Carl will be with them?"

"I hope so. Problem is with him dropping out of communication after that call from Seattle, we don't really have any idea what might have happened."

"Name of the game, buddy. No promises. No guarantees."

"Knowing it doesn't help."

"Hell, I wish I could make it right."

"Tell me to quit moaning," Schwarz said. "I know we'll find him. We'll probably regret it, but we'll find him."

WHEN THE VEHICLES stopped for the second time Lyons started to take notice. They had drawn together in the base of an undulating fissure that might at some distant time have been a riverbed. Now it was a dry ravinelike formation straggling across the landscape. There was some tangled foliage in among the rock piles, and the sloping banks hid the three 4×4s from immediate view.

Lyons was left alone in the vehicle he had been sharing with Tetrow and Teeler. Even Warner and Sutherland had exited the vehicle, joining the others as they gathered for what looked like a council of war. Lyons didn't fool himself into believing he had been left unsupervised. His vehicle was in plain view of the Militia Men, and there was no way he could have gotten out without being seen.

He concentrated on his bound hands and feet.

From past experience of handling plastic cuffs Lyons knew how tough the loops were. The principle of the strap going through the notched block and the ridged surface locking tight was one of those simple but frighteningly effective inventions. No amount of struggling would loosen the thing. It only resulted in chafing the skin with the plastic and adding self-inflicted wounds. So Lyons didn't struggle.

He studied the problem and decided the only way to get out of the loop was to cut it. It was an easy solution not so easily carried out. To cut the plastic required some kind of abrasive or keen metal edge. He checked out the interior of the vehicle. Nothing showed immediately. Lyons scanned the area around him with patient deliberation. All he saw were leather seat covers, rubber floor mats, padded door panels. New models of vehicles were built with safety as the byword. Nothing was left to chance. The word was driver-passenger comfort. The inside of the 4×4 looked like something out of a marshmallow factory.

Soft, rounded, puffy. So safe you could let a baby roll around inside it without getting hurt.

Lyons leaned back, lips set in a taut line. He forced himself to breathe steadily. If he hadn't, he might have lost. He was getting angry, close to losing it. Frustration piled on helplessness. Carl Lyons hated both those feelings. He wasn't a man used to sitting back in a helpless mode. He wanted—needed—to be able to strike out at the men who held him captive. He was no passive hostage, about to sit still and let his captors dictate the terms. Carl Lyons made the terms, no matter what the situation. That was how he had run his life, and he saw no good reason to change it now.

Lyons glanced out the window and watched the Militia Men as they decided their tactics. Okay, he thought, we can all do that.

There was nothing inside the vehicle he could use. That meant he was going to have to try something with one of his captors. They all carried weapons. Maybe there was a chance he could grab one and... Lyons paused. In his present condition even that would present him with a challenge. So? Weren't challenges something he thrived on? There was no use coming up with a plan if he didn't have the guts to carry it through. He dismissed the thought that his captors were armed to a man. What did he expect? They were planning a violent, armed raid, so the presence of weapons had to accepted and taken into account. That didn't have to mean there was nothing he could do. There was always *something* to be gleaned from any situation, no matter how bleak it looked.

He watched and waited. The thin fall of snow began to increase. The flakes became larger, pushed about by the wind as it got stronger. Within a few minutes the fall had become seriously heavy. Lyons studied it with interest. If it continued it would provide good cover for someone on the move. He had every intention to be that someone. All he needed was the opportunity to get out of his bonds and get his hands on a weapon.

Turning his head, Lyons saw the group was breaking up. A single figure was approaching the 4×4. He couldn't make out who it was until the figure reached the vehicle and walked around to the driver's door. The 4×4 rocked as the figure climbed in and started the engine. Lyons stayed silent, watching and listening.

The 4×4 was turned, then reversed, moving away from the other vehicles. It came to a stop a few moments later. The figure behind the wheel turned, shoving back the hood of his parka as he leaned over to look at Lyons.

It was Joe Warner.

"You got people curious, Jag. Worried, as well. See, they don't know if you told anybody about us. Problem is they want to know. And they want to know now. So I guess you are in for a hurtin' time."

"Nice of you to tell me."

Warner's face hardened. "Don't fuck with me, you pile of shit. You tried to screw us. Stop what we're doing. I tell you, Jag, you ain't got any friends out there. Given the chance, they'd all come and put a bullet in you right now."

Lyons didn't push the point.

"I got to get you outside. Let you chill out a little so you might feel more inclined to talk."

Warner climbed outside and moved around to Lyons's side of the vehicle. He yanked open the door.

Lyons rolled on his back, and as Warner leaned in to grab him the Able Team commando drove his bound feet forward in a brutal kick that caught Warner full in the face. The militia man gave a stunned groan as his face burst like an overripe tomato. He slumped sideways, falling against the open door. He would have fallen to the ground if the door hadn't been there.

Wriggling across the seat, Lyons reached out and grabbed the edge of the door frame, hauling himself out of the 4×4. He almost fell because of his strapped ankles, but fought to stay on his feet. Turning toward Warner, who was still recovering from the crushing kick, Lyons reached out with his bound hands and took hold of Warner's hair. He slammed Warner's head against the door frame, hard and often, not allowing the man the chance to recover. Blood spattered the door glass and Lyons's clothes.

Warner's knees buckled and he dropped, half-turning in his adversary's direction, fumbling blindly for the pistol in his belt. Lyons caught hold of the edge of the open door and used every ounce of his pent-up strength to slam the door on Warner's head. The heavy door pinned the man's skull between it and the frame making an ugly, bone-cracking sound. Warner's legs kicked out, quivering. His free arm flailed about for a few seconds before the weight of his body dragged him to the ground.

Lyons bent over Warner. He searched him quickly, finding a folding knife in a pocket. The Able Team leader fumbled a little with his bound hands until he opened the blade. The first thing he did was sever the plastic loops around his ankles. Then he reversed the knife and patiently sawed at the wrist loop until it parted and fell away. He flexed his fingers to get the circulation going. Closing the knife, Lyons stuffed it into a back pocket, then reached down and took the pistol from Warner. It was a stainless-steel Smith & Wesson .45ACP. He checked for extra mags and found two, then clicked off the safety.

He was far from safe yet, and to prove the point he heard someone yell in his direction. He recognized Rick Teeler's voice. Lyons grinned, the expression that of a caged animal back on the loose and ready to take on anything that came his way.

Dark figures moved toward Lyons's position, armed and determined. He backed away, seeking a better place to make his stand. The Militia Men didn't know it yet, but the war had started, and they had no idea what was coming.

"THEY'RE OVER the water," Grimaldi announced.

"Too far to hit them with a missile?" McCarter asked.

"Way too far."

"Pity. If we could drop them in the drink, it would solve all our problems."

Grimaldi smiled. "Life just ain't that easy, buddy."

"Tell me about it."

They were flying into a solid fall of gusting snow. Despite *Dragon Slayer*'s constant velocity and stabilized flight, the heavy wind could be felt as it banged against the combat chopper. The electronic guidance system kept them on course, but the flight was less than smooth.

The Hind, ahead of them, was making good time despite the weather. Grimaldi had a great deal of admiration for the pilot, whoever he was. The Hind wasn't equipped to anywhere near *Dragon Slayer*'s standard so the pilot was flying by his own hand, and that impressed Jack Grimaldi. Flying without the aid of sophisticated equipment backup was hazardous enough in good weather. Riding through the eye of an Arctic snowstorm was no kind of picnic.

The com set came online. It was Stony Man.

"Your target is closing on the U.S. coast," Kurtzman informed them. "Storm is not, I repeat not, letting up. Able Team is within striking distance of the Militia Men."

"Update appreciated," McCarter said. "This part of the world not recommended for vacation time. Bloody inhospitable, and the natives have a habit of shooting at us."

"We get anything else I'll patch it through."

"Thanks. Over and out."

"Only one we don't seem to hear about is Carl," Grimaldi said.

McCarter nodded. "They always say no news is

good news, don't they? In this case I don't bloody well agree with that sentiment.''

THE FIRST VOLLEY HIT the hood of the of the 4×4, piercing the metal and bursting the radiator. The Militia Men had disabled one of its own vehicles and denied Lyons a possible means of escape.

Wild yelling followed when it was realized what had happened. Lyons took the opportunity to move away from the all-terrain vehicle. He plunged through the brittle undergrowth, aware that unlike the Militia Men he wasn't clad in full protective clothing. The thought was fleeting and vanished from his conscious mind. He had more pressing things to worry about.

Like staying alive.

He picked up the crash of bodies tramping through the undergrowth, following the marks he had left in the snow.

Lyons reached a steep slope. He glanced around and saw there was no other way forward he could use in time. His pursuers were closing fast. Time to make a decision. Never one for taking too long in that department, Lyons did a swift about-face, bringing up the S&W in a two-handed grip. The moment the first militia man showed, emerging from the snow, Lyons locked on and fired. The powerful .45-caliber slug took him dead center in the chest, the impact knocking him off his feet. He struck hard, twisting over in agony. The ACP round had torn its way deep into his body, wreaking havoc on its journey, and the militia man found he was coughing up gouts of blood from a punctured lung. The impacted slug continued on to fragment against his spine, tearing it apart.

The sound of the shot made the others pause, spreading apart before they stepped into the open. Lyons ran forward, staying low, and snatched up the M-16 from the limp hand of the man he had just put down. He turned aside, starting to circle, and his rapid move brought him in from the left. He saw blurred forms emerging from the undergrowth, passing whispered commands back and forth. The Militia Men were confused. Events had changed too quickly. They were supposed to be carrying out a sneak attack on the radar facility, possibly facing a few construction workers or security guards. No one had told them they might have to go hunting an undercover agent in the Alaskan wilderness. One who was shooting back.

Lyons checked that the M-16 was ready for use. He raised the weapon and raked the area ahead with a short burst, shifting his aim and his position even as he pulled the trigger. He fired again. This time someone gave a pained cry, and there was some thrashing in the undergrowth. Lyons didn't fall back. He was in no mood for any kind of retreat. He picked his targets and fired the moment they were in his sights. He put down two men before the others backed off in confusion. The crackle of the M-16 followed their retreat.

Retracing his steps, Lyons located the first man he had shot. There were no signs of life left. Lyons dragged the heavy parka off the body and struggled into it. He closed the zip and pulled the hood over his head. He found two extra magazines for the M-16 in the deep pockets of the parka.

Reasonably well armed and protected from the weather, Lyons started to move back to where he had run from. He knew that Hubbard Tetrow wasn't going to pack up and go home because of what had happened. The Militia Men had come to Alaska for a purpose. They were in deadly earnest in their intentions, and Tetrow would keep right on going until the end.

Carl Lyons's job was to stop him.

CHAPTER FIFTEEN

Alaska

The coastline lay an hour behind them. In the predawn light, misted by the blinding snow, the Hind skimmed the Alaskan landscape with feet to spare. Inside the closed cabin the strike force was unable to see how low they were flying. If they had they might have been less calm than they were. With the LZ fast approaching, they were making final preparations. Each man, in addition to his AK-74, carried personal weapons and grenades. They had all been supplied, courtesy of Malinchek, with 9 mm Beretta handguns and plenty of additional ammunition. Also on board were two cases of RPG-7 rocket launchers.

Toward the rear of the helicopter Yat Sen Took sat alone. He had isolated himself by choice, wanting to spend some time preparing for what he needed to do on arrival. The Russians would clear the way for him, entering the facility and making certain there were no hostiles remaining alive. Once the site had been secured he would leave the Hind, backpacking the nuclear device. He had taken the stolen warhead and removed the critical section, bypassing the original detonation circuit and wiring the device to a timer of his own design. The adapted device was sitting on the floor of the Hind, resting against his left leg. Took was rather pleased with himself. His skills with explosive devices, nuclear or HE, were well documented. His credentials were of the highest degree. It was why he alone had been chosen for this mission. The North Korean regime needed someone on the ground who would make certain that the device detonated correctly and achieved its purpose. If they succeeded in destroying the American facility, it would leave them unchallenged for some considerable time. During that period, they would be able to press on with their own missile program, bringing out the next generation of intermediate and long-range nuclear missiles. It would give them a great deal of leverage in future discussions and would undoubtedly allow them to tell the Americans what to do.

So because of the importance of the mission, the North Korean military council had chosen Yat Sen Took. He was their most dependable man. If anyone could carry out the mission with success, it was Yat Sen Took, and success was what the Korean government needed. Despite talks and meetings and PR visits, the North Korean government maintained the internal missile program. There was a ready market for the range of weapons they produced, as well as their own requirements. To cripple the American defense systems would bring home to the rest of the world that America wasn't invincible, and would be even less so without its much vaunted Slingshot program.

It had been like a gift from heaven when news of the Militia Men and their campaign against their own government had reached the ears of the Russians and the Koreans. The Chinese had put in their hand with Shun Wei. She had brought much needed technical information, originally stolen by Chinese agents working in America. The complex plan of action, using the Militia Men as unwitting pawns, had gone well until a series of misfortunes put the whole thing in jeopardy. There was the information collected by the man called Kranski, who worked in partnership with a Chinese dissident named Mei Anna. Added to that was Shun Wei's increasing bid for power. The woman had become an embarrassment to her own people, as well as to the Koreans. She had already been placed under a death sentence when her own stupidity got her killed during the assassination of Kranski.

Took let his mind wander, sifting through all the strands that made up the picture. It was a strange concoction. So many different people, all working toward the same goal, but each for their own agenda. And every one of them believing that theirs was the most important.

The Korean smiled at the absurdity of it all. He felt the heavy pack at his feet move as the Hind was buffeted by the wind. Only his solution would gain the most. The nuclear device would detonate and wipe the radar facility off the map. The radiation created by the blast would leave an area irradiated for many years. That would leave the lasting impression. When all the other factors were long gone and the day forgotten, the poisoned earth would remain and remind the Americans that they were just as vulnerable as any.

Yat Sen Took leaned back and waited for the flight to end. When it did, *his* work would begin.

"JESUS," HUBBARD TETROW yelled. "One man! One fuckin' man and you let him get away."

"He's got a gun," one of the men said.

"I know he's got a gun. Didn't I hear the damn thing? Forget about the guy. We came here to do a job. Let's get back to it."

Yesinovich interrupted Tetrow's outburst.

"We should start for the site now," he said. "We cannot waste time on this foolishness."

"Foolishness my ass, Boris," Teeler said. "We've got a Fed on the loose with an M-16. Now, he ain't about to go away. If we leave him alone, he's going to stay on our tail and bite the hell out of us."

"Rick, take Deke. Go find that mother and deal with him. Rest of you Militia Men with me. Make sure your weapons are loaded and ready. Let's move out."

Sutherland joined Teeler. They checked their weapons, then backtracked until they picked up Lyons's tracks from where he left the vehicle and Warner's body. Sutherland was ready to explode, and it took Teeler a few minutes to calm him down.

"Look, I know you and Joe were together a good time. Even before you joined the Militia Men. But we got to go after Jag with a clear head. This guy is no beginner. He knows what he's doing."

They moved away from the 4×4 and picked up the trail where it wound in among rock and undergrowth. Teeler spotted where the vegetation had been damaged as someone forced his way through. He pointed it out to Sutherland.

"Where the hell is he going to go, Rick? This place is nothing. Just a mess of snow and freezing wind. He can't hide out forever."

"Just long enough to put you down," Lyons's voice said from the drifting snow.

Sutherland turned sharply, his M-16 snapping to his shoulder.

"Show yourself, you son of a bitch."

"You should have killed me when you had the chance. Now it's my turn."

An M-16 fired once, the 5.56 mm slug coring through Sutherland's chest and into his heart. The man twisted under the impact and fell on his side, his only protest a slight jerky movement in his left arm.

Rick Teeler turned and fired off a burst in the direction the shot had come from. He imagined he saw a shadow move from left to right, but couldn't be certain because of the falling snow.

"Bastard," Teeler yelled. "I'm going to kill you."

"No chance," Lyons said very quietly, and Teeler realized he could hear because Lyons was very close.

In fact Lyons was right behind the man. He stood motionless until Teeler turned. The militia man found he was staring into a pair of eyes colder than any of the snow and ice around them.

Carl Lyons even managed a smile as he pulled the trigger on Rick Teeler. The Militia Men's second in command was dead before he hit the ground, his M-16 spilling from his nerveless fingers.

"Teeler, I quit," Lyons said.

He turned away and began his hunt for the rest of the Militia Men.

BOONE PUT the Bell JetRanger down three hundred yards outside the perimeter fence surrounding the construction site. he reduced power so that the chopper was idling. He didn't want to close down fully in case they needed a quick liftoff.

"I shut down it's going to take time to whip her up to max again."

"Good thinking," Schwarz said.

He and Blancanales had pulled thick, insulated jackets over their combat fatigues. From a zippered carryall Blancanales pulled out a pair of 9 mm Uzis. They already held double magazines for fast reloading. Extra magazines went into the large side pockets of the jackets. Under the jackets they carried their Beretta handguns in shoulder rigs. They each pulled on a combat harness and clipped stun and fragmentation grenades to the hooks.

"You guys were serious about shooting," Boone said.

"It happens," Blancanales replied.

"Can I help?" Boone asked. "I don't wear this gun for show."

"You ever shot anyone?"

Boone stared at Schwarz. "Truth be told, I ain't. Have you?"

Schwarz just nodded. He didn't need to elaborate.

Boone recognized the look in his eyes, the expression of a man who had walked to the door of hell and seen what was on the other side.

"Looks like we arrived early," Blancanales said.

"Boone, you know anyone in there?" Schwarz asked.

"Sure do."

"Okay, we need to talk to whoever is in charge."

"No problem."

TEN MINUTES LATER Blancanales and Schwarz were inside the facility. The office of the security chief was one of the few completed rooms inside the main building. The chief, a bullnecked, powerful man named Renwick, listened to what the Able Team warriors had to say.

"Lee said okay to whatever these guys want?" Renwick asked Boone.

The young state trooper nodded. "This comes all the way from Washington. Sounds like a damn war's about to start the way they tell it."

"Well, we ain't equipped to handle anything like that," Renwick said. "Christ, all we do is work for the construction company. My boys ain't Delta Force."

"We have more of our own people on the way," Blancanales said. "Problem is, we can't pin it down to when they might arrive."

"So what the hell do we do?"

"Boone, get your chopper inside the perimeter fence. Put her down somewhere away from the main gate. Renwick, get all your men inside here. Arm yourselves with whatever you have. Hopefully it won't come to that. If it dies, give it your best shot.''

Renwick scratched his broad forehead. ''I'll be askin' the company for one hell of a bonus after this.''

They pulled the whole security crew into the office and explained what might happen. The security guards weren't particularly impressed. They were caught up in something out of their normal business, and no one could blame them for being thrown by the details.

''We need a couple of your jackets and caps,'' Blancanales said.

''What have you got in mind?'' Renwick asked.

''These people are going to do it by the book, military style,'' Blancanales said. ''They'll assume the checkpoint will be manned, so seeing people in the hut won't throw them. First thing they'll do will be to take out the guards, then come in through the gate. We'll be there to try and hold them back until our people show up.''

''You'll need one of these,'' Renwick said, handing Schwarz a swipe card. ''It opens the door on the hut.''

''We can keep in contact using the phone in the hut,'' Schwarz said.

He and Blancanales turned for the door.

''Good luck, guys,'' Boone said.

Blancanales glanced at him, grinning briefly. ''Luck doesn't have a thing to do with it.''

BIRYENKO CAME through from the flight deck.

''Get ready. We touch down in a few minutes.

When we land, you know what to do. Follow the plan of operation. We have trained for this. The facility here is the same as the one we used back home. You all know you places in the operation. Keep to them. Be aware there may be opposition. We can deal with that, too.

"Our priority is to take over the site so that Took can plant his nuclear device. Remember, too, that our American comrades will be around, too."

Someone laughed at that.

"Who is helping who?" Bering asked.

"As far as the Militia Men are concerned, we are joining them in a strike against the U.S. government. Let me go on believing that. Once we have planted the device, hopefully without their knowledge, we make our retreat. If they discover the device, they will not be able to stop it. If they stay around, they will die when it detonates. Either way I am not worried by them. They are idiots, and idiots usually get what they deserve. Just remember that if we make contact, be nice to them. Agree with their opinions. Tell them how we are brothers in a war against tyranny. They will love that. You have permission to be ill later."

"Thank you for that at least."

The Hind began to sink to the ground. It veered to the left, making almost a complete circle before there was a slight impact and the heavy gunship settled.

"THERE," YESINOVICH said, indicating the Hind.

"They damn well made it," Tetrow said.

"Did you doubt they would?" the Russian asked.

"What? Hell, no."

"Let us go and greet them."

Tetrow nodded. The Militia Men surged forward, and the group made its way over the snow-covered ground to where the Hind sat, Rotors slowing as the power was reduced. As they neared the helicopter, the side door slid open and a tall, broad man stood in the opening.

Yesinovich stepped forward, holding out his arms as the man jumped to the ground. They embraced, hugging each other. Yesinovich stepped back.

"Welcome to America, Vladimir," he said in Russian.

Biryenko nodded. "I think I would have been happier if they had built this damn station in California."

"Vladimir, we should talk in English in respect of our American friends."

Biryenko looked over Yesinovish's shoulder. "These are the patriots?"

"Yes."

"Then they should change the words to 'God *help* America.'"

Ignoring Yesinovich's look of disapproval, Biryenko stepped around him, reaching out with a large hand.

"It is good to meet you, my comrades," he said in English. "Today we strike a blow for freedom, yes?"

Hubbard Tetrow nodded, taking his hand. "Damn right we do. Good to meet someone who understands our commitment."

"Yes," Biryenko said. "Now we must begin. There are some American commandos who have followed us from Russia. We have to complete what we need to do as quickly as possible.''

"You have your people ready?'' Tetrow asked.

"Yes. We have trained for this and know the layout of the facility. We will break in and then you can join us for the main assault. We have special explosives and trained men to use them.''

"I can't wait,'' Tetrow said.

Biryenko produced a scale map of the immediate area that showed the radar facility, with details of approaches.

"Here we have the approach road. Checkpoint. Main gate. My demolition team will blow the door of the hut and dispose of the two guards inside. From the hut we can open the main gate. Once inside we handle the security crew and then we can move to destroy the whole site. You approve?''

Tetrow nodded. "You want us to cover you as you go in?''

"That will be good. If our backs are protected, we can concentrate on getting inside.''

"We'll meet inside the compound,'' Tetrow said.

"Boris has copy of the map. He will show you where to assemble your men while we deal with the guards in the hut.''

"Good luck,'' Tetrow said.

Biryenko watched Tetrow lead his men in Yesinovich's direction. The Russian go-between took them off to where they would wait for the signal to go.

"If the Americans following us had the brains of

these idiots, we would have nothing to worry about," Biryenko said as he rejoined his team inside the Hind.

He sat alongside Bering. "We'll wait until Yesinovich informs us he has the Militia Men settled. Just remember. Once you leave here, you work to the plan. Nothing more, nothing less. No damn heroics. Nothing but the plan. Understood? *Understood?*"

His loud use of the word startled even the most hardened and they turned to stare at him.

"I don't want to lose any of you. So let's do what we came to and then we can go home."

CHAPTER SIXTEEN

The Radar Facility

Biryenko was at the door, releasing the latch and pushing it open before the Hind touched down.

"Go-go-go!" he yelled, slapping each man on the shoulder as he exited the helicopter.

Snow billowed in through the open hatch, swirling wildly under the rotor wash. The Russians hit the ground running, moving quickly in the direction of the construction site. Despite the snowfall they made for the approach road and the checkpoint, following exactly the route they had practiced over and over at the mock-up in Siberia. The Hind had touched down within yards of the precise spot marked on the operation plan. It gave the strike team access to the entrance to the radar facility.

They moved forward in formation, each group covering the ground it had been assigned, allowing the next team to move on while the first provided cover. The operation had been planned with military thoroughness, and the Russians trained to follow that plan without hesitation.

Each man was equipped with a headset and microphone, able to contact any team member and also Biryenko. The few words spoken were sharp, abrupt, to the point. There was no wasted effort.

"Section One, area contained."

"Section Two, perimeter covered."

"Section Three, approaching checkpoint. Two armed security guards identified."

"Leader to Section Three. Disable security guards with utmost prejudice."

Section Three was composed of four men. They moved forward, confident that the other sections were covering them and had the area contained. Their task was to take out the two guards at the checkpoint, clearing the way for the main group to breach the gates and move onto the site.

They split into pairs, guiding each other with hand signals. Due to the weather conditions they would need to speak via the headset-microphone equipment they wore. Visibility was down to a few yards. It would hamper them slightly but not enough to cause too many problems.

The checkpoint was a hut constructed from metal, with the upper half high-impact glass. The door, solid metal, could only be opened with swipe cards that were carried by the guards. The information supplied to them by the American, Paul Curtis, told them that the guards were well armed. Each guard carried an automatic pistol, and there were automatic rifles and shotguns racked inside the hut. There was an alarm system inside the hut, connected to the main office on the site. More guards were based there, again well armed. This had all been assimilated by the Russians, who also knew that the security guards were employees of the construction company and therefore weren't professional soldiers. They were simply there as a precaution until the site reached a certain level in its construction. Then the military would take over and the radar facility would come under their jurisdiction.

Two civilian guards, warm and comfortable within their steel cocoon, wouldn't present much of a problem to the highly trained and motivated Russian strike force. The main complement within the site might put up more of a fight, unless it could be taken by surprise. Which was why it was important to disable the pair at the checkpoint quickly and silently, preventing them from sounding any alarm.

According to the roster supplied by Curtis, the guards on duty would have been on the job for the past three hours. By now they would be reaching boredom point. Lack of activity, lulled by the warmth inside their hut, the pair would be less than alert. They were ready to be taken down.

THE FIRST TWO Russians reached the hut. Flat on the ground, blending in with the snow, they crawled the final yards and crouched below the level of the windows. In position they signaled the second pair to join them. With the advance section reunited at the checkpoint hut, Biryenko was ready to deploy his other teams at their most forward positions, where they would be ready to move in fast. All it needed was for the guards in the hut to be disposed of. Biryenko gave the order. The teams moved into position and passed the word back. Biryenko contacted his advance team and gave the order.

"Take out the guards!"

Two of the advance team moved around to the secured door of the hut. The procedure they started had been gone over numerous times during the training sessions. A small, powerful explosive charge would be fitted to the door directly over the locking mechanism. The explosive compound would direct the blast inward, through the door, and take out the lock. With the door freed the team would enter the hut and dispose of the security guards. The action would take no longer than ten seconds from the moment the charge detonated. The guards, disorientated by the blast would offer little resistance. With the hut secured, the rest of the strike force would move forward and use another charge to blow the main gate and make their entry into the compound.

Attaching the charge to the door and staying well below the visible area of the windows, the two Russians ran their final check, then backed off. The small detonation unit was activated, a dull red light indicating that it was ready. The button was pressed and the charge went off with a sharp explosion.

The second pair moved in quickly. The damaged door received a hefty kick that drove it open and back against the inner wall of the hut. The Russians stormed the opening, weapons up and ready as they went in.

They were met by a burst of autofire that drove them back out of the door, bodies punctured and bleeding. One man went down immediately. His partner stumbled to his knees, shock registering on his face for a split second before a second volley put him down permanently.

The pair who had set and detonated the charge snatched their weapons into line, fingers on the triggers. A small canister flew out of the hut, bouncing as it hit the ground. It exploded with a sharp crack and a blinding flash that left the pair dazed and with blurred vision. Neither man really saw the armed figures who came out of the hut, firing as they moved. Both Russians died under a hail of shots from the Heckler & Koch MP-5s.

BLANCANALES WAS a step behind his partner as they left the checkpoint hut. They swung around the structure, flattening against the steel wall. Schwarz kept an eye on the approach road, knowing that somewhere close the rest of the Russian strike force was waiting. Once they realized something had gone wrong with the attempt to disable the checkpoint guards, they were going to move in quickly. With the element of surprise lost the Russians would attempt to right the situation.

Activating his com set, Blancanales spoke to McCarter on board *Dragon Slayer.*

"How much longer we got to hold on here?" he asked.

"Making our approach now, mate," McCarter said. "Just give… Okay, we can see the Hind. Be on the ground any minute."

"Glad you could join us," Blancanales said. "We're behind the checkpoint hut. The advance team has been taken out, but the rest of these guys are going to be pretty well pissed off by now...."

MCCARTER PICKED UP the sudden crackle of gunfire as Blancanales stopped talking.

"Jack, we need to be on the ground now. Get that bleeding hatch open."

McCarter unclipped his seat belt and scrambled out of his seat, moving into the rear compartment.

"Saddle up, mates, it's time to go to work."

"How is it down there?" Manning asked.

"As far as I can tell, Gadgets and Pol have started the ball rolling. They kicked back the team trying for the checkpoint hut, but now they have the rest of the Russians coming at them."

"The Militia Men?" Encizo asked.

"They'll be showing their ugly mugs somewhere, so it's eyes-in-the-back-of-the-head time."

"What about this Korean with the nuclear device?" Manning asked. "We need to find him. If the Russians decide they can't get right to the main target, they might set the damn thing off anyway. The long-term effect will be the same."

"Don't remind me," McCarter said.

Over his shoulder he called, "Bugger landing at a safe distance. Jack, put us down as close as you can to the fireworks. I don't want to leave Able on its own any longer than we need to."

"You got it," Grimaldi said.

The side hatch hissed as the pilot released the pressure. It slid open, filling the interior with chill air and swirling snowflakes.

"Welcome to Alaska," Grimaldi said cheerfully. "Fun-filled, action-packed, freeze-off-your-*cojones* Alaska."

Dragon Slayer swept in to ground level, Grimaldi holding it stationary no more than a couple of feet clear.

Turning his head, he caught a brief glimpse of the men of Phoenix Force as they exited the aircraft. The moment the last man disappeared from sight, Grimaldi kicked in the power and took the helicopter to a safe height. He touched the switch that closed the hatch, shutting out the sound of the wind and the low temperature.

THEY COULD SEE the perimeter lights mounted on the chain-link fence. The approach road that led up to the checkpoint hut was crowded with figures clad in white protective clothing. They were all armed. As Phoenix Force dropped from *Dragon Slayer,* fanning out across the road, a number of the white-clad figures turned, alerted by the sound of the helicopter. Orders were snapped out in Russian.

"Let's do it," McCarter yelled.

The pale dawn light, brightening with every passing minute, allowed each side to see their targets, and the sound of gunfire filled the air.

Initially the advantage belonged to Phoenix Force. They had come out of nowhere, dropping to the rear of the Russian force, and having that moment allowed them to establish position and first fire. Two Russians went down in the first volley. The others scattered. Those who had turned around returned fire, the harsh crack of the AK-74s mingling with the sustained bursts of the MP-5s.

McCarter and Hawkins led the charge, Manning and Encizo on their right flank, Calvin James the left. They pushed forward with relentless speed, making no concessions to any of the Russians. They, in turn, stood their ground, returning fire against the barrage of shots from Phoenix Force.

With Blancanales and Schwarz at their rear the Russians were in a hot fire zone and they finally broke, leaving the road area and plunging into the spread of construction materials and machinery that stood to one side of the facility.

BIRYENKO CLICKED the switch on his headset and spoke to Yesinovich.

"Bring them in now, Boris. We need their backup. The Americans have arrived. They have boxed in my people, and I want the Militia Men to hit them now. If we can't distract the Americans, Took will not be able to place his device."

"Very well," Yesinovich said. "They are on their way."

"OUR RUSSIAN compatriots need your support, Hubbard. We need to draw the Americans away so the gates to the site can be breached."

Hubbard Tetrow raised his M-16.

"It's time we showed these federal bastards how real Americans fight, boys. Let's go. I want this place razed to the ground. This is our day. For the Militia Men and Old Glory."

The ragtag group, armed and ready, followed Tetrow in the direction of the firefight. They moved with purpose, believers in their own ability to change the destiny of a nation by challenging the might of the federal government.

In the wasteland that surrounded the Tetrow ranch in Dakota they had practiced maneuvers, shot their weapons and carried out all kinds of combat simulations. The earnest show of force was expected to earn them a place in history. Many long nights had been spent discussing tactics, the reaction to any given situation and the possible ways out of them. The dry fields around the Tetrow ranch were a far cry from a freezing Alaska where the targets fired back.

That was the bitter experience they endured as they came into contact with Phoenix Force. The Militia Men, unused to the dedicated ferocity of *real* combat, were outclassed from the start. The clumsiness of their approach was heard and the lack of discipline among their ranks proved their undoing.

Manning picked up on the shapes emerging from the snowfall at Phoenix Force's rear and warned the others with a short call over his com set.

The Canadian's words drew McCarter's attention to the Militia Men's entry into the conflict. He spoke into his mike.

"Cal, you and Rafe fall back. Don't let these buggers get too close. The rest of us will stay with the Russians."

It was all that was needed. James and Encizo stayed put as the others continued their harassment of the

Russian strike force, following them into the construction site.

James snapped a fresh magazine into his MP-5, moving quickly to the side of the approach road and dropped to his knees beside a metal spotlight pylon. On the other side of the road Encizo bellied down in a shallow dip and snugged his weapon to his shoulder.

The bunched Militia Men loomed out of the drifting snow, breaking into a trot as they made out the hazy forms of Phoenix Force ahead of them. Shouted commands drifted back and forth as they raised their weapons.

James and Encizo triggered their own weapons, laying a deadly volley of shots that dropped three of the Militia Men instantly and sent the rest scattering. Some ran a few yards, then stopped to raise their weapons again, despite the fact they had no clear targets. James fired a short burst that put a tight group of 9 mm slugs into the chest of one defiant man. The guy collapsed, groaning against the sudden pain, pawing at his chest. A second gunner went down, spinning in an erratic arc as Encizo's shots tore his side open, spilling his blood across the snowy ground. The man refused to go down. He turned his M-16 in Encizo's direction, having seen a slight movement in the Cuban's position. Before he could fire, James targeted him and placed a solid burst into his skull. The guy pitched over, leaking bloody debris from his shattered head.

Plucking a grenade from his harness, Encizo pulled the pin and tossed the missile in an overarm throw. It detonated with a sharp explosion, spreading its deadly force among a dispersing group of the Militia Men, shredding clothing and flesh in a moment of searing terror.

The sudden about-turn, from dedicated intention to the realization that combat was no moment of patriotic excitement, filled the minds of the Militia Men with the awful truth. They weren't about to destroy the radar installation and march home proudly showing the flag of victory. In truth many of them were going to die, ending up as some of their brothers already had—torn and bloody, bodies damaged beyond repair, flesh and bone shattered. The specter of death had never been so clear in their eyes, and the ease with which healthy men were turned into pathetic victims would haunt them for a long time.

They weren't ready for the unrelenting reality of close combat. It was a bloody, violent experience, something that couldn't be trained into anyone. The only true way of gaining combat skills was by engaging in combat, coming through unscathed in body, while the mind had to come to terms with an unpleasant aspect of the human experience. There was no room for anything but fighting the fight, hoping to stay alive while the enemy died. The means of his death didn't matter. Emotion and moral concerns had to be pushed aside in the heat of combat. One split second of hesitation was all that was needed to lose the battle. The Militia Men were out of their league— but the realization was too late coming.

LYONS HAD SEEN the dark shape of the Hind looming out of the falling snow, and had watched the tail end of the Russian strike force leaving and slipping away into the snowfall. Lyons crouched and studied the helicopter. No one else left it. He could see the open door in the side, faint light showing, and after a moment he saw the figure of a tall, broad-shouldered man framed in the opening. Lyons could the man's lips moving as he spoke into a microphone, but the wind carried away any sound.

Moments after Lyons heard the muted blast of an explosive device. It wasn't long after that the sound of a firefight reached his ears. The exchange of gunfire was fast, furious and continuous.

He peered out from the hood of his parka and studied the Hind again. It was obvious that the helicopter had brought in a hostile force to make an attempt on the radar facility. Hubbard Tetrow's Russian allies? It would be ready to carry them away after the attack. Lyons wondered how many were left on board. Pilot and copilot? Someone directing the strike team?

Lyons's decision was a natural one. He was close to the Hind and he was armed. It was a logical move from that to his choice of action.

He checked the M-16. He had ample shots from the magazine, plus the spare ones in the pockets of his parka.

The Able Team leader circled the gunship, coming in on its blind side, away from the open door. Taking his time, he closed in, low on the ground, easing beneath the fuselage until he was directly under the open door. Lyons crawled out from under the Hind, moving to one side of the opening, and paused to listen for sound from inside. He picked up a low mur-

mur of voices. Someone was speaking in Russian, listening, then replying. Lyons guessed that the speaker was in touch with someone over a com link, possibly the man he had seen in the door opening speaking to the strike team.

Lyons gave the M-16 a final check. Pushing upright, he peered in through the open door and scanned the interior of the Hind. There was little to see at first. The cabin area was empty. He saw the benches set in the center of the floor area. The basic layout of the military aircraft. Austere to the point of dullness. The Hind, like any military-specified construction, was designed and built to do a job. It wasn't built for comfort. It was there to ferry troops or cargo, to fly to a combat zone and deliver people or death from the use of its armament.

Somewhere behind Lyons the crack of grenades added their sound to the gunfire. The battle for the radar facility was well and truly under way. The thought spurred him on, and Lyons hauled himself up into the Hind, his M-16 tracking ahead of him.

The first person he saw was Yat Sen Took. The North Korean had started to rise from his seat at the far end of the cabin, his right hand reaching for the pistol holstered at his waist.

"Your choice," Lyons warned. "Touch it and you're dead."

Took moved his hand away from the weapon, holding it clear of his body. Lyons made his way down to him and quickly removed the pistol, tucking it in his own belt.

"Sit down. Hands on top of your head."

Took did as he was told. He could see the hard look in the man's blue eyes. This one would kill without hesitation. He was professional in the best sense of the word, a man who knew his work and did it well.

"You carrying any other weapons? Make it the right answer because it won't be repeated."

Took shook his head. "Only the pistol."

"How many more on board?"

"The pilot and the strike force commander."

Lyons moved to the opposite side of the cabin, his back to the bulkhead. The muzzle of the M-16 remained on Took.

"What's in the pack?" Lyons asked.

Took saw no reason to lie. All the American had to do was to open the backpack for himself, which he would do if he thought Took was trying to fool him.

"A nuclear device."

Lyons digested the information, his mind going over the possible need for such a weapon. He reached the conclusion Took knew he would very quickly.

"You were going to set that off at the radar site? Wipe the place out and turn the installation into a no-go area?"

Took simply nodded. He didn't say anything after seeing the dangerous change in the American's eyes.

"Leave the place dirty for the next hundred years? Is that the idea? You bastards are sick."

"Is it any worse than using a gun? War is not a game where you decide that one way of killing is better than the next. The object is to kill the enemy. Or have I missed something?"

"Don't try that philosophical bullshit on me," Lyons snapped.

"No! Let him try this!" someone yelled.

Lyons snapped his head around and saw the tall Russian coming toward him from the front of the cabin. The man had a pistol in his hand, and the moment he had Lyons in his sights he pulled the trigger.

CHAPTER SEVENTEEN

The Radar Facility

The daylight was spreading, shadows vanishing so that it wasn't so easy to hide. The falling snow, twisting and eddying due to the wind, still allowed a degree of concealment, but not as much as the darkness.

Phoenix Force pushed forward, using every skill at its command to prevent the Russians from grouping together and making a stand. The firefight was hard and brutal, neither side giving any kind of quarter.

McCarter and Hawkins had driven three of the Russian invaders into the cover of a large earthmoving machine. The hulking yellow piece of equipment had tires on it that stood taller than a man. The machine weighed many tons, constructed as it was from thick, solid steel, and now that impenetrable bulk defied the bullets fired at it by McCarter and Hawkins. The Russians had taken cover behind the massive road wheels, knowing that even they would stop a bullet.

Crouching, McCarter and Hawkins studied the huge machine.

"We can't get at them. *They* can't hit us," Hawkins said. "We could be here all damn day, boss."

"Not in this bloody awful temperature," McCarter grumbled. "I want them cleared out soon as."

He was still studying the machine.

"Let's try something," the Briton said.

He raised his H&K to his shoulder, taking careful aim, then fired off a single shot. Hawkins heard it clang against the underside of the machine's huge dumper body, spotted the telltale plume of dust where it struck. It bounced off with a whine. One of the Russians moved suddenly as the flattened bullet chunked into the ground inches from him.

"I get it," Hawkins said.

The Phoenix Force pair began to fire bullets against the underside of the body, the ricochets sending them groundward at an angle. It was only a matter of time before one of them found flesh.

One of the Russians stumbled into view, pawing at the top of his left shoulder where one of the deformed bullets had ripped through flesh and muscle. The moment he came into view, McCarter brought his H&K down and laid a 9 mm slug in the man's chest, knocking him off his feet.

Another burst of fire directed at the flat body drove the other Russians into the open. They came out firing, the AK-74s sending a stream of slugs at the Phoenix Force duo. McCarter and Hawkins shifted position, then tracked in on the moving targets, catching them in the open.

As Phoenix Force's weapons started to fire, the Russians went belly down, pushing their own weapons forward, and engaged in a vicious cross fire. There was no questioning the Russians' courage or combat skills. These were experienced men, possibly ex-Soviet military. They didn't understand the concept of failure. Surrender wasn't an option, so the end result of the conflict had to be the wounding or death of the opposition.

With the crack of the AK-74s sending 5.45 mm slugs at them, McCarter and Hawkins found they were facing worthy opponents. Whether the Russians felt the same would never be known. McCarter especially didn't give a damn. All he wanted was to end the firefight and move on. His concern was the nuclear device the Russians had shipped in. If the invaders decided they weren't going to win the battle for the radar facility, the next-best thing would be to plant the device nearby, arm it, then make a strategic retreat. It might not achieve the full symbolism as placing it in the middle of the construction site, but the end result would still be horrific and the aftereffects certainly something that would linger.

Hawkins, returning the Russian gunfire, moved a little to one side as he ejected his empty magazine and reached for a fresh one. He made the mistake of raising his left shoulder a little as he turned his body. It was a slight move that lasted little more than a few seconds.

It was enough.

One of the Russians caught the exposure and quickly shifted his aim. His Kalashnikov cracked sharply. McCarter saw Hawkins arch up, saw the dark flecks burst from his shoulder and heard the gasp as Hawkins slumped back.

McCarter stayed flat, wriggling to his partner's side.

"T.J.? You okay?"

"That hurt, boss," the younger man said.

His shoulder gleamed as blood began to swell through the ragged tear in his combat jacket. Below the torn material McCarter could see the expanded hole in the flesh, paler inner tissue and muscle against the pulse of blood. He took a quick look and saw the bone was exposed, but didn't appear damaged. Hawkins had been lucky. The wound was deep and ragged. It was going to hurt like hell, and he'd be very sore for a while.

"David, they're coming! Look out for yourself!"

Hawkins's warning preceded the crash of heavy boots on the hard ground. McCarter rolled away from where he lay beside Hawkins. He dragged his MP-5 around, jamming it against his hip as he came up on one knee and found himself face-to-face with the two Russians. They were charging in his direction, faces taut from the effort as they pounded toward him.

The AK-74s cracked out their shots, the slugs chewing at the hard ground around McCarter.

He ignored the danger, leaning slightly forward as he opened up with his own weapon, short, well-placed bursts that hit one man, then the other at waist level. The 9 mm rounds punctured the white combat suits, the dark holes welling with blood that began to spread in irregular patches. McCarter raised his muzzle, laying a final burst into the Russians at chest height.

They ran on for a few faltering steps before crashing to the ground hard, twisting and thrashing out their final seconds.

McCarter turned back to Hawkins, snapping words into his mike.

"Jack, T.J.'s down. It's a shoulder wound, and it's bleeding pretty heavily."

"Where are you?"

"North side of approach road to site, where construction materials are kept. You can't miss it. There are pieces of heavy machinery parked there. Opposition is wearing white combat gear."

"On my way."

GRIMALDI THROTTLED back, swinging *Dragon Slayer* in a wide arc that brought him in from behind McCarter's position. He activated the 30 mm chain gun, making sure it was locked into his IHDS helmet configuration, and took the combat helicopter in a long dive, bringing the machine over the area at no more than ten feet.

Ahead of him he saw the sprawl of construction material, the stationary earthmovers. Twenty feet in front of the area he saw two figures down on the ground, one of them waving in his direction.

"I see you," Grimaldi said into his mike.

"Well, don't waste time taking a bloody picture," McCarter grumbled.

Grimaldi smiled. He was about to reply when he caught signs of movement beyond McCarter's position. White-clad figures were moving out from cover.

"Hang fire, pal," Grimaldi said, and eased *Dragon*

Slayer around a few degrees. He touched the firing button, and the 30 mm cannon spewed a long burst of rapid fire in the direction of the Russians. The concentrated fire chewed up anything in its path, splintering stone and earth, cleaving bodies, and sent the stunned Russians—those still on their feet—scrambling for cover.

Dropping back, Grimaldi opened the crew hatch and swung the helicopter around to cover McCarter as he hauled Hawkins off the ground and pushed him inside.

"Get him inside the compound. There should be security people in there who can look after him. Go, Jack, get the hell out of here!"

Grimaldi pushed *Dragon Slayer* up and away. He closed the hatch, glancing over his shoulder.

"Hold on, T.J. I'll have you fixed up in no time."

He hauled the helicopter over the high, heavy chain-link fence, skimming the main building. As he hovered, he saw a Bell JetRanger on the ground. It bore the insignia of the Alaska state troopers. Grimaldi put *Dragon Slayer* down just beyond the JetRanger, cutting the power. He unbuckled his belt and opened the hatch as he went to Hawkins's aid.

"You still with us, T.J.?"

Hawkins opened his eyes. "Hi, Jack, thanks for the ride."

"Let's get you out of here."

Grimaldi eased Hawkins to the hatch, climbed down and helped his friend out.

"Hold it right there," a voice commanded.

Grimaldi turned to see a young state trooper aiming a pistol at him.

"Sonny, you put that away before I forget my manners. I got a wounded man here who needs attention."

"How do I—?"

"My buddies are out there trying to stop you from being invaded. Now, let's get inside before my guy bleeds to death."

Boone put away his gun and helped Grimaldi get Hawkins inside the building. They took him to where the security men had established themselves.

"Anybody got medic training?" Grimaldi demanded.

"Yeah, that's my job," a sandy-haired man said.

"I got you a patient. He took a 5.45 mm slug in his shoulder. Do what you can for him, then we'll fly him to the nearest hospital."

Renwick, the chief of security, caught Grimaldi's arm.

"Sounds like World War III's going on out there."

"We're trying to stop it becoming World War III, chief."

"They going to break in?"

Grimaldi couldn't hold back a grin. "Chief, if they do, you'll be the first to know."

Renwick glared at him for a moment, then laughed.

"Yeah, I guess we will be."

Grimaldi crossed to where Hawkins had been laid out on a table. The medic was cutting away his clothing prior to looking at his wound.

"See you soon, hotshot."

Hawkins nodded. "Thanks for the ride."

"No sweat, buddy."

GRIMALDI MADE his way back out of the building and returned to his helicopter. He settled back in his seat, firing up the engines. He increased the power and took the black aircraft up and out of the compound.

Reaching altitude, he scanned the area below. The snowfall still hampered his vision. As he overflew the zone, he was able to see figures moving back and forth, pick out the flash of gunfire and the burst of grenades.

He made a wider sweep, going beyond the combat zone. He backtracked, and after a mile or so, saw three 4×4 all-terrain vehicles partly hidden. He contacted Blancanales and established that the Militia Men had made the trip in using such vehicles.

"Well, they're not going to use them again," Grimaldi said.

He brought *Dragon Slayer* into range and clicked on his weapons selection. He fired off one HE missile, adjusted position and fired a second. The sleek missiles, trailing flame, left the pod and impacted against the three vehicles. The resulting explosion sent fire and smoke into the air. One of the 4×4s lifted off the ground and flipped over on its side, twisted and scorched. Debris rained over a wide area, and burning fuel hissed as it struck the snow-covered earth. As the rumble of the explosions drifted away, Grimaldi turned the helicopter back in the direction of the radar facility.

He remembered he had a Russian Hind gunship to find.

CARL LYONS FELT the bullet gouge his left side. The sudden pain was unexpected and made him gasp. He automatically turned in the direction of the shooter and saw the tall Russian running toward him.

BIRYENKO HAD FIRED on the move, shooting the moment he set eyes on Lyons, something he might not have done under different circumstances. He was concerned for his men, aware of the possibility that the mission wasn't going exactly to plan, and those factors had contributed to his early pull on the trigger. A couple of inches to the right, and he would have scored a perfect hit. It was a momentary lapse that cost him dearly.

He saw the blond man turn, pulling back slightly under the impact of the bullet. He slumped against the bulkhead, hung there for a moment, then reacted with much faster reflexes than Biryenko could have expected.

Lyons shoved himself away from the bulkhead, diving toward the floor, the M-16 snapping out shots even as he was in the air. The shots were wild, missing Biryenko by inches, but they were enough to make him veer off track.

As Lyons hit the deck plates, he twisted his body in a frantic roll, ignoring the pain from his side and the jarring impact of landing. He slithered across the deck, crashing up against the opposite bulkhead. He almost lost his grip on the M-16. Grasping it tightly, he turned the muzzle in Biryenko's direction, sensing the big Russian closing on him.

Both fired simultaneously. The interior of the Hind

echoed to the racket of shots as the two men triggered shot after shot.

Lyons felt the deck plates quiver under the impact as 9 mm slugs drilled into the metal. He felt slivers sting his cheek and slice across the top of his right hand. Others tugged at his clothing.

Biryenko felt something punch his stomach. It was a strange sensation, and for a moment nothing else happened. He felt a second blow, this time higher up his body, and there was a sudden restriction to his breathing. He kept moving and shooting, only he abruptly realized that he wasn't actually doing those things. He was on his knees, watching the Beretta slip from his fingers, and when he looked down he could see blood welling from holes in his clothing. He tried to draw breath and his mouth took on the brassy tang of blood. It burst from his lips. Biryenko slid back, stopping only when he lodged against the bulkhead. He saw the blond man pushing slowly to his feet, holding his own hand over the wound in his side, and behind the American he could make out Yat Sen Took's lean form moving up behind him. It was the last he ever saw.

Carl Lyons pressed his left hand against the bleeding wound in his side. With Biryenko dead he turned to deal with the Korean.

Took sprang forward, his right foot swinging up in a kick that struck Lyons over the heart. The force of the blow spun him sideways, banging him against the bulkhead. The M-16 slipped from his grasp. Lyons drew breath, finding his lungs almost paralyzed from the heavy blow. He tried to resist Took's follow-up blow. It struck his raised arm, numbing it, and when Took aimed a third blow Lyons was unable to stop it. The boot smacked his head, and Lyons was thrown to the deck. He lay semiconscious, a heaviness rising in him that persisted even though he tried to fight it off.

Out of soft darkness threatening to engulf him Lyons heard the Korean say something. The words weren't clear. Lyons didn't have the strength to concentrate. He made a supreme effort to stand, got as far as his knees before a sudden rush warned of Took moving in again. This time the blow seemed to tear his head off his shoulders. Lyons was slammed against the bulkhead, the side of his face scraping against the rough surface. He dropped to the deck, unconscious, plunged into total, unrelenting darkness.

THE MILITIA MEN WERE moving back in the direction of the radar site, refusing to retreat, still led by a defiant Hubbard Tetrow.

"The crazy bastards won't quit," Blancanales said as he snapped a fresh magazine into his Uzi.

Behind them a grenade burst filled the air with noise.

"Pol, you there?" Manning said over the com link.

"Yeah."

"Couple of the Russians heading your way."

"Okay."

"Pol, watch yourselves. These guys are nasty."

"Wait until they see the kind of mood I'm in."

When Manning had gone off-line, Blancanales called Schwarz.

"Pair of white Russians on our patch."

"I heard."

Blancanales swung around, checking the area. He saw nothing at first, then picked out the two white-clad figures emerging from the misty near distance. One was carrying an RPG-7 cradled against his chest.

"What the hell is he going to do with that?" Schwarz asked.

"I'm not that hot on finding out," Blancanales said.

He pushed to his feet and closed in on the Russians. Neither saw him until he was within Uzi range. Blancanales stopped and leveled his weapon. He hit the closer Russian with a short burst, putting the man facedown in the snow.

The second man yelled something that was whipped away by the wind and began to raise the RPG-7. It was then that Blancanales saw he was wounded, blood staining the side of his combat suit. As the RPG-7 leveled out, Blancanales turned the Uzi on him. His finger began to put pressure on the trigger, then he heard Schwarz's voice through his headset.

"On your left! Two coming in!"

Blancanales dropped to a crouch, turning his upper body, and saw two Militia Men rushing in his direction, their M-16s moving into target acquisition. Blancanales didn't wait. He triggered the Uzi, moving the muzzle back and forth between the two. His line of fire was low, catching them midthigh, the 9 mm slugs tearing bloody holes in the gunners' limbs, ravaging flesh and bone. The Militia Men tumbled to the ground, weapons abandoned as they clutched at their legs with hands turned red.

Close by, Blancanales heard another Uzi chattering. He turned his head and saw the second Russian reel back as Schwarz's burst punctured his chest.

The Russian let the RPG-7 slip from his shoulder, the tip of the rocket angled at the ground between his feet. His finger nudged the trigger and the missile burst from the launcher, the firing blowback searing his face, burning the flesh. He had no time to register any pain as the rocket impacted with the ground and went off with a burst of flame and smoke. The detonation created a ragged crater in the earth and threw the lacerated, charred remains of the Russian aside like a rag doll.

Blancanales pushed to his feet, staring around. The area was clear for the moment. He spotted Schwarz moving in his direction, using the time to reload his Uzi. Before he could speak to his partner, Blancanales heard a click in his headset. Jack Grimaldi's voice came through.

"I spotted the Hind, guys. What do I do? Take her out or what?"

CHAPTER EIGHTEEN

Stony Man Farm, Virginia

"Anything?" Brognola asked.

"Hard to get any clear images at the moment," Huntington Wethers said. "The weather has closed in. There's heavy snow, and wind, and communications have gone crazy. It'd say too much is being transmitted by the teams for us to make much sense."

"Background noise isn't helping," Carmen Delahunt added. "Lots of noise out there. I'd say they're right in the middle of a firefight."

"Damn!" Brognola said. "Right now we're no use to them."

"Don't be hard on yourself," Wethers said. "We all feel the same, Hal. Let's face it. Once the guys get into a firefight situation, our job is done anyhow. When they get down and dirty, all we can do is wait and hope."

"Don't I know it," Brognola said. "That doesn't make me feel any better."

"Take a break, Hal," Delahunt said. "When was the last time you actually had some sleep?"

"Late '98, I think," Brognola said. "At least that's what it feels like."

"Then you are due some," Delahunt said. "Go take a break."

"Hal, if anything big breaks we'll let you know," Wethers promised.

Brognola accepted that and turned to leave. He made his way along the passage to where one of the rooms had been fitted with a few military-type cots for emergencies. The cots were nothing to shout about, but when Brognola sank down on one it felt good. He dragged the blanket over himself and was asleep in minutes.

WETHERS LOGGED ON as one of the orbiting satellites came into position. He checked that it was free for a while, then keyed in the coordinates that would image the area of Alaska they were interested in. The satellite made its course correction and aimed its image scanners at the designated spot on Earth.

Using his computer, Wethers tapped in the commands that pinpointed the area he needed to look at. The image faded and emerged again at a higher resolution.

He didn't say anything at first. Not until he had gained something worth looking at.

Manipulating the camera setup on the satellite, Wethers zoomed in on the radar site. He managed to focus in on the construction unit outside the high steel security fence. Then he started to pick up figures moving about. He tried thermal imaging. He spotted occasional flashes, which he took to be grenades.

There was a heat source that showed larger than any of the others when he picked up on it. Wethers checked on the configuration. It could only be the Hind. The scale size he had in the computer database would have shown *Dragon Slayer* to have been smaller by comparison. Wethers moved around the area. Heat sources showed again. They had to be people moving around. He watched two of the tiny blips moving in the direction of the Hind and wondered who they were.

Alaska

THE WIND WAS gusting now, dragging at their clothing as Blancanales and Schwarz located and attempted to reach the Hind. None of the Russian team was in the vicinity. The Able Team commandos closed in on the gunship.

"Just as ugly as everyone tells you," Blancanales said as he and Schwarz crawled under the fuselage of the Hind and rested for a moment.

"Hey, what's the plan on this one?" Schwarz asked. "We just going to hijack the damn thing, or what?"

"Something like that," Blancanales said. "The main thing is to get our hands on that nuclear device if it's still on board."

"Let's do it."

They moved out, weapons ready. They saw the open door and moved along the fuselage, positioning themselves on either side.

Blancanales turned to the opening, peering over the

edge of the frame. The interior of the Hind was dimly lit. There was enough light for Blancanales to see something that brought him up cold.

Carl Lyons lay slumped against the bulkhead, battered and bloody, barely able to move against the plastic loops tethering him to a metal frame by his wrists. Lyons was looking directly at his teammate, recognition in his eyes.

Blancanales was about to call out when he sensed movement to his right. He saw a lean Asian, pistol in one hand, hauling a backpack with his free hand as he stepped right up to the door.

The man was Yat Sen Took. He was staring out through the open door, his eyes on the distant radar site, and hadn't seen Blancanales, who had pulled back from the opening. Took braced himself against the pull of the wind, feeling the cold snow driven into his face.

On the other side of the door Schwarz spotted the Korean with the backpack. It was on his side, and all he had to do was reach out for it as Took rested it on the lip of the door frame.

Schwarz moved instantly. He lunged forward and grabbed the backpack, curling his fingers around a dangling strap. He yanked the pack toward him, taking its weight as it fell out of the Hind. Dropping to his knees, Schwarz rolled back under the fuselage, pulling the heavy pack with him.

Took gave a yell of frustration, leaning out of the door, his pistol thrust forward. He saw a dark shape move to one side as Blancanales covered his partner.

Took jerked the pistol around and fired, triggering swift shots.

Blancanales felt the bullets drill into the ground close by. He turned and fired back, his 9 mm slugs glancing off the fuselage. He stepped away from cover to get a better angle for his shots, and as he did he saw the door sliding shut. For a brief moment he saw Lyons, still curled up against the inner bulkhead, then the door slid and cut off his view. Blancanales could only see Took's left hand and arm curled around the edge of the door as he hauled it shut. The Able Team commando fired more in frustration, and saw his shots impact against Took's hand and arm. Bloody chunks erupted from the Korean's exposed hand and arm, blood streaming across the dull matte paint of the door. The shattered limb was pulled inside and the door slammed shut.

"Pol! Let's get the hell out of here. We hit the jackpot," Schwarz yelled from beneath the fuselage.

"No!" Blancanales said. "Carl's in there. I saw him."

The Hind's rotors were picking up speed, the sound of the powerful engines filling the air, whipping up snow and debris.

Schwarz scrambled out from under the gunship. He was dragging the backpack, flap open to expose the nuclear device.

"What?"

"He's on board," Blancanales yelled against the noise.

"Carl? Are you sure?"

"Do I look like I'm imagining it?"

The Hind lurched suddenly as the pilot made an early attempt at getting off the ground. The power was still on the low side and the massive helicopter sideslipped, almost hitting the Able Team duo. They pulled back, slipping and stumbling across the snow-covered ground.

"We have to stop it," Blancanales shouted. "We can't let him get away. Not with Carl on board."

The Hind swung wildly, the pilot pouring on the power now. A blinding swirl of snow lashed the two men, knocking them off their feet, and by the time they were able to see again the Hind was twenty feet up and climbing, drawing away from them quickly.

Blancanales staggered upright, raising his Uzi. He would have fired if Schwarz hadn't pushed his weapon aside.

"What the hell are you doing?" Blancanales shouted.

"You can't," Schwarz said. "If you did manage to hit it, what about Carl? If that Hind goes down, you'll kill him for certain."

They faced each other, anger, frustration and helplessness etched on their faces. Lyons was getting farther away with every passing moment, and there was nothing they could do to stop it.

Sound filled their headsets, words that only increased the feeling of loss, as Jack Grimaldi's voice reached them

"Hind in sight. She's heading away from the zone. I have it covered and locked in. I can take her down with one shot."

Schwarz activated his mike.

"Jack, don't do it! Carl is on board. I repeat, Carl Lyons is on board that chopper. Do not fire!"

There was a long pause and Schwarz was certain he heard Grimaldi give a sigh.

"Confirm that last message."

"Carl is on board the Hind. Do not intercept. Do not engage," Schwarz repeated. "Jack, tell me you heard."

"Jesus, I heard. Understood. No problem. Weapons system stood down, guys."

"Can you follow? Maintain contact with the Hind?"

"Will do," Grimaldi acknowledged.

GRIMALDI SET his course. He had the Hind on his radar, and occasionally he spotted the gunship as it broke out of the snowfall. He eased off and settled into a steady pursuit mode.

He unclipped his helmet and took it off, running a hand through his hair. He could feel a thin sheen of sweat on his face. It had come close, he realized. Too damn close. He might have fired on the Hind at any second prior to speaking to Schwarz.

That was scary. The fact that he hadn't known Lyons was on board failed to ease his discomfort.

He leaned forward and contacted Stony Man. Barbara Price acknowledged his transmission.

"Am in pursuit of Russian Hind gunship," Grimaldi said. "Carl Lyons is on board. I'll try and maintain contact."

"Okay, Jack. Any news on the nuclear device?"

"Gadgets called me about Carl. Sounds like they must have been in close contact with the Hind. Maybe they can update you."

"Jack, you okay? You sound strange."

"I came close to shooting down that Hind."

"You couldn't have known," Price said. "Things must be pretty hectic out there. None of us knew where Carl was."

"I guess you're right," Grimaldi said.

"Talking of close, you keep that Hind in sight. I'll see if Aaron can get a fix on it, as well. Where is it heading at the moment?"

"Back toward the coast. She's making a run back to Russia."

"Jack, I need to speak to the others. Call you soon."

Stony Man Farm, Virginia

IT TOOK Price a little time to establish contact with Able Team despite the satellite communication setup.

"Pol? Give me an update. I just spoke to Jack, and he told me about Carl. He's following the Hind."

"We have the device. From what we can see, it's safe. The arming unit is attached but hasn't been activated."

"We'll have to get a NEST team up to you. Get that bomb deactivated. Pol, don't let that damn thing out of your sight. I won't feel safe until it's been dealt with."

"*You* won't feel safe?" Blancanales said. "Barb,

I'm practically sitting on the thing. If we're wrong, I can kiss my ass goodbye.''

"What a lovely picture you paint, Pol.''

Aboard the Hind

YAT SEN TOOK HAD DONE what he could to stem the bleeding. His left hand was in a mess. He had lost two fingers, and the outer edge of his palm was lacerated and showed ragged shards of splintered bone. He had also been hit just below the left elbow. He bore the pain in silence. The Hind's first-aid kit had provided him with bandages and sterilized dressings. There were also painkillers. He had injected himself. The painkiller took some time to work, reducing the severe pain to a heavy throb. He strapped his arm to his body, eliciting the pilot's help for the final tying of the sling.

"We don't have any choice,'' Took told the pilot. "We have to be practical. Sacrificing ourselves will not help the others.''

"You don't have to convince me,'' the pilot said. "They hired me to fly this thing for them. I did it for money. If I stayed behind and got shot or put in an American jail, that money wouldn't have done me any good.''

"Can you get us back?'' Took asked.

"I don't see why not. It might be a rough ride. This weather isn't slacking off. We should be fine once we get across the water. At least we'll be on home ground.''

"I will go and see how our passenger is.''

"Question?"

"Yes?"

"What are you going to do with him?"

Took smiled. "Take him back to Korea with me. He is obviously an American agent. My superiors will be interested in what he might know. Until he is questioned, it is impossible to gauge the depth of his knowledge. He may have connections with the Slingshot project. We will find out eventually."

The pilot considered Took's reply. "If it was me, I think I'd rather be dropped over the side and take my chances. No offense, Comrade Took, but I don't think he'll like what he finds in your country."

"Oh, I'm sure he won't," Took said. "I will be disappointed if he doesn't."

Alaska

THE GROUND BATTLE continued.

The Russians had attempted to force the advance toward the radar facility, with the splintered Militia Men doing their best to back them.

McCarter had teamed up with James, Manning and Encizo and they had pushed the invading force back from the approach road. In the confusion of battle, Phoenix Force maintained its solidarity while the opposition seemed to be having trouble staying together.

After the initial, furious struggle, the battle had become an exchange of fire intent, on both sides, on wearing down the other side.

The weather remained constant. Heavy snow and wind reduced visibility. It did nothing to help anyone.

In the end both sides settled into a shot-for-shot stand-off.

McCarter took the opportunity and contacted Stony Man. What he heard both pleased and angered him.

The taking of the nuclear device by Able Team was a relief, but it was tempered by the news that the retreating Hind had taken Carl Lyons with it.

"Jack is in pursuit," Price explained. "We're tracking, as well."

"Don't lose that bloody chopper, Barb."

"What do think we're doing here, David? Sitting on our hands waiting for the phone to ring?"

"How do I know what you're doing? I'm stuck out in the middle of bloody Alaska getting shot at."

"It isn't much fun back here, either, pal."

They both cut the connection at the same time. McCarter settled back at his firing position, muttering to himself.

"You two have words?" James asked.

McCarter glanced at him, his face dark with anger. He took a breath.

"You don't think it's love, do you?" he asked.

"In your dreams," James said.

"Thank God for that," McCarter said. "I don't think I could handle it."

"Hey, you two," Manning said, "do you mind getting back to reality. I think our friends are making a move."

THE RUSSIANS HAD broken cover and were making for Phoenix Force's position. They opened fire as soon as they commenced their assault, laying down a heavy covering fire for two of their number who were carrying RPG-7s. The pair split, moving to left and right, using whatever cover they could as they closed on Phoenix Force.

"Pick your targets, lads," McCarter said, "and watch those blokes with the rocket launchers."

Manning, the team's marksman, leveled his H&K, set for single shot. He snugged the weapon to his shoulder and followed the first of the RPG men. The Russian paused to lay the launcher across his shoulder, peering across his sights, his finger already on the trigger. He began his squeeze.

Manning held his aim, waiting for the target to settle, then fired. His 9 mm slug hit the Russian over the heart. The impact jogged his body, but he was able to complete his trigger pull.

The RPG-7 gushed fire and smoke, the projectile shooting from the tube. It howled over the heads of the Stony Man team and struck the abandoned checkpoint hut, destroying it.

The Russian slumped to the ground a fraction of a second before Rafael Encizo matched Manning's shot and took out the second RPG-7 carrier. The Russian fell to his knees, the launcher dropping from his dead fingers.

THE REST of the Russians continued their headlong charge, weapons firing on full-auto, peppering the ground above Phoenix Force's position. There was a reckless intent in their move, as if they had realized that whatever else, the attack on the radar facility wasn't about to succeed but they had to at least follow through.

The men of Phoenix Force had no wish to go down for any such thoughts. In their minds the defense of the radar site was top priority, with their own survival ranking alongside it. Suicide missions weren't an option as such, though they might have often looked at a mission brief and considered it as total insanity. The Stony Man team had too much respect for their own lives to let them be placed in jeopardy without first considering the legitimacy of any cause first.

Regardless they fought back with their usual tenacity, refusing to allow themselves to be defeated by the Russian force.

The concentrated fire from their weapons reduced the advancing Russians to the minimum. Two of the invaders actually reached their position unscathed, only to be faced by McCarter's Browning Hi-Power, the Briton having exhausted his H&K's ammunition.

As the first Russian sprang over the lip of the depression concealing Phoenix Force, McCarter hit him with two 9 mm slugs that drilled into the man's head. He pitched forward, crashing down beside the Phoenix Force leader. The stoic Briton calmly turned and fired again, his target this time the second Russian who had reached their position. McCarter's single shot was just ahead of a burst from Calvin James. The Russian spun awkwardly, losing his coordination and sprawling over his downed companion. The stuttering autofire slackened, became ragged and stopped.

Manning reloaded, glancing around.

"Game and match," he said quietly.

"I don't think so," Encizo replied. "Our Militia Men don't seem ready to quit yet."

He indicated where the Militia Men were working their way around to the radar site's perimeter fence.

McCarter borrowed a fresh magazine for his H&K. He ejected the spent one and reloaded, cocking the weapon.

"Then they've got one hell of a surprise coming to them," he snapped.

CHAPTER NINETEEN

Alaska

"Spread out," McCarter said as he led Phoenix Force to intercept the Militia Men.

His team formed a line, with distance between each as they closed on the determined group moving ahead of them.

The Militia Men were down to a hard core of seven, Hubbard Tetrow leading them as they pushed across the open ground, going directly for the main gate. As well as their regular weapons, two of the Militia Men carried a number of AT-4s.

"You see what they're carrying?" Manning asked. "They could still do some damage."

McCarter raised his MP-5 and triggered a burst that drew the attention of the Militia Men.

"Tetrow, it's time to stand down," McCarter yelled. "Give it up now. The game's over. Your Russian pals are dead. The nuke has been taken, so let's end it here."

Tetrow turned. "What the are fuck you talkin' about? Nuke? What nuke?"

Realization hit McCarter as he digested Tetrow's query. The man was genuine. It showed in his voice.

"They didn't tell you? Bloody hell, pal, did they take *you* for a ride."

"What's he saying, Hub?" one of the Militia Men asked.

"What he's saying is you've been had," James said. "Suckered all the way down the line."

"What's the black boy crowin' about?"

McCarter ignored the racist gibe.

"Tetrow, the Russians had nothing to do with a militia group. They just told you that to get in bed with you, use your knowledge. They were using you for their own purpose."

Tetrow turned and faced one of his group.

"Boris?"

The Russian stood suddenly alone as the others moved away from him, leaving him exposed.

"I ain't heard you tell me he's lying, Boris," Tetrow said.

Yesinovich inclined his head. "Forget the bomb. We can still do it," he said gently, lowering his voice so that only Tetrow could here. "You still have the LAWs."

Tetrow moved with sudden violence, using the butt of his M-16 to strike Yesinovich in the face. The Russian went down, blood gleaming against his flesh.

"Bad enough my own fuckin' government treats me like crap. Now I got the goddamn Russkies doin' it."

His M-16 suddenly cracked as Tetrow triggered a burst into Yesinovich's chest.

"We're surrounded by Feds and fuckin' Russians, and they all want to take us down! Jesus Christ, the whole damn world is goin' crazy."

The rising pitch in Tetrow's voice warned McCarter what was coming. He knew but he could not stop it.

"Hit that fuckin' radar site," Tetrow screamed.

The Militia Men carrying the AT-4s ran forward, opening up the tubes and arming the rocket launchers.

"Oh, shit," McCarter said. "Stop them."

Manning and Encizo ran forward, shouldering their weapons and firing on single-shot cycle. Manning hit his first target on the second shot, pitching the guy facedown with a 9 mm round between the shoulders. As the hardman hit the ground, the LAW bounced from his hand and fired its missile. The rocket screeched across the ground, exploding when it struck an outcropping.

Encizo took a little longer to track his man. The Cuban would have been the first to admit his sniper skills were below Manning's. When he fired, his 9 mm slug struck the target in the lower back, causing the man to stumble but remain on his feet. Encizo muttered under his breath and went after him. The guy swayed as he shouldered the LAW, still trying to achieve his goal. He lined up on the radar site and pulled the trigger. The rocket soared toward the high fence and punched a hole through it about ten feet up. He was reaching for a second tube when Encizo opened up on full-auto. The shot man went down hard and stayed still, his right side a mass of glistening blood and tissue.

THE MOMENT he had given the order, Hubbard Tetrow turned his own weapon on McCarter and James. He advanced across the snow-covered ground, his M-16 on single shot, firing shot after shot at the two men. Behind him his surviving three gunners fell into position, their own weapons ready.

Neither McCarter nor James was in the mood for a prolonged firefight. McCarter yanked the pin of his last grenade and sprang the lever. He held for long seconds, then hurled the projectile into the advancing group. The grenade blew two of them off their feet, one losing a lower leg. The other caught shrapnel in his face and throat, and fell in a moaning heap on the ground where he lay bleeding.

"Okay! Okay, I quit. This is fuckin' crazy," the last man yelled. He tossed his weapon aside and thrust his hands in the air.

Hubbard Tetrow closed his ears to the racket going on around him. He was beyond reason now. His world had collapsed. Betrayal from all sides had brought about his downfall. He saw nothing ahead of him. Not any longer. Yet he remained defiant, refusing to back down. The only way he had now was to maintain his stance, whatever the cost.

Hubbard Tetrow took the only way out and did it with the rifle in his hands, raising it to fire.

The cost was his life. A burst of fire from the weapons of the men he still considered his enemy and the cold earth of Alaska drained the warmth from his bleeding body. He died still not fully understanding how it had all gone wrong.

BLANCANALES PICKED up a call from McCarter.

"You can come in now, ladies. It's safe. Just promise me you haven't been playing around with that bloody bomb."

"Of course we haven't," Blancanales said. "Only, should it be making a ticking sound?"

"I've a good mind to leave you out there."

Phoenix Force helped get the wounded inside the compound, where the most severe cases were loaded into Boone's helicopter. The medic from the security team went along to keep an eye on them. Hawkins was one of the injured.

Boone radioed ahead, informing the hospital they were on their way. Two of the security men went along to keep an eye on the patients.

Stony Man had been informed, and agents from the FBI were en route to take charge of the case now that it had come under their jurisdiction. Brognola would have endless meetings with them, ironing out the complexities of the case, but he had the satisfaction of having the White House behind him if things became too hot.

The Pentagon had also been told that their new baby had almost died at birth. It spurred them into action, and a contingent of infantry was being flown in to take charge of the site.

WITH THE AREA secure Phoenix Force and Able Team made contact with Stony Man to ask the question that had been with them since they had learned about Carl Lyons's abduction.

"Let's have the update," McCarter said.

They were alone in the communication office inside the main building. McCarter put the speaker on so that they could all hear what was said.

"Last we heard from Jack, he was still in pursuit. The problem is the weather and the fact he's starting to get low on fuel. He has another hour at best before he has to turn back," Barbara Price told them. "Sorry, guys."

"What about Aaron? Can't he keep tracking them?" McCarter asked.

"We're doing what we can. You know the situation regarding satellite time. We're begging, stealing and borrowing from every bird we can."

"Any thoughts on where the Hind is headed?" Schwarz asked.

"Once it hit Russian airspace, it turned south. Looks like it's moving along the coast. If it keeps on that heading, it'll eventually reach China."

"Or North Korea," McCarter suggested.

"Can't Hal get help from the Air Force? Get the AWACS to see if they can find the damn thing," James said. "Come on, Barb, they owe us that much."

"Hal's already talking to the military brass and the President."

"The problem with that is," McCarter snapped, "the military likes to talk too much. We need some bloody action here."

"We're pulling in every favor we can," Price said. "Considering our status, we can't exactly go on national TV and ask for it, guys. As soon as we ask, people want to know who we are and how we were involved in the Alaska deal. This is thin ice we are skating on here."

"Okay, we get the message," James said. "We don't like it, but we understand."

"Look, once the military takes over in Alaska, we'll get you back to base. Maybe by then we'll have better news. It will also give us all the opportunity to cool down. Agreed?" Price paused, then added, "Agreed, *David?*"

McCarter glanced up at the mention of his name. He stared at the speaker.

"Agreed, Barbara."

CHAPTER TWENTY

Moscow

"Are we safe to talk?"

Nikolai Gagarin sat forward as he recognized the voice coming over the line.

"Yes," he said.

"You have heard about the mission failure?"

"Bad news travels fast. My people informed me a little while ago."

"And?"

"Naturally I am extremely disappointed. At least your man got out. And with a prize, I believe?"

"That is why I am calling. You expressed interest in the American agency thought responsible for earlier disappointments. The capture of this individual could be useful, don't you think?"

"Exactly my own thoughts."

"Would you be interested in becoming involved in his interrogation?"

"Very."

"It would mean traveling to where we are holding him."

"No problem."

"Good. I will arrange things. It may take a few days. I believe you will find a great deal to interest you when you arrive. Although the failed mission presents us with certain problems, we do have other considerations. Your thoughts would be much appreciated."

"Anything I can do to help."

"Then I will be in touch."

Gagarin replaced the receiver. He sat for a while, replaying the conversation in his head. It had been interesting to say the least. Considering the catastrophic events over the past week, anything that could salvaged had to be better than nothing. What should have been a straightforward mission had turned out to be a costly fiasco.

He gave brief thought to the losses *he* had incurred and the price he had paid. Biryenko and his team. Yesinovich and Nureyev. All dead. The most irritating part was that Malinchek was still alive. Gagarin had been tempted to leave him and his band of gangsters to freeze in the Siberian wastes. But a rescue team had already pulled them out. Malinchek, though he wasn't aware of it, was living on borrowed time. His involvement had proved costly, and he knew too much. There was an urgent need to take care of the problem. It had taught Gagarin a lesson—never to employ people like Malinchek ever again. In this instance his needs had dictated his actions. Malinchek had contacts in the area, and he was able to supply weapons at short notice. It hadn't been enough.

Using contacts and favors, Gagarin had managed

to have a MiG fighter sent after the American helicopter. That ended in disaster. Due to financial cutbacks, the fighter hadn't been equipped with a full complement of missiles. The American machine *had*, and brought down the expensive MiG, killing the pilot in the process. It was another score Gagarin had to settle with the Americans.

He pushed back in his seat, watching snow fall outside the window. The weather matched his mood. Dark and bleak for the moment. He allowed himself the bitter reflection only for a short time. Wallowing in self-pity achieved nothing at all. He needed a way forward, and the conversation he had just had would do that for him. He could see something positive coming from his involvement with the North Koreans. They were an uncompromising people. Extremely fixated when they set out on a path. They were utterly convinced that the Slingshot project was nothing more than a device to conceal the real intentions of the American military. The USA was viewed as having militaristic tendencies toward Asia.

North Korea, despite overtures to the West, and even South Korea, was still an isolated nation, inward looking and highly suspicious. Those in charge of the country's destiny maintained a stoic indifference to world disapproval of their policies. They continued with the development of their missile program. Despite the country suffering from lack of food and medical supplies, the administration went ahead with greater and more ambitious plans. Their missiles were open for sale to anyone with the money to buy. If they could eliminate the American defense shield, it would place them in an extremely strong position.

Gagarin liked the idea. A weaker America would benefit them all. An America under the gun, so to speak, would be even better. It would curb their expansionist tendencies. The thought pleased Gagarin. He pushed to his feet and crossed to the locked cabinet standing against the wall. He unlocked it and took out a bottle of Jack Daniel's whiskey, pouring himself a healthy glassful. He raised the glass and studied the mellow liquid, smiling to himself. Even the Americans were able to get *something* right.

Stony Man Farm, Virginia

THE MOOD at the Farm was subdued. Phoenix Force and Able Team had been back for three days. Hawkins was in hospital after being flown back from Alaska. His wound was healing due to the excellent care he was receiving.

The rest of the men were suffering bruises and scratches. Their problems were less physical and more cerebral.

None of them could get Carl Lyons out of their thoughts. His disappearance in the Russian Hind stayed with them during waking and sleep. They were, at once, angry, full of remorse at not being there when he had needed them, and increasingly impatient at the seeming lack of progress.

Jack Grimaldi had returned from his abortive pursuit, nursing *Dragon Slayer* along on fumes. The tanks were to all intents empty. He had put down outside the radar facility, shutting down the combat helicopter and walking in to meet the teams with a look on his face that warned them not to say much. Grimaldi needn't have worried. They were all exhibiting the same emotions.

Carl Lyons was one of them. When one member of the teams was injured or in a threatening situation they all felt it. Though the inner feelings they had for one another were kept hidden most of the time, there was no embarrassment when it came to showing how they really felt.

Lyons, despite his often snappy nature, impatience and lack of tact, was one of them. They had all shared desperate times together. Struggled and fought side by side. Come close to the edge, and hauled one another out of trouble countless times. The invisible bond holding them together was never stronger than at times when one of them was in trouble.

Kurtzman and his cyberteam had taken over when Grimaldi had to abandon his pursuit. Despite everything, they had managed to get a lock on the Hind. They saw it land twice, most probably to refuel, and had tracked it via Khabarovsk and Vladivostok. From there it continued south and eventually put down in North Korea.

A high-flying Air Force AWACS out of Japan had spotted and tracked the Hind to its North Korean touchdown, confirming Kurtzman's satellite images. Shortly after that the contact had been lost. No amount of scanning had picked it up again.

In the end the search was abandoned. If Lyons was

in Korea, he would have been moved around by other means and invisible to surveillance.

Debriefing completed, the Stony Man teams were stood down, which almost resulted in a mutiny. They refused to leave the Farm until they had something solid concerning Lyons. Combining forces, they badgered Brognola until he set up a meeting in the War Room. Everyone was present for the meeting, and the mood wasn't suggestive of it being a pleasant one.

Hal Brognola sat down, clearing his throat and swallowing a couple of antacid tablets. He was going to need them, he decided, after seeing the look on McCarter's face.

"Okay, guys, I know you all have something to say. I also know I'm going to be the bad guy. So let's have it."

"What's being done about Carl?" McCarter asked. "No bullshit, Hal."

"Okay, straight. The usual checks. All our people in the area have been asked to go to their sources. The problem is it takes time. There isn't much more we can do."

Blancanales wasn't impressed. "That it? Hal, we're talking about Carl here. One of our own. We don't walk away. You're telling us nothing is being done."

"I told you exactly what's being done," Brognola said. "If you can come up with something better, let me hear it."

"Have you spoken to the President?" James asked.

"I was with him late last night. He's just as concerned as we are. He's doing all he can on the diplomatic front. But it's limited. The only response we have from the North Koreans is a total denial. They've never heard of Lyons. According to them, no American is being held anywhere in the country.''

"We know that's a damn lie," James said. "They've got Carl. We know it and so do they.''

"Do we?" Katz asked, his low tone a direct contrast to the angry voices around him.

"What's that mean?" McCarter asked testily.

"Let's put emotions aside. You're all concerned and rightly so. But we have to look at this objectively. What proof do we have that the North Koreans are holding Carl? Solid proof.''

"He was on that damn Hind when it left Alaska," Blancanales said. "I saw him in it.''

"Okay," Yakov Katzenelenbogen said. "Carl was on board when the Hind took off from Alaska. So we assume he was still on board when it landed to refuel. Was he on board when it took off again? If he was, what about the second time it landed? Carl could have been removed from the helicopter on either landing. Am I right? Convince me he was still on board the Hind when it landed in North Korea.''

"You know we can't do that," McCarter said, his impatience starting to wear.

"So how do you know he was on the Hind when it reached North Korea?" Katz kept his repeated question low-key. "Perhaps the Russians took him off during one of the fuels stops.''

"No," Encizo said. "The Koreans would have hung on to him. He'd be a big prize to them.''

"Maybe he's dead," Katz suggested, "and they jettisoned his body while they were over the water."

"Dammit, Katz," Blancanales growled, rising from his seat.

"Hey, back off, guys," Price warned. "Let's cool it, huh? What are you trying to prove, Katz?"

"Just that there are more ways than one to look at any scenario. You could all be right. The probability is that you are and Carl *is* being held in North Korea. But you have to be certain before anything can be done. Go charging off in the wrong direction and all you do is waste precious time and effort."

The door opened then, and Aaron Kurtzman rolled his wheelchair into the War Room. He was holding up a number of photographs.

"Figured you guys would want to see these," he said.

He rolled up to the table and spread the images across the surface.

"We pulled these from the database of a surveillance run from an agency recon satellite. They do work for one of the strategic analysis departments in the Pentagon. Don't ask me how I got in there, Hal, because I'll deny everything. The thing is, they run regular checks on certain regimes, checking up on defense-offense capabilities. All this is fed into some program that crunches it all down into readable figures for the Defense Department. The images here were from a scan two days ago. That would be about the time that Hind reached North Korea."

Kurtzman jabbed a finger at a black-and-white

photo that showed a series of time-lapse images taken over a period of two to three minutes.

"This is a North Korean facility known to be into all kinds of missile development work. Pretty isolated as are most of these places. Here you can see what looks very much to me like a helicopter. Pretty big. Configuration matches the Hind according to our database. Check the sequence. Door opens, one guy gets out. Does that look like a strapped-up left arm? You said you hit the Korean before the Hind took off, Pol?"

"Yeah. Left hand and arm."

"Next image has two more people stepping out. Am I seeing things or does that guy there have blond hair? We enlarged it as much as we could. The guy isn't bald. It is blond hair, and it looks like the one behind him has a weapon."

The teams crowded around the spread of photographs. Kurtzman eased his chair out of the way and left them to it.

"Looks pretty definite to me," Brognola said.

"Aaron, you are a miracle worker," Price said.

"It was nothing."

"Yes, it was," Katz said. "And I'm glad to be proved wrong."

"We've still got one hell of a problem on our hands," Brognola said. "How do we keep these guys from invading North Korea now?"

EPILOGUE

North Korea

He woke again from a restless sleep, body stiff from lying on a bare stone floor. It was cold and damp. The walls allowed water to seep through and there were pools on the floor. The barred window, which looked out across the inner compound, let the chill air into the cell. The nights were bitter and if it rained or snowed, it drifted into the cell. The air smelled damp. Sour.

He could hear sound coming from outside—men moving around the compound, vehicles coming and going. The barred window was too high for him to look out of. All he could ever see were the four stone walls and the heavy door of the cell. The small view slot in the door was kept closed.

For most of the time he was kept isolated. Once a day he received a bowl of watery rice and vegetables, and a tin can of cold water. It was just enough to keep him nourished. A hole in the floor in one corner of the cell served as his toilet.

Before they threw him in the cell on the first day, he was stripped and a doctor tended the wound in his side. He was given a crude uniform of sacklike material and a pair of basic sandals. His watch was taken from him, so he had no real sense of time passing.

The first day he had been left completely alone. They started to feed him from the second day.

He tried to keep a record in his head of the days, and by his reckoning he had been in the cell for four days before anyone came to see him. Before that his only human contact had been another captive who brought him his food and water every day. The man never spoke, never even looked at him. He simply came in and placed the food and water by the door, then stepped out so the door could be closed and barred from the outside.

Sometimes at night Lyons heard movement, a door being opened, someone being dragged from what he guessed to be a cell like his own. He heard protests, then the sound of blows. Then silence. Later he would be disturbed by the return of the one who had been dragged away. A cell door would be opened, and a body would be thrown to the floor before the door was slammed and bolted. This happened most nights. No one ever came near his cell.

On the fourth day he heard footsteps. They reached his door. It was unbolted and thrown open. A pair of armed North Korean soldiers came in. They signaled for him to stand up. He was escorted out of the cell, along a stone passage that had a number of doors identical to that of his cell.

A door at the end of the passage led to the outside. The fresh air tasted good. It was cold. Snow was falling. His escort took him across the wide compound. There was a number of soldiers around, all armed. He saw vehicles, too. It was hard to look because his eyes were taking time to adjust to the brightness of the day. It made him realize how gloomy it was in his cell.

On the far side of the compound was a long two-story building. He saw aerials on the roof. His escort took him inside and up some steps to the next floor. A door was opened and he was pushed inside. The door closed behind him, the armed soldiers remaining outside.

He was in an office, which was long and well furnished. A computer and printer sat on a wooden desk. At the far end of the room a log fire burned in a stone hearth. Large armchairs were ranged in front of the fire.

He stood just inside the door, waiting, unsure what was going to happen. He was content for the moment to allow the room's warmth to engulf him.

A man stood up from where he had been seated in one of the armchairs. He wore a well-cut military uniform. When he turned, he was revealed as Yat Sen Took. His left arm and hand were still heavily bandaged. He stepped around the armchair, a slight smile on his lips. He gestured to one of the chairs.

"Please join us, Mr. Jag."

Carl Lyons moved forward and sat down, watching Took closely. He didn't trust the man. His attention was caught by the presence of a second man, seated in another of the armchairs, across from Lyons.

He was studying Lyons carefully, making silent assessments. He was a good-looking man, his thick gray hair brushed back from his forehead. He had a strong face, lined with age. Lyons judged him to be in his early sixties. There was nothing frail about him. He wore a plain, expensive dark suit, with a white shirt and dark tie.

"Nikolai Gagarin," the man said. His Russian accent was strong. He made no attempt to disguise it. "You are a hard man to kill, Jag. And what a strange name. I understand it is not your own. Just something you used to infiltrate those sad dissidents. Are you ready to tell us your real name?"

"What do you think?" Lyons said.

Gagarin made a slight movement with his head.

"Time enough for that. Would you like something to drink? Coffee perhaps? Or tea?"

"Whichever you prefer," Took said from somewhere behind Lyons.

"Okay. Coffee. Black. No sugar," Lyons said.

Lyons sat and waited. He heard Took cross the room and leave by a door at the far end. He tried to stay alert, but it was difficult. His weary body craved rest. The heat from the fire lulled him, and Lyons let it flow over him. He felt dirty, unshaven. He was stiff from his long night lying on the hard stone floor of his cell. The uniform he was wearing chafed his skin. The material was coarse, uncomfortable.

"Those cells are terrible places," Gagarin said. "Cold and damp. I'm sure the floor is very hard."

Lyons met the Russian's gaze and held it.

"Is this the pitch for my sympathy? Next you'll be telling me it doesn't have to be this way. I can have a warm bed and clean clothes. Even some proper food. Only I have to give you something in return?"

"Something like that," Gagarin admitted. "On the

other hand we could have you taken outside and shot within the next few minutes."

Lyons managed a crooked smile. "You haven't brought me all this way just to shoot me. If I was just excess baggage, Took would have dumped me in the sea and let me drown."

"You may be right. Perhaps Took and I are just a pair of sadists. We enjoy doing things like this for our amusement."

"You said it."

Took returned. He carried a mug in his right hand and handed it to Lyons. The smell of rich coffee rose from the mug. Lyons held the mug and watched as Took crossed to one of the armchairs and sat down.

"Please, drink it," Took said. "It has not been doctored with anything."

Gagarin leaned forward. "A dilemma for you, Jag. Is Took telling the truth? Or is he using his explanation to cover the fact that the coffee has actually been drugged? Everything comes down to choice. Just like your situation here. In the end you will have to make a choice. Whether to tell us what we need to know, or refuse and undergo the consequences. For us the choice is whether we believe anything you tell us, or ignore your words and torture you anyway. In the end we are all left with choices."

Lyons raised the coffee and drank. He was careful not to swallow too much. His stomach needed time to absorb the hot liquid after being deprived for so long. Despite everything the coffee tasted good.

"So, Jag, is there anything else you require?"

"A one-way ticket back to the U.S.?"

"Unfortunately that is not on the list," Took said.

"You and your colleagues, by your interference, have caused us a great deal of inconvenience." Gagarin's voice was still conversational, friendly. "I hope you realize how much effort went into our mission."

Lyons lowered his mug.

"Did you expect us to stand by while you mounted an armed invasion on American soil?"

"Oh, hardly an invasion."

"Call it what the hell you like. What were we expected to do, roll over and pretend nothing was happening?"

"I suppose not." Gagarin considered his next statement. "As far as we are concerned, your actions were nothing short of a terrorist act. That alone could get you an extremely long prison sentence. And you would not like that experience. The Korean prison facilities are nothing like those you have in America."

"Consider your current accommodation as five-star," Took said. "Anything else will be of a much lower standard."

"If you're trying to scare me, you've done it," Lyons said. "I don't have any illusions about you bastards. I know I'm in trouble. I'd be a fool not to realize that. On the other hand I'm thinking what it is you want from me. I don't have anything to tell you because I don't know anything. So if you're going to kick the shit out of me, get on with it."

"Naturally you are trained to resist," Gagarin said. "I understand that. My own people were given the same indoctrination. However, it has been proved that in the end no one can resist forever. There comes a time when you will talk. You will tell us anything we want to know. And probably things we have not asked about. Because it will please you to tell us."

Lyons drained the coffee mug.

"The coffee was fine," he said. "I'm not so sure about the company."

"Why not save yourself a great deal of discomfort?" Took asked, taking the mug away. He stood with his back to the fire. "There is no reason why you have to be uncomfortable. You could be transferred to better accommodations immediately. Have the opportunity to take a bath. Wear clean clothes. Be given good food."

Lyons smiled, glancing at Gagarin.

"I have said something to amuse you?" Took asked.

"We had this conversation while you were getting the coffee," Gagarin explained. "Our friend has suspicions that raise the question about our kindly motives."

"Coercion takes many forms," Took said. "A sound beating against the promise of comfort and less aggression. It is up to the individual to take whichever path he desires."

"You see, Jag. Choices again," Gagarin said. "Full circle."

"Talking of choices," Lyons said. "Any chance of another mug of coffee?"

Took shook his head.

"Not this time. Perhaps next time we talk. This was only the first of our discussions, Jag. Just to lay down the rules. Really to give you an opportunity to understand what we want from you."

He snapped out a command in Korean. The door opened and the armed escort stepped inside.

"Time to go back," Took said. "You need time to consider what we have discussed today. I hope next time we meet, your attitude will have changed."

As he turned to leave, Lyons glanced at Gagarin. The Russian was watching him closely, a distant look in his eyes.

The escort returned Lyons to his cell. The door crashed shut, bolts sliding into place. Silence returned. Lyons crossed to squat against the wall, his gaze fixed on the door. He had a feeling he wouldn't be alone for very long.

They came for him two hours later, took him from his cell and along the passage. A door was opened, and he was pushed inside a room that looked very much like his cell, except that there was a heavy wooden chair in the center of the room, bolted to the floor. There were wrist and ankle restraints on the chair. The wood and the floor around the chair were dark with dried blood.

The door closed behind Lyons. There were three Korean soldiers in the room, and none of them had any armament. They all carried long bamboo staves. The three moved so that Lyons was in their midst. Without any kind of signal they began to beat him with the staves. The blows were hard and painful. They took their time, making sure that each blow delivered the maximum pain. They concentrated on his legs and body. When Lyons tried to ward off the blows, his arms took the punishment. The beating went on for some time. Lyons refused to go down. He took the punishment in silence, his mind elsewhere, trying to focus on something other than the beating. His body screamed for relief.

When they had finished with the staves, the Koreans moved in closer and used their fists on his face. They were expert. The blows hurt. Blood flowed. But nothing was broken. They were hurting him without turning him into a cripple.

For the moment. The real damage would come later.

Lyons realized that this was just to show him what they could do. If this failed to convince him all they had to do was raise the level. When they had finished they had to drag Lyons back to his cell because he was too stiff to walk. They threw him down on the floor and left him.

Lyons didn't move for a long time. The moment he did, his body begged him not to. He ignored it and crawled to his usual spot against the wall.

His whole body hurt. His face was swollen and distorted. Blood filled his mouth from where his inner cheeks had been cut. Lyons raised his head and looked in the direction of the cell door. The small slot was open, and someone was watching him. All Lyons could see were the eyes. He recognized them. They belonged to Yat Sen Took. Lyons refused to turn away. After a few minutes the slot was closed.

The rest of the day passed in a haze of pain. Lyons stayed exactly where he was until it got dark, then he struggled to his feet and began to walk around the cell, moving his arms in time to his motion. He walked for hours, fighting the stiffness in his body. The walking stopped him from seizing up. Later he sat down again and fell into a disturbed sleep.

It was light when he opened his eyes. He heard his cell door being opened. The same escort stood there. They led him out of the cell and across the compound, into the same building and up the steps. The door was opened and Lyons was pushed back inside the same room.

Took and Gagarin were waiting for him again. The Russian waved him to a chair. Lyons sat down, waiting. It was their game, he decided, let them start.

"So, Jag, you have experienced both sides of the coin," Gagarin said in that quiet, benevolent tone. "Last night will have given you time to reconsider."

Lyons glanced up at the Russian.

"Sure," he said.

"So do you have anything to say?"

Lyons nodded.

"Coffee. Black. No sugar…"

* * * * *

The heart-stopping action
concludes in ROGUE STATE,
Book II of THE SLINGSHOT PROJECT,
Available October 2002.

THE Destroyer™

FATHER TO SON

As the long road to the rank of Reigning Master of the venerable house of assassins nears its end, the *Time of Succession* ritual begins. But there is a storm cloud on the horizon of Chiun's retirement and Remo's promotion: a dark nemesis has been reborn from the fires of evil and has unleashed his plot for vengeance. He won't stop until he has fulfilled a prophecy of doom that even Chiun may not be able to thwart: the death of the Destroyer.

Available in October 2002 at your favorite retail outlet.

TAKE 'EM FREE

2 action-packed novels plus a mystery bonus

NO RISK

NO OBLIGATION TO BUY

James Axler
Outlanders®

DRAGONEYE

Deep inside the moon two ancient beings live on—the sole
survivors of two mighty races whose battle to rule earth and
mankind is poised to end after millennia of struggle and subterfuge.
Now, in a final conflict, they are prepared to unleash a blood
sacrifice of truly monstrous proportions, a heaven-shaking
Armageddon that will obliterate earth and its solar system. At last
Kane, Grant and Brigid Baptiste will confront the true architects
of mankind: their creators…and now, ultimately, their destroyers.

In the Outlands, the shocking truth is humanity's last hope.

DEATH LANDS®

Amazon Gate

Adventure and suspense in the midst of a new reality

JAMES AXLER

DEATH LANDS

THE ILLUMINATED ONES BOOK!

Amazon Gate

*Available in
September 2002
at your favorite retail outlet.*

In the radiation-blasted heart of the Northwest, Ryan and his companions form a tenuous alliance with a society of women warriors in what may be the stunning culmination of their quest. After years of searching, they have found the gateway belonging to the pre-dark cabal known as the Illuminated Ones—and perhaps their one chance to reclaim the future from the jaws of madness. But they must confront its deadly guardians: what is left of the constitutional government of the United States of America.